# EVERYONE LOVES
# THE LAST UNICORN

"Beagle has extraordinary inventive powers, and they make page after page a delight. . . . The book is rich not only in comic bits but also in passages of uncommon beauty. Beagle is a true magician with words, a master of prose and a deft practitioner in verse. He has been compared, not unreasonably, with Lewis Carroll and J.R.R. Tolkien, but he stands squarely and triumphantly on his own feet.

—*The Saturday Review*

"THE LAST UNICORN flows onward in a fine blend of sheer fantasy and shameless fun, in an alteration of rough parody and tender purity. Beagle plays with a lively prose that has a habit of turning unexpectedly—and effectively—into a poetry that is sometimes sensuous, sometimes nonsensical. . . . A wild, whimsical, and, in the end, wonderfully touching fairy tale. It is magic with a touch of majesty."

—Louis Untermeyer

"Peter Beagle illuminates with his own particular magic such commonplace matters as ghosts, unicorns, and werewolves. For years a loving readership has consulted him as an expert on those heart's reasons that reason does not know."

—Ursula K. Le Guin

love and magic are their own rewards.

appearances - the nature of true magic
nothing men can do can change the
universe. we are insignificant. making
choices is what it's all about.

more magical to be mortal and make
choices than to be immortal and unable
to choose.

Book to unobsess people with the idea of
death. It's [important to still]
make good, [loving and magical]
experiences despite the obvious insignificance

# THE
# LAST
## A NOVEL OF CHOICE!!
# UNICORN

The true magic in life is the magic of love
Red Bull is manageable w/ less fear.
Red Bull is death, fear of taking chances
caring and loving. He is vanquished not
vanished. **Peter S. Beagle** (fear of love
and true magic - unicorns). evil in that sense

Lir has to come to grips w/ loving and
losing. "Never knew I was empty to feel
so good. now - Schmendrick

Plot is simple, but allegory is great.
allegory - comparison - strained
  every character stands for an idea

characters exist on one level. open-
ended

**DEL REY**

A Del Rey Book

**BALLANTINE BOOKS • NEW YORK**

Sea represents commonly freedom
but here ironically means
imprisonment.

60's writers concerned w/dehumanization
and manipulation. everything controlled by
something above/beyond. fear was strong
of being yourself, natural
There was danger in way people were
conspiring to plans to ruin the human
spirit.

A Del Rey Book
Published by Ballantine Books

Library of Congress Catalog Card Number: 68-16075

ISBN 0-345-30037-8

This edition published by arrangement with
The Viking Press, Inc.

Manufactured in the United States of America

First U.S. Printing: February 1969
Twenty-first U.S. Printing: June 1983

Cover art by Darrell K. Sweet

Red Bull - fear / universal dream of
masculinity annihilation
sun's animal


Unicorn - feminine (lightness) dream of beauty
moon's animal perfection
ideals of the 60's. dreams
Embodiment of wonder. helps comprehension
of death, and mortality. her humanness
shows beauty of " - fragile hold on
time. love, though brief, is beautiful

To the memory of Dr. Olfert Dapper, who saw a
wild unicorn in the Maine woods in 1673,
and for Robert Nathan, who has seen
one or two in Los Angeles

King Haggard -




Prince Lir -




Princess

Schmendrick - maker. antagonist
chooses to do magic well. wants magic
to be useful and practical


Mommy Fortuna - offers an evil art that
makes people gullible. antagonist
chooses black magic.


Molly Grue

# THE LAST UNICORN

# I

THE UNICORN LIVED in a lilac wood, and she
lived all alone. She was very old, though she did
not know it, and she was no longer the careless
color of sea foam, but rather the color of snow falling
on a moonlit night. But her eyes were still clear and
unwearied, and she still moved like a shadow on the
sea.

She did not look anything like a horned horse, as
unicorns are often pictured, being smaller and cloven-
hoofed, and possessing that oldest, wildest grace that
horses have never had, that deer have only in a shy, thin
imitation and goats in dancing mockery. Her neck was
long and slender, making her head seem smaller than it
was, and the mane that fell almost to the middle of her
back was as soft as dandelion fluff and as fine as cirrus.
She had pointed ears and thin legs, with feathers of
white hair at the ankles; and the long horn above her
eyes shone and shivered with its own seashell light even
in the deepest midnight. She had killed dragons with it,
and healed a king whose poisoned wound would not
close, and knocked down ripe chestnuts for bear cubs.

Unicorns are immortal. It is their nature to live alone
in one place: usually a forest where there is a pool clear

1

enough for them to see themselves—for they are a little vain, knowing themselves to be the most beautiful creatures in all the world, and magic besides. They mate very rarely, and no place is more enchanted than one where a unicorn has been born. The last time she had seen another unicorn the young virgins who still came seeking her now and then had called to her in a different tongue; but then, she had no idea of months and years and centuries, or even of seasons. It was always spring in her forest, because she lived there, and she wandered all day among the great beech trees, keeping watch over the animals that lived in the ground and under bushes, in nests and caves, earths and treetops. Generation after generation, wolves and rabbits alike, they hunted and loved and had children and died, and as the unicorn did none of these things, she never grew tired of watching them.

One day it happened that two men with long bows rode through her forest, hunting for deer. The unicorn followed them, moving so warily that not even the horses knew she was near. The sight of men filled her with an old, slow, strange mixture of tenderness and terror. She never let one see her if she could help it, but she liked to watch them ride by and hear them talking.

"I mislike the feel of this forest," the elder of the two hunters grumbled. "Creatures that live in a unicorn's wood learn a little magic of their own in time, mainly concerned with disappearing. We'll find no game here."

"Unicorns are long gone," the second man said. "If,

2

indeed, they ever were. This is a forest like any other."

"Then why do the leaves never fall here, or the snow? I tell you, there is one unicorn left in the world—good luck to the lonely old thing, I say—and as long as it lives in this forest, there won't be a hunter who takes so much as a titmouse home at his saddle. Ride on, ride on, you'll see. I know their ways, unicorns."

"From books," answered the other. "Only from books and tales and songs. Not in the reign of three kings has there been even a whisper of a unicorn seen in this country or any other. You know no more about unicorns than I do, for I've read the same books and heard the same stories, and I've never seen one either."

The first hunter was silent for a time, and the second whistled sourly to himself. Then the first said, "My great-grandmother saw a unicorn once. She used to tell me about it when I was little."

"Oh, indeed? And did she capture it with a golden bridle?"

"No. She didn't have one. You don't have to have a golden bridle to catch a unicorn; that part's the fairy tale. You need only to be pure of heart."

"Yes, yes." The younger man chuckled. "Did she ride her unicorn, then? Bareback, under the trees, like a nymph in the early days of the world?"

"My great-grandmother was afraid of large animals," said the first hunter. "She didn't ride it, but she sat very still, and the unicorn put its head in her lap and fell asleep. My great-grandmother never moved till it woke."

3

"What did it look like? Pliny describes the unicorn as being very ferocious, similar in the rest of its body to a horse, with the head of a deer, the feet of an elephant, the tail of a bear; a deep, bellowing voice, and a single black horn, two cubits in length. And the Chinese—"

"My great-grandmother said only that the unicorn had a good smell. She never could abide the smell of any beast, even a cat or a cow, let alone a wild thing. But she loved the smell of the unicorn. She began to cry once, telling me about it. Of course, she was a very old woman then, and cried at anything that reminded her of her youth."

"Let's turn around and hunt somewhere else," the second hunter said abruptly. The unicorn stepped softly into a thicket as they turned their horses, and took up the trail only when they were well ahead of her once more. The men rode in silence until they were nearing the edge of the forest, when the second hunter asked quietly, "Why did they go away, do you think? If there ever were such things."

"Who knows? Times change. Would you call this age a good one for unicorns?"

"No, but I wonder if any man before us ever thought his time a good time for unicorns. And it seems to me now that I have heard stories—but I was sleepy with wine, or I was thinking of something else. Well, no matter. There's light enough yet to hunt, if we hurry. Come!"

They broke out of the woods, kicked their horses to a gallop, and dashed away. But before they were out of sight, the first hunter looked back over his shoulder and called, just as though he could see the unicorn standing in shadow, "Stay where you are, poor beast. This is no world for you. Stay in your forest, and keep your trees green and your friends long-lived. Pay no mind to young girls, for they never become anything more than silly old women. And good luck to you."

The unicorn stood still at the edge of the forest and said aloud, "I am the only unicorn there is." They were the first words she had spoken, even to herself, in more than a hundred years.

That can't be, she thought. She had never minded being alone, never seeing another unicorn, because she had always known that there were others like her in the world, and a unicorn needs no more than that for company. "But I would know if all the others were gone. I'd be gone too. Nothing can happen to them that does not happen to me."

Her own voice frightened her and made her want to be running. She moved along the dark paths of her forest, swift and shining, passing through sudden clearings unbearably brilliant with grass or soft with shadow, aware of everything around her, from the weeds that brushed her ankles to insect-quick flickers of blue and silver as the wind lifted the leaves. "Oh, I could never leave this, I never could, not if I really were the only unicorn in the world. I know how to live here, I know how everything smells, and tastes, and is. What could I ever search for in the world, except this again?"

But when she stopped running at last and stood still, listening to crows and a quarrel of squirrels over her head, she wondered, But suppose they are riding togeth-

*unicorns utopia coming apart from curiosity*

er, somewhere far away? What if they are hiding and waiting for me?

From that first moment of doubt, there was no peace for her; from the time she first imagined leaving her forest, she could not stand in one place without wanting to be somewhere else. She trotted up and down beside her pool, restless and unhappy. Unicorns are not meant to make choices. She said no, and yes, and no again, day and night, and for the first time she began to feel the minutes crawling over her like worms. "I will not go. Because men have seen no unicorns for a while does not mean they have all vanished. Even if it were true, I would not go. I live here."

But at last she woke up in the middle of one warm night and said, "Yes, but now." She hurried through her forest, trying to look at nothing and smell nothing, trying not to feel her earth under her cloven hoofs. The animals who move in the dark, the owls and the foxes and the deer, raised their heads as she passed by, but she would not look at them. I must go quickly, she thought, and come back as soon as I can. Maybe I won't have to go very far. But whether I find the others or not, I will come back very soon, as soon as I can.

Under the moon, the road that ran from the edge of her forest gleamed like water, but when she stepped out onto it, away from the trees, she felt how hard it was, and how long. She almost turned back then; but instead she took a deep breath of the woods air that still drifted to her, and held it in her mouth like a flower, as long as she could.

The long road hurried to nowhere and had no end. It

6

*unicorn becomes aequainted with the real (outer) world.*

ran through villages and small towns, flat country and mountains, stony barrens and meadows springing out of stones, but it belonged to none of these, and it never rested anywhere. It rushed the unicorn along, tugging at her feet like the tide, fretting at her, never letting her be quiet and listen to the air, as she was used to do. Her eyes were always full of dust, and her mane was stiff and heavy with dirt.

Time had always passed her by in her forest, but now it was she who passed through time as she traveled. The colors of the trees changed, and the animals along the way grew heavy coats and lost them again; the clouds crept or hurried before the changing winds, and were pink and gold in the sun or livid with storm. Wherever she went, she searched for her people, but she found no trace of them, and in all the tongues she heard spoken along the road there was not even a word for them any more.

Early one morning, about to turn off the road to sleep, she saw a man hoeing in his garden. Knowing that she should hide, she stood still instead and watched him work, until he straightened and saw her. He was fat, and his cheeks jumped with every step he took. "Oh," he said. "Oh, you're beautiful."

When he tugged off his belt, made a loop in it, and moved clumsily toward her, the unicorn was more pleased than frightened. The man knew what she was, and what he himself was for: to hoe turnips and pursue something that shone and could run faster than he could. She sidestepped his first lunge as lightly as though the wind of it had blown her out of his reach. "I have been hunted with bells and banners in my time,"

7

she told him. "Men knew that the only way to hunt me was to make the chase so wondrous that I would come near to see it. And even so I was never once captured."

"My foot must have slipped," said the man. "Steady now, you pretty thing."

"I've never really understood," the unicorn mused as the man picked himself up, "what you dream of doing with me, once you've caught me." The man leaped again, and she slipped away from him like rain. "I don't think you know yourselves," she said.

"Ah, steady, steady, easy now." The man's sweating face was striped with dirt, and he could hardly get his breath. "Pretty," he gasped. "You pretty little mare."

*"Mare?"* The unicorn trumpeted the word so shrilly that the man stopped pursuing her and clapped his hands to his ears. "Mare?" she demanded, "I, a horse? Is that what you take me for? Is that what you see?'

"Good horse," the fat man panted. He leaned on the fence and wiped his face. "Curry you up, clean you off, you'll be the prettiest old mare anywhere." He reached out with the belt again. "Take you to the fair," he said. "Come on, horse."

"A horse," the unicorn said. "That's what you were trying to capture. A white mare with her mane full of burrs." As the man approached her, she hooked her horn through the belt, jerked it out of his grasp, and hurled it across the road into a patch of daisies. "A horse, am I?" she snorted. "A horse, indeed!"

For a moment the man was very close to her, and her great eyes stared into his own, which were small and tired and amazed. Then she turned and fled up the road, running so swiftly that those who saw her exclaimed, "Now *there's* a horse! There's a real horse!" One old man said quietly to his wife, "That's an Ayrab horse. I was on a ship with an Ayrab horse once."

From that time the unicorn avoided towns, even at night, unless there was no way at all to go around them. Even so, there were a few men who gave chase, but always to a wandering white mare; never in the gay and reverent manner proper to the pursuit of a unicorn. They came with ropes and nets and baits of sugar lumps, and they whistled and called her Bess and Nellie. Sometimes she would slow down enough to let their horses catch her scent, and then watch as the beasts reared and wheeled and ran away with their terrified riders. The horses always knew her.

"How can it be?" she wondered. "I suppose I could understand it if men had simply forgotten unicorn or if they had changed so that they hated all unicorns now and tried to kill them when they saw them. But not to see them at all, to look at them and see something else—what do they look like to one another, then? What do trees look like to them, or houses, or real horses, or their own children?"

Sometimes she thought, "If men no longer know what they are looking at, there may well be unicorns in the world yet, unknown and glad of it." But she knew beyond both hope and vanity that men had changed, and the world with them, because the unicorns were gone. Yet she went on along the hard road, although each day she wished a little more that she had never left her forest.

Then one afternoon the butterfly wobbled out of a

breeze and lit on the tip of her horn. He was velvet all over, dark and dusty, with golden spots on his wings, and he was as thin as a flower petal. Dancing along her horn, he saluted her with his curling feelers. "I am a roving gambler. How do you do?"

The unicorn laughed for the first time in her travels. "Butterfly, what are you doing out on such a windy day?" she asked him. "You'll take cold and die long before your time."

"Death takes what man would keep," said the butterfly, "and leaves what man would lose. Blow, wind, and crack your cheeks. I warm my hands before the fire of life and get four-way relief." He glimmered like a scrap of owl-light on her horn.

"Do you know what I am, butterfly?" the unicorn asked hopefully, and he replied, "Excellent well, you're a fishmonger. You're my everything, you are my sunshine, you are old and gray and full of sleep, you're my pickle-face, consumptive Mary Jane." He paused, fluttering his wings against the wind, and added conversationally, "Your name is a golden bell hung in my heart. I would break my body to pieces to call you once by your name."

"Say my name, then," the unicorn begged him. "If you know my name, tell it to me."

"Rumpelstiltskin," the butterfly answered happily. "Gotcha! You don't get no medal." He jigged and twinkled on her horn, singing, "Won't you come home, Bill Bailey, won't you come home, where once he could not go. Buckle down, Winsocki, go and catch a falling star. Clay lies still, but blood's a rover, so I should be called kill-devil all the parish over." His eyes were gleaming scarlet in the glow of the unicorn's horn.

She sighed and plodded on, both amused and disappointed. It serves you right, she told herself. You know better than to expect a butterfly to know your name. All they know are songs and poetry, and anything else they hear. They mean well, but they can't keep things straight. And why should they? They die so soon.

The butterfly swaggered before her eyes, singing, "One, two, three o'lairy," as he whirled; chanting, "Not, I'll not, carrion comfort, look down that lonesome road. For, oh, what damned minutes tells he o'er who dotes, yet doubts. Hasten, Mirth, and bring with thee a host of furious fancies whereof I am commander, which will be on sale for three days only at bargain summer prices. I love you, I love you, oh, the horror, the horror, and aroint thee, witch, aroint thee, indeed and truly you've chosen a bad place to be lame in, willow, willow, willow." His voice tinkled in the unicorn's head like silver money falling.

He traveled with her for the rest of the waning day, but when the sun went down and the sky was full of rosy fish, he flew off her horn and hovered in the air before her. "I must take the A train," he said politely. Against the clouds she could see that his velvet wings were ribbed with delicate black veins.

"Farewell," she said. "I hope you hear many more songs"—which was the best way she could think of to say good-by to a butterfly. But instead of leaving her, he fluttered above her head, looking suddenly less dashing and a little nervous in the blue evening air. "Fly away," she urged him. "It's too cold for you to be out." But the butterfly still dallied, humming to himself.

"They ride that horse you call the Macedonai," he intoned absent-mindedly; and then, very clearly, "Unicorn. Old French, *unicorne*. Latin, *unicornis*. Literally, one-horned: *unus*, one and *cornu*, a horn. A fabulous animal resembling a horse with one horn. Oh, I am a cook and a captain bold and the mate of the *Nancy* brig. Has anybody here seen Kelly?" He strutted joyously in the air, and the first fireflies blinked around him in wonder and grave doubt.

The unicorn was so startled and so happy to hear her name spoken at last that she overlooked the remark about the horse. "Oh, you do know me!" she cried, and the breath of her delight blew the butterfly twenty feet away. When he came scrambling back to her, she pleaded, "Butterfly, if you really know who I am, tell me if you have ever seen anyone like me, tell me which way I must go to find them. Where have they gone?"

"Butterfly, butterfly, where shall I hide?" he sang in the fading light. "The sweet and bitter fool will presently appear. Christ, that my love were in my arms, and I in my bed again." He rested on the unicorn's horn once more, and she could feel him trembling.

"Please," she said. "All I want to know is that there are other unicorns somewhere in the world. Butterfly, tell me that there are still others like me, and I will believe you and go home to my forest. I have been away so long, and I said that I would come back soon."

"Over the mountains of the moon," the butterfly began, "down the Valley of the Shadow, ride, boldly ride."

Then he stopped suddenly and said in a strange voice, "No, no, listen, don't listen to me, listen. You can find your people if you are brave. They passed down all the roads long ago, and the Red Bull ran close behind them and covered their footprints. Let nothing you dismay, but don't be half-safe." His wings brushed against the unicorn's skin.

"The <u>Red Bull</u>?" she asked. "What is the Red Bull?"

The butterfly started to sing. "Follow me down. Follow me down. Follow me down. Follow me down." But then he shook his head wildly and recited, "His firstling bull has majesty, and his horns are the horns of a wild ox. With them he shall push the peoples, all of them, to the ends of the earth. Listen, listen, listen quickly."

"I am listening," the unicorn cried. "Where are my people, and what is the Red Bull?"

But the butterfly swooped close to her ear, laughing. "I have nightmares about crawling around on the ground," he sang. "The little dogs, Tray, Blanche, Sue, they bark at me, the little snakes, they hiss at me, the beggars are coming to town. Then at last come the clams."

For a moment more he danced in the dusk before her; then he shivered away into the violet shadows by the roadside, chanting defiantly, "It's you or me, moth! Hand to hand to hand to hand to hand ..." The last the unicorn saw of him was a tiny skittering between the trees, and her eyes might have deceived her, for the night was full of wings now.

At least he did recognize me, she thought sadly. That means something. But she answered herself, No, that means nothing at all, except that somebody once made up a song about unicorns, or a poem. But the Red Bull. What could he have meant by that? Another song, I suppose.

She walked on slowly, and the night drew close about her. The sky was low and almost pure black, save for one spot of yellowing silver where the moon paced behind the thick clouds. The unicorn sang softly to herself, a song she had heard a young girl singing in her forest long ago.

> "Sparrows and cats will live in my shoe,
> Sooner than I will live with you.
> Fish will come walking out of the sea,
> Sooner than you will come back to me."

She did not understand the words, but the song made her think longingly of her home. It seemed to her that she had heard autumn beginning to shake the beech trees the very moment that she stepped out into the road.

At last she lay down in the cold grass and fell asleep. Unicorns are the wariest of all wild things, but they sleep soundly when they sleep. All the same, if she had not been dreaming of home, she would surely have roused at the sound of wheels and jingling coming closer through the night, even though the wheels were muffled in rags and the little bells wrapped in wool. But she was very far away, farther than the soft bells could go, and she did not wake.

There were nine wagons, each draped in black, each drawn by a lean black horse, and each baring barred sides like teeth when the wind blew through the black hangings. The lead wagon was driven by a squat old woman, and it bore signs on its shrouded sides that said in big letters; MOMMY FORTUNA'S MIDNIGHT CARNIVAL. And below, in smaller print: *Creatures of night, brought to light.*

When the first wagon drew even with the place where the unicorn lay asleep, the old woman suddenly pulled her black horse to a stop. All the other wagons stopped too and waited silently as the old woman swung herself to the ground with an ugly grace. Gliding close to the unicorn, she peered down at her for a long time, and then said, "Well. Well, bless my old husk of a heart. And here I thought I'd seen the last of them." Her voice left a flavor of honey and gunpowder on the air.

"If he knew," she said and she showed pebbly teeth as she smiled. "But I don't think I'll tell him." She looked back at the black wagons and snapped her fingers twice. The drivers of the second and third wagons got down and came toward her. One was short and dark and stony, like herself; the other was a tall thin man with an air of resolute bewilderment. He wore an old black cloak, and his eyes were green.

"What do you see?' the old woman asked the short man. "Rukh, what do you see lying there?

"Dead horse," he answered. "No, not dead. Give it to the manticore, or the dragon." His chuckle sounded like matches striking.

"You're a fool," Mommy Fortuna said to him. Then to the other, "What about you, wizard, seer, thauma~turge? What do you see with your sorcerer's sight?" She joined with the man Rukh in a ratchety roar of laugh-

*Mommy Fortuna casts a sleep spell on the unicorn.*

ter, but it ended when she saw that the tall man was still staring at the unicorn. "Answer me, you juggler!" she snarled, but the tall man did not turn his head. The old woman turned it for him, reaching out a crablike hand to yank his chin around. His eyes fell before her yellow stare.

"A horse," he muttered. "A white mare."

Mommy Fortuna looked at him for a long time. "You're a fool too, magician," she snickered at last, "but a worse fool than Rukh, and a more dangerous one. He lies only out of greed, but you lie out of fear. Or could it be kindness?" The man said nothing, and Mommy Fortuna laughed by herself.

"All right," she said. "It's a white mare. I want her for the Carnival. The ninth cage is empty."

"I'll need rope," Rukh said. He was about to turn away, but the old woman stopped him.

"The only rope that could hold her," she told him, "would be the cord with which the old gods bound the Fenris-wolf. That one was made of fishes' breath, bird spittle, a woman's beard, the miaowing of a cat, the sinews of a bear, and one thing more. I remember—mountain roots. Having none of these elements, nor dwarfs to weave them for us, we'll have to do the best we can with iron bars. I'll put a sleep on her, thus," and Mommy Fortuna's hands knitted the night air while she grumbled a few unpleasant words in her throat. There was a smell of lightning about the unicorn when the old woman had finished her spell.

"Now cage her," she said to the two men. "She'll sleep till sunrise, whatever racket you make—unless, in your accustomed stupidity, you touch her with your

16

hands. Take the ninth cage to pieces and build it around her, but beware! The hand that so much as brushes her mane turns instantly to the donkey's hoof it deserves to be." Again she gazed mockingly at the tall, thin man. "Your little tricks would be even harder for you than they already are, wizard," she said, wheezing. "Get to work. There's not much dark left."

When she was well out of earshot, sliding back into the shadow of her wagon as though she had just come out to mark the hour, the man named Rukh spat and said curiously, "Now I wonder what's worrying the old squid. What would it matter if we touched the beast?"

The magician answered him in a voice almost too soft to be heard. "The touch of a human hand would wake her out of the deepest sleep the devil himself could lay on her. And Mommy Fortuna's no devil."

"She'd like us to think so," the dark man sneered. "Donkey hoofs! Gahhh!" But he thrust his hands deep into his pockets. "Why would the spell be broken? It's just an old white mare."

But the magician was walking away toward the last of the black wagons. "Hurry," he called over his shoulder. "It will be day soon."

It took them the rest of the night to pull down the ninth cage, bars and floor and roof and then to put it back together around the sleeping unicorn. Rukh was tugging at the door to make sure that it was securely locked, when the gray trees in the east boiled over and the unicorn opened her eyes. The two men slipped hurriedly away, but the tall magician looked back in

time to see the unicorn rise to her feet and stare at the
iron bars, her low head swaying like the head of an old
white horse.

# II

THE NINE BLACK wagons of the Midnight Carnival seemed smaller by daylight and not menacing at all, but flimsy and fragile as dead leaves. Their draperies were gone, and they were now adorned with sad black banners cut from blankets, and stubby black ribbons that twitched in the breeze. They were arranged strangely in a scrubby field: a pentacle of cages enclosing a triangle, and Mommy Fortuna's wagon lumping in the center. This cage alone retained its black veil, concealing whatever it contained. Mommy Fortuna was nowhere to be seen.

The man named Rukh was leading a straggling crowd of country folk slowly from one cage to the next, commenting somberly on the beasts within. "This here's the manticore. Man's head, lion's body, tail of a scorpion. Captured at midnight, eating werewolves to sweeten its breath. Creatures of night, brought to light. Here's the dragon. Breathes fire now and then—usually at people who poke it, little boy. Its inside is an inferno, but its skin is so cold it burns. The dragon speaks seventeen languages badly, and is subject to gout. The satyr. Ladies keep back. A real troublemaker. Captured under curious circumstances revealed to gentlemen

19

only, for a token fee after the show. Creatures of night." Standing by the unicorn's cage, which was one of the inner three, the tall magician watched the procession proceeding around the pentacle. "I shouldn't be here," he said to the unicorn. "The old woman warned me to stay away from you." He chuckled pleasantly. "She has mocked me from the day I joined her, but I have made her nervous all that time."

The unicorn hardly heard him. She turned and turned in her prison, her body shrinking from the touch of the iron bars all around her. No creature of man's night loves cold iron, and while the unicorn could endure its presence, the murderous smell of it seemed to turn her bones to sand and her blood to rain. The bars of her cage must have had some sort of spell on them, for they never stopped whispering evilly to one another in clawed, pattering voices. The heavy lock giggled and whined like a mad monkey.

"Tell me what you see," said the magician, as Mommy Fortuna had said it to him. "Look at your fellow legends and tell me what you see."

Rukh's iron voice came clanging through the wan afternoon. "Gatekeeper of the underworld. Three heads and a healthy coat of vipers, as you can see. Last seen aboveground in the time of Hercules, who dragged him up under one arm. But we lured him to light again with promises of a better life. Cerberus. Look at those six cheated red eyes. You may look into them again one day. This way to the Midgard Serpent. This way."

The unicorn stared through the bars at the animal in the cage. Her eyes were wide with disbelief. "It's only a dog," she whispered. "It's a hungry, unhappy dog with only one head and hardly any coat at all, the poor thing. How could they ever take it for Cerberus? Are they all blind?"

"Look again," the magician said.

"And the satyr," the unicorn continued. "The satyr is an ape, an old ape with a twisted foot. The dragon is a crocodile, much more likely to breathe fish than fire. And the great manticore is a lion—a perfectly good lion, but no more monstrous than the others. I don't understand."

"It's got the whole world in its coils," Rukh was droning. And once more the magician said, "Look again."

Then, as though her eyes were getting used to darkness, the unicorn began to perceive a second figure in each cage. They loomed hugely over the captives of the Midnight Carnival, and yet they were joined to them: stormy dreams sprung from a grain of truth. So there was a manticore—famine-eyed, slobber-mouthed, roaring, curving his deadly tail over his back until the poison spine lolled and nodded just above his ear—and there was a lion too, tiny and absurd by comparison. Yet they were the same creature. The unicorn stamped in wonder.

It was so in all the other cages. The shadow-dragon opened his mouth and hissed harmless fire to make the gapers gasp and cringe, while Hell's snake-furred watchdog howled triple dooms and devastations down on his betrayers, and the satyr limped leering to the bars and beckoned young girls to impossible delights, right there in public. As for the crocodile, the ape, and the sad dog, they faded steadily before the marvelous phantoms until they were only shadows themselves, even to the unicorn's undeceived eyes. "This is a strange sorcery," she said softly. "There's more meaning than magic to this."

The magician laughed with pleasure and great relief. "Well said, well said indeed. I knew the old horror wouldn't dazzle *you* with her twopenny spells." His voice grew hard and secret. "She's made her third mistake now," he said, "and that's at least two too many for a tired old trickster like herself. The time draws near."

"The time draws near," Rukh was telling the crowd, as though he had overheard the magician. "Ragnarok. On that day, when the gods fall, the Serpent of the Midgard will spit a storm of venom at great Thor himself, till he tumbles over like a poisoned fly. And so he waits for Judgment Day, and dreams about the part he'll play. It may be so—I couldn't say. Creatures of night, brought to light."

The cage was filled with snake. There was no head to it, and no tail—nothing but a wave of tarnished darkness rolling from one end of the cage to the other, leaving no room for anything but its own thunderous breathing. Only the unicorn saw, coiled in a corner, a baleful boa; brooding, perhaps, over its own Judgment on the Midnight Carnival. But it was tiny and dim as the ghost of a worm in the Serpent's shadow.

A wondering gawk stuck up his hand and demanded of Rukh, "If this big snake do be coiled around the world, as you say, how come you to be having a piece of it in your wagon? And if it can shatter the sea just by stretching of itself, what's to keep it from crawling off wearing your whole show like a necklace?" There were murmurs of agreement, and some of the murmurers began to back warily away.

"I'm glad you asked me that, friend," Rukh said with a scowl. "It just so happens that the Midgard Serpent exists in like another space from ours, another dimension. Normally, therefore, he's invisible, but dragged into our world—as Thor hooked him once—he shows clear as lightning, which also visits us from somewhere else, where it might look quite different. And naturally he might turn nasty if he knew that a bit of his tummy slack was on view daily and Sundays in Mommy Fortuna's Midnight Carnival. But he don't know. He's got other things to think about than what becomes of his belly button, and we take our chances—as do you all—on his continued tranquillity." He rolled and stretched the last word like dough, and his hearers laughed carefully.

"Spells of seeming," the unicorn said. "She cannot make things."

"Nor truly change them," added the magician. "Her shabby skill lies in disguise. And even that knack would be beyond her, if it weren't for the eagerness of those gulls, those marks, to believe whatever comes easiest. She can't turn cream into butter, but she can give a lion the semblance of a manticore to eyes that want to see a manticore there—eyes that would take a real manticore for a lion, a dragon for a lizard, and the Midgard Serpent for an earthquake. And a unicorn for a white mare."

The unicorn halted in her slow, desperate round of the cage, realizing for the first time that the magician understood her speech. He smiled, and she saw that his face was frighteningly young for a grown man—untraveled by time, unvisited by grief or wisdom. "I know you," he said.

The bars whispered wickedly between them. Rukh was leading the crowd to the inner cages now. The unicorn asked the tall man, "Who are you?"

"I am called Schmendrick the Magician," he answered. "You won't have heard of me."

The unicorn came very near to explaining that it was hardly for her to have heard of one wizard or another, but something sad and valiant in his voice kept her from it. The magician said, "I entertain the sightseers as they gather for the show. Miniature magic, sleight of hand—flowers to flags and flags to fish, all accompanied by persuasive patter and a suggestion that I could work more ominous wonders if I chose. It's not much of a job, but I've had worse, and I'll have better one day. This is not the end."

But the sound of his voice made the unicorn feel as though she were trapped forever, and once more she began pacing her cage, moving to keep her heart from bursting with the terror of being closed in. Rukh was standing before a cage that contained nothing but a small brown spider weaving a modest web across the bars. "Arachne of Lydia," he told the crowd. "Guaranteed the greatest weaver in the world—her fate's the proof of it. She had the bad luck to defeat the goddess Athena in a weaving contest. Athena was a sore loser, and Arachne is now a spider, creating only for Mommy Fortuna's Midnight Canival, by special arrangement.

Warp of snow and woof of flame, and never any two the same. Arachne."

Strung on the loom of iron bars, the web was very simple and almost colorless, except for an occasional rainbow shiver when the spider scuttled out on it to put a thread right. But it drew the onlookers' eyes—and the unicorn's eyes as well—back and forth and steadily deeper, until they seemed to be looking down into great rifts in the world, black fissures that widened remorselessly and yet would not fall into pieces as long as Arachne's web held the world together. The unicorn shook herself free with a sigh, and saw the real web again. It was very simple, and almost colorless.

"It isn't like the others," she said.

"No," Schmendrick agreed grudgingly. "But there's no credit due to Mommy Fortuna for that. You see, the spider believes. She sees those cat's-cradles herself and thinks them her own work. Belief makes all the difference to magic like Mommy Fortuna's. Why, if that troop of witlings withdrew their wonder, there'd be nothing left of all her witchery but the sound of a spider weeping. And no one would hear it."

The unicorn did not want to look into the web again. She glanced at the cage closest to her own, and suddenly felt the breath in her body turning to cold iron. There sat on an oaken perch a creature with the body of a great bronze bird and a hag's face, clenched and deadly as the talons with which she gripped the wood. She had the shaggy round ears of a bear; but down her scaly shoulders, mingling with the bright knives of her plumage, there fell hair the color of moonlight, thick and youthful around the hating human face. She glittered, but to look at her was to feel the light going out of the sky. Catching sight of the unicorn, she made a queer sound like a hiss and a chuckle together.

The unicorn said quietly, "This one is real. This is the harpy Celaeno."

Schmendrick's face had gone the color of oatmeal. "The old woman caught her by chance," he whispered, "asleep, as she took you. But it was an ill fortune, and they both know it. Mommy Fortuna's craft is just sure enough to hold the monster, but its mere presence is wearing all her spells so thin that in a little time she won't have power enough left to fry an egg. She should never have done it, never meddled with a real harpy, a real unicorn. The truth melts her magic, always, but she cannot keep from trying to make it serve her. But this time—"

"Sister of the rainbow, believe it or not," they heard Rukh braying to the awed onlookers. "Her name means 'the Dark One,' the one whose wings blacken the sky before a storm. She and her two sweet sisters nearly starved the king Phineus to death by snatching and befouling his food before he could eat it. But the sons of the North Wind made them quit that, didn't they, my beauty?" The harpy made no sound, and Rukh grinned like a cage himself.

"She put up a fiercer fight than all the others put together," he went on. "It was like trying to bind all hell with a hair, but Mommy Fortuna's powers are great enough even for that. Creatures of night, brought to light. Polly want a cracker?" Few in the crowd laughed. The harpy's talons tightened on her perch until the wood cried out.

"You'll need to be free when she frees herself," the magician said. "She mustn't catch you caged."

"I dare not touch the iron," the unicorn replied. "My horn could open the lock, but I cannot reach it. I cannot get out." She was trembling with horror of the harpy, but her voice was quite calm.

Schmendrick the Magician drew himself up several inches taller than the unicorn would have thought possible. "Fear nothing," he began grandly. "For all my air of mystery, I have a feeling heart." But he was interrupted by the approach of Rukh and his followers, grown quieter than the grubby gang who had giggled at the manticore. The magician fled, calling back softly, "Don't be afraid, Schmendrick is with you. Do nothing till you hear from me!" His voice drifted to the unicorn, so faint and lonely that she was not sure whether she actually heard it or only felt it brush against her.

It was growing dark. The crowd stood in front of her cage, peering in at her with a strange shyness. Rukh said, "The unicorn," and stepped aside.

She heard hearts bounce, tears brewing, and breath going backward, but nobody said a word. By the sorrow and loss and sweetness in their faces she knew that they recognized her, and she accepted their hunger as her homage. She thought of the hunter's great-grandmother, and wondered what it must be like to grow old, and to cry.

"Most shows," said Rukh after a time, "would end here, for what could they possibly present after a genuine unicorn? But Mommy Fortuna's Midnight Carnival holds one more mystery yet—a demon more destructive than the dragon, more monstrous than the manticore, more hideous than the harpy, and certainly more universal than the unicorn." He waved his hand toward the last wagon and the black hangings began to wriggle open, though there was no one pulling them. "Behold her!" Rukh cried. "Behold the last, the Very End! Behold Elli!"

Inside the cage, it was darker than the evening, and cold stirred behind the bars like a live thing. Something moved in the cold, and the unicorn saw Elli—an old, bony, ragged woman who crouched in the cage rocking and warming herself before a fire that was not there. She looked so frail that the weight of the darkness should have crushed her, and so helpless and alone that the watchers should have rushed forward in pity to free her. Instead, they began to back silently away, for all the world as though Elli were stalking them. But she was not even looking at them. She sat in the dark and creaked a song to herself in a voice that sounded like a saw going through a tree, and like a tree getting ready to fall.

> "What is plucked will grow again,
> What is slain lives on,
> What is stolen will remain—
> What is gone is gone."

"She doesn't look like much, does she?" Rukh asked. "But no hero can stand before her, no god can wrestle her down, no magic can keep her out—or in, for she's no prisoner of ours. Even while we exhibit her here, she is walking among you, touching and taking. For Elli is Old Age."

The cold of the cage reached out to the unicorn, and

wherever it touched her she grew lame and feeble. She felt herself withering, loosening, felt her beauty leaving her with her breath. Ugliness swung from her mane, dragged down her head, stripped her tail, gaunted her body, ate up her coat, and ravaged her mind with remembrance of what she had once been. Somewhere nearby, the harpy made her low, eager sound, but the unicorn would gladly have huddled in the shadow of her bronze wings to hide from this last demon. Elli's song sawed away at her heart.

> "What is sea-born dies on land,
> Soft is trod upon.
> What is given burns the hand—
> What is gone is gone."

The show was over. The crowd was stealing away, no one alone but in couples and fews and severals, strangers holding strangers' hands, looking back often to see if Elli were following. Rukh called plaintively, "Won't the gentlemen wait to hear the story about the satyr?" and sent a sour yowl of laughter chasing their slow flight. "Creatures of night, brought to light!" They struggled through the stiffening air, past the unicorn's cage, and on away, with Rukh's laughter yapping them home, and Elli still singing.

This is illusion, the unicorn told herself. This is illusion—and somehow raised a head heavy with death to stare deep into the dark of the last cage and see, not Old Age, but Mommy Fortuna herself, stretching and snickering and clambering to the ground with her old eerie ease. And the unicorn knew then that she had not become mortal and ugly at all, but she did not feel beautiful again. Perhaps that was illusion too, she thought wearily.

"I enjoyed that," Mommy Fortuna said to Rukh. "I always do. I guess I'm just stagestruck at heart."

"You better check on that damn harpy," Rukh said. "I could *feel* her working loose this time. It was like I was a rope holding her, and she was untying me." He shuddered and lowered his voice. "Get rid of her," he said hoarsely. "Before she scatters us across the sky like bloody clouds. She thinks about it all the time. I can feel her thinking about it."

"Fool, be still!" The witch's own voice was fierce with fear. "I can turn her into wind if she escapes, or into snow, or into seven notes of music. But I choose to keep her. No other witch in the world holds a harpy captive, and none ever will. I would keep her if I could do it only by feeding her a piece of your liver every day."

"Oh, that's nice," Rukh said. He sidled away from her. "What if she only wanted your liver?" he demanded. "What would you do then?"

"Feed her yours anyway," Mommy Fortuna said. "She wouldn't know the difference. Harpies aren't bright."

Alone in the moonlight, the old woman glided from cage to cage, rattling locks and prodding her enchantments as a housewife squeezes melons in the market. When she came to the harpy's cage the monster made a sound as shrill as a spear, and spread the horrid glory of its wings. For a moment it seemed to the unicorn that the bars of the cage began to wriggle and run like rain; but Mommy Fortuna crackled her twiggy fingers and the bars were iron again, and the harpy sank down on its perch, waiting.

"Not yet," the witch said. "Not yet." They stared at each other with the same eyes. Mommy Fortuna said, "You're mine. If you kill me, you're mine." The harpy did not move, but a cloud put out the moon.

"Not yet," Mommy Fortuna said, and she turned toward the unicorn's cage. "Well," she said in her sweet, smoky voice. "I had you frightened for a little while, didn't I?" She laughed with a sound like snakes hurrying through mud, and strolled closer.

"Whatever your friend the magician may say," she went on, "I must have some small art after all. To trick a unicorn into believing herself old and foul—that takes a certain skill, I'd say. And is it a twopenny spell that holds the Dark One prisoner? No other till I—"

The unicorn replied, "Do not boast, old woman. Your death sits in that cage and hears you."

"Yes," Mommy Fortuna said calmly. "But at least I know where it is. You were out on the road hunting for your own death." She laughed again. "And I know where that one is, too. But I spared you the finding of it, and you should be grateful for that."

Forgetting where she was, the unicorn pressed forward against the bars. They hurt her, but she did not draw back. "The Red Bull," she said. "Where can I find the Red Bull?"

Mommy Fortuna stepped very close to the cage. "The Red Bull of King Haggard," she muttered. "So you know of the Bull." She showed two of her teeth. "Well, he'll not have you," she said. "You belong to me."

The unicorn shook her head. "You know better," she

answered gently. "Free the harpy, while there is time, and set me free as well. Keep your poor shadows, if you will, but let us go."

The witch's stagnant eyes blazed up so savagely bright that a ragged company of luna moths, off to a night's revel, fluttered straight into them, and sizzled into snowy ashes. "I'd quit show business first," she snarled. "Trudging through eternity, hauling my homemade horrors—do you think *that* was my dream when I was young and evil? Do you think I chose this meager magic, sprung of stupidity, because I never knew the true witchery? I play tricks with dogs and monkeys because I cannot touch the grass, but I know the difference. And now you ask me to give up the sight of you, the presence of your power. I told Rukh I'd feed his liver to the harpy if I had to, and so I would. And to keep you I'd take your friend Schmendrick, and I'd—" She raged herself to gibberish, and at last to silence.

"Speaking of livers," the unicorn said. "Real magic can never be made by offering up someone else's liver. You must tear out your own, and not expect to get it back. The true witches know that."

A few grains of sand rustled down Mommy Fortuna's cheek as she stared at the unicorn. All witches weep like that. She turned and walked swiftly toward her wagon, but suddenly she turned again and grinned her rubbly grin. "But I tricked you twice, anyway," she said. "Did you really think that those gogglers knew you for yourself without any help from me? No, I had to give you an aspect they could understand, and a horn they could see. These days, it takes a cheap carnival witch to make folk recognize a real unicorn.

You'd do much better to stay with me and be false, for in this whole world only the Red Bull will know you when he sees you." She disappeared into her wagon, and the harpy let the moon come out again.

# III

SCHMENDRICK CAME BACK a little before dawn, slipping between the cages as silently as water.

Only the harpy made a sound as he went by. "I couldn't get away any sooner," he told the unicorn. "She's set Rukh to watching me, and he hardly ever sleeps. But I asked him a riddle, and it always takes him all night to solve riddles. Next time, I'll tell him a joke and keep him busy for a week."

The unicorn was gray and still. "There is magic on me," she said. "Why did you not tell me?"

"I thought you knew," the magician answered gently. "After all, didn't you wonder how it could be that they recognized you?" Then he smiled, which made him look a little older. "No, of course not. You never would wonder about that."

"There has never been a spell on me before," the unicorn said. She shivered long and deep. "There has never been a world in which I was not known."

"I know exactly how you feel," Schmendrick said eagerly. The unicorn looked at him out of dark, endless eyes, and he smiled nervously and looked at his hands. "It's a rare man who is taken for what he truly is," he said. "There is much misjudgment in the world. Now I

34

knew you for a unicorn when I first saw you, and I know that I am your friend. Yet you take me for a clown, or a clod, or a betrayer, and so must I be if you see me so. The magic on you is only magic and will vanish as soon as you are free, but the enchantment of error that you put on me I must wear forever in your eyes. We are not always what we seem, and hardly ever what we dream. Still I have read, or heard it sung, that uncorns when time was young, could tell the difference 'twixt the two—the false shining and the true, the lips' laugh and the heart's rue." His quiet voice lifted as the sky grew lighter, and for a moment the unicorn could not hear the bars whining, or the soft ringing of the harpy's wings.

"I think you are my friend," she said. "Will you help me?"

"If not you, no one," the magician answered. "You are my last chance."

One by one, the sad beasts of the Midnight Carnival came whimpering, sneezing, and shuddering awake. One had been dreaming of rocks and bugs and tender leaves; another of bounding through high, hot grass; a third of mud and blood. And one had dreamed of a hand scratching the lonely place behind its ears. Only the harpy had not slept, and now she sat staring into the sun without blinking. Schmendrick said. "If she frees herself first, we are lost."

They heard Rukh's voice nearby—that voice always sounded nearby—calling, "Schmendrick! Hey, Schmendrick, I got it! It's a coffeepot, right?" The magician began to move slowly away. "Tonight," he murmured to the unicorn. "Trust me till dawn." And was gone with

35

a flap and a scramble, seeming as before to leave part of himself behind. Rukh loped by the cage a moment later, all deadly economy. Hidden in her black wagon, Mommy Fortuna grumbled Elli's song to herself.

> "Here is there, and high is low;
> All may be undone.
> What is true, no two men know—
> What is gone is gone."

Soon a new catch of spectators began to come sauntering up to see the show. Rukh called them in, crying, "Creatures of night!" like an iron parrot, and Schmendrick stood on a box and did tricks. The unicorn watched him with great interest and a growing uncertainty, not of his heart, but of his craft. He made an entire sow out of a sow's ear; turned a sermon into a stone, a glass of water into a handful of water, a five of spades into a twelve of spades, and a rabbit into a goldfish that drowned. Each time he conjured up confusion, he glanced quickly at the unicorn with eyes that said, "Oh, but *you* know what I really did." Once he changed a dead rose into a seed. The unicorn liked that, even though it did turn out to be a radish seed.

The show began again. Once more Rukh led the crowd from one of Mommy Fortuna's poor fables to another. The dragon blazed, Cerberus howled for Hell to come and help him, and the satyr tempted women until they wept. They squinted and pointed at the manticore's yellow tusks and swollen sting; grew still at the thought of the Midgard Serpent; and wondered at Arachne's new web, which was like a fisherman's net with the dripping moon in it. Each of them took it for a real web, but only the spider believed that it held the real moon.

This time, Rukh did not tell the story of King Phineus and the Argonauts; indeed, he hurried his sightseers past the harpy's cage as quickly as he could, gabbling only her name and the meaning of it. The harpy smiled. Nobody saw her smile except the unicorn, and she wished that she had chanced to be looking somewhere else at the time.

When they stood in front of her cage, gazing silently in at her, the unicorn thought bitterly, Their eyes are so sad. How much sadder would they be, I wonder, if the spell that disguises me dissolved and they were left staring at a common white mare? The witch is right—not one would know me. But then a soft voice, rather like the voice of Schmendrick the Magician, said inside her, But their eyes are so sad.

And when Rukh shrieked, "Behold the Very End!" and the black hangings slithered back to reveal Elli, mumbling in the cold and the darkness, the unicorn felt the same helpless fear of growing old that set the crowd to flight, even though she knew that it was only Mommy Fortuna in the cage. She thought, The witch knows more than she knows she knows.

Night came quickly, perhaps because the harpy hurried it on. The sun sank into dirty clouds like a stone into the sea, and with about as much chance of rising again, and there was no moon, or any stars. Mommy Fortuna made her gliding rounds of the cages. The harpy did not move when she drew near, and that made the old woman stand and stare at her for a long while.

"Not yet," she muttered at last, "not yet," but her voice was weary and doubtful. She peered briefly at the unicorn, her eyes a stir of yellow in the greasy gloom. "Well, one day more," she said in a crackling sigh, and turned away again.

There was no sound in the Carnival after she was gone. All the beasts were asleep, save the spider, who wove, and the harpy, who waited. Yet the night creaked tighter and tighter, until the unicorn expected it to split wide open, ripping a seam down the sky, to reveal— More bars, she thought. Where is the magician?

At last he came hurrying through the silence, spinning and dancing like a cat in the cold, stumbling over shadows. When he reached the unicorn's cage, he made a joyful bow to her and said proudly, "Schmendrick is with you." In the cage nearest to hers, the unicorn heard the edged shivering of bronze.

"I think we have very little time," she said. "Can you truly set me free?"

The tall man smiled, and even his pale, solemn fingers grew merry. "I told you that the witch has made three great mistakes. Your capture was the last, and the taking of the harpy the second, because you are both real, and Mommy Fortuna can no more make you hers than she can make the winter a day longer. But to take me for a mountebank like herself—that was her first and fatal folly. For I too am real. I am Schmendrick the Magician, the last of the red-hot swamis, and I am older than I look."

"Where is the other?" the unicorn asked.

Schmendrick was pushing back his sleeves. "Don't

worry about Rukh. I asked him another riddle, one that has no answer. He may never move again."

He spoke three angled words and snapped his fingers. The cage disappeared. The unicorn found herself standing in a grove of trees—orange and lemon, pear and pomegranate, almond and acacia—with soft spring earth under her feet, and the sky growing over her. Her heart turned light as smoke, and she gathered up the strength of her body for a great bound into the sweet night. But she let the leap drift out of her, untaken, for she knew, although she could not see them, that the bars were still there. She was too old not to know.

"I'm sorry," Schmendrick said, somewhere in the dark. "I would have liked it to be that spell that freed you."

Now he sang something cold and low, and the strange trees blew away like dandelion down. "This is a surer spell," he said. "The bars are now as brittle as old cheese, which I crumble and scatter, so." Then he gasped and snatched his hands away. Each long finger was dripping blood.

"I must have gotten the accent wrong," he said hoarsely. He hid his hands in his cloak and tried to make his voice light. "It comes and goes."

A scratching of flinty phrases this time, and Schmendrick's bloody hands flickering across the sky. Something gray and grinning, something like a bear, but bigger than a bear, something that chuckled muddily, came limping from somewhere, eager to crack the cage like a nut and pick out bits of the unicorn's flesh with its claws. Schmendrick ordered it back into the night, but it wouldn't go.

The unicorn backed into a corner and lowered her head; but the harpy stirred softly in her cage, ringing, and the gray shape turned what must have been its head and saw her. It made a foggy, globbering sound of terror, and was gone.

The magician cursed and shivered. He said, "I called him up one other time, long ago. I couldn't handle him then either. Now we owe our lives to the harpy, and she may yet come to call for them before the sun rises." He stood silent, twisting his wounded fingers, waiting for the unicorn to speak. "I'll try once more," he said finally. "Shall I try once more?"

The unicorn thought that she could still see the night boiling where the gray thing had been. "Yes," she said.

Schmendrick took a deep breath, spat three times, and spoke words that sounded like bells ringing under the sea. He scattered a handful of powder over the spittle, and smiled triumphantly as it puffed up in a single silent flash of green. When the light had faded, he said three more words. They were like the noise bees might make buzzing on the moon.

The cage began to grow smaller. The unicorn could not see the bars moving, but each time Schmendrick said "Ah, no!" she had less room in which to stand. Already she could not turn around. The bars were drawing in, pitiless as the tide or the morning, and they would shear through her until they surrounded her heart, which they would keep a prisoner forever. She had not cried out when the creature Schmendrick had summoned came, grinning, toward her, but now she made a sound. It was small and despairing, but not yet yielding.

Schmendrick stopped the bars, though she never knew how. If he spoke any magic, she had not heard it; but the cage stopped shrinking a breath before the bars touched her body. She could feel them all the same, each one like a little cold wind, miaowing with hunger. But they could not reach her.

The magician's arms fell to his sides. "I dare no more," he said heavily. "The next time, I might not be able ..." His voice trailed miserably away, and his eyes were as defeated as his hands. "The witch made no mistake in me," he said.

"Try again," the unicorn said. "You are my friend. Try again."

But Schmendrick, smiling bitterly, was fumbling through his pockets in search of something that clicked and clinked. "I knew it would come to this," he muttered. "I dreamed it differently, but I knew." He brought out a ring from which dangled several rusty keys. "You deserve the services of a great wizard," he said to the unicorn, "but I'm afraid you'll have to be glad of the aid of a second-rate pickpocket. Unicorns know nought of need, or shame, or doubt, or debt—but mortals, as you may have noticed, take what they can get. And Rukh can only concentrate on one thing at a time."

The unicorn was suddenly aware that every animal in the Midnight Carnival was awake, making no sound, but watching her. In the next cage, the harpy began to stamp slowly from one foot to the other. "Hurry," the unicorn said. "Hurry."

Schmendrick was already fitting a key into the snickering lock. At his first attempt, which failed, the lock fell silent, but when he tried another key it cried out loudly, "Ho-ho, some magician! Some magician!" It had Mommy Fortuna's voice.

"Ah, turn blue," the magician mumbled, but the unicorn could feel him blushing. He twisted the key, and the lock snapped open with one last grunt of contempt. Schmendrick swung the cage door wide and said softly, "Step down, lady. You are free."

The unicorn stepped lightly to the ground, and Schmendrick the Magician drew back in sudden wonder. "Oh," he whispered. "It was different when there were bars between us. You look smaller, and not as—oh. Oh my."

She was home in her forest, which was black and wet and ruined because she had been gone so long. Someone was calling to her from a long way off but she was home, warming the trees and waking the grass.

Then she heard Rukh's voice, like a boat bottom gritting on pebbles. "Okay, Schmendrick, I give up. Why *is* a raven like a writing desk?" The unicorn moved away into deepest shadow, and Rukh saw only the magician and the empty, dwindled cage. His hand jumped to his pocket and came away again. "Why, you thin thief," he said, grinning iron. "She'll string you on barbed wire to make a necklace for the harpy." He turned then and headed straight for Mommy Fortuna's wagon.

"Run," the magician said. He made a frantic, foolish,

flying leap and landed on Rukh's back, hugging the dark man dumb and blind with his long arms. They fell together, and Schmendrick scrambled up first, his knees nailing Rukh's shoulders to the earth. "Barbed wire," he gasped. "You pile of stones, you waste, you desolation, I'll stuff you with misery till it comes out of your eyes. I'll change your heart into green grass, and all you love into a sheep. I'll turn you into a bad poet with dreams. I'll set all your toenails growing inward. You mess with me."

Rukh shook his head and sat up, hurling Schmendrick ten feet away. "What are you talking about?" He chuckled. "You can't turn cream into butter." The magician was getting to his feet, but Rukh pushed his back down and sat on him. "I never did like you," he said pleasantly. "You give yourself airs, and you're not very strong." Heavy as night, his hands closed on the magician's throat.

The unicorn did not see. She was out at the farthest cage, where the manticore growled and whimpered and lay flat. She touched the point of her horn to the lock, and was gone to the dragon's cage without looking back. One after another, she set them all free—the satyr, Cerberus, the Midgard Serpent. Their enchantments vanished as they felt their freedom, and they leaped and lumbered and slithered away into the night, once more a lion, an ape, a snake, a crocodile, a joyous dog. None of them thanked the unicorn, and she did not watch them go.

Only the spider paid no mind when the unicorn called softly to her through the open door. Arachne was busy with a web which looked to her as though the

Milky Way had begun to fall like snow. The unicorn whispered, "Weaver, freedom is better, freedom is better," but the spider fled unhearing up and down her iron loom. She never stopped for a moment, even when the unicorn cried, "It's really very attractive, Arachne, but it's not art." The new web drifted down the bars like snow.

Then the wind began. The spiderweb blew across the unicorn's eyes and disappeared. The harpy had begun to beat her wings, calling her power in, as a crouching wave draws sand and water roaring down the beach. A bloodshot moon burst out of the clouds, and the unicorn saw her—swollen gold, her streaming hair kindling, the cold, slow wings shaking the cage. The harpy was laughing.

In the shadow of the unicorn's cage, Rukh and Schmendrick were on their knees. The magician was clutching the heavy ring of keys, and Rukh was rubbing his head and blinking. Their faces were blind with terror as they stared at the rising harpy, and they leaned together in the wind. It blew them against one another, and their bones rang.

The unicorn began to walk toward the harpy's cage. Schmendrick the Magician, tiny and pale, kept opening and closing his mouth at her, and she knew what he was shrieking, though she could not hear him. "She will kill you, she will kill you! Run, you fool, while she's still a prisoner! She will kill you if you set her free!" But the unicorn walked on, following the light of her horn, until she stood before Celaeno, the Dark One.

For an instant the icy wings hung silent in the air, like clouds, and the harpy's old yellow eyes sank into the unicorn's heart and drew her close. "I will kill you if you set me free," the eyes said. "Set me free."

The unicorn lowered her head until her horn touched the lock of the harpy's cage. The door did not swing open, and the iron bars did not thaw into starlight. But the harpy lifted her wings, and the four sides of the cage fell slowly away and down, like the petals of some great flower waking at night. And out of the wreckage the harpy bloomed, terrible and free, screaming, her hair swinging like a sword. The moon withered and fled.

The unicorn heard herself cry out, not in terror but in wonder, "Oh, you are like me!" She reared joyously to meet the harpy's stoop, and her horn leaped up into the wicked wind. The harpy struck once, missed, and swung away, her wings clanging and her breath warm and stinking. She burned overhead, and the unicorn saw herself reflected on the harpy's bronze breast and felt the monster shining from her own body. So they circled one another like a double star, and under the shrunken sky there was nothing real but the two of them. The harpy laughed with delight, and her eyes turned the color of honey. The unicorn knew that she was going to strike again.

The harpy folded her wings and fell like a star—not at the unicorn, but beyond her, passing so close that a single feather drew blood from the unicorn's shoulder; bright claws reaching for the heart of Mommy Fortuna, who was stretching out her own sharp hands as though to welcome the harpy home. "Not alone!" the witch howled triumphantly at both of them. "You never could have freed yourselves alone! I held you!" Then the harpy reached her, and she broke like a dead stick and fell. The harpy crouched on her body, hiding it from sight, and the bronze wings turned red.

The unicorn turned away. Close by, she heard a child's voice telling her that she must run, she must run. It was the magician. His eyes were huge and empty, and his face—always too young—was collapsing into childhood as the unicorn looked at him. "No," she said. "Come with me."

The harpy made a thick, happy sound that melted the magician's knees. But the unicorn said again, "Come with me," and together they walked away from the Midnight Carnival. The moon was gone, but to the magician's eyes the unicorn was the moon, cold and white and very old, lighting his way to safety, or to madness. He followed her, never once looking back, even when he heard the desperate scrambling and skidding of heavy feet, the boom of bronze wings, and Rukh's interrupted scream.

"He ran," the unicorn said. "You must never run from anything immortal. It attracts their attention." Her voice was gentle, and without pity. "Never run," she said. "Walk slowly, and pretend to be thinking of something else. Sing a song, say a poem, do your tricks, but walk slowly and she may not follow. Walk very slowly, magician."

So they fled across the night together, step by step, the tall man in black and the horned white beast. The magician crept as close to the unicorn's light as he dared, for beyond it moved hungry shadows, the shadows of the sounds that the harpy made as she destroyed the little there was to destroy of the Midnight Carnival.

46

moon = imagination, freedom, madness
"
unicorn - maybe can lead past wasteland
or to madness - maybe same thing

## THE LAST UNICORN

But another sound followed them long after these had
faded, followed them into morning on a strange road—
the tiny, dry sound of a spider weeping.

TRANSCENDENTAL EXPERIENCE
- living on higher plane

47

# IV

IKE A NEWBORN CHILD, the magician wept for a long time before he could speak. "The poor old woman," he whispered at last. The unicorn said nothing, and Schmendrick raised his head and stared at her in a strange way. A gray morning rain was beginning to fall, and she shone through it like a dolphin. "No," she said, answering his eyes. "I can never regret."

He was silent, crouched by the road in the rain, drawing his soaked cloak close around his body until he looked like a broken black umbrella. The unicorn waited, feeling the days of her life falling around her with the rain. "I can sorrow," she offered gently, "but it's not the same thing."

When Schmendrick looked at her again he had managed to pull his face together, but it was still struggling to escape from him. "Where will you go now?" he asked. "Where were you going when she took you?"

"I was looking for my people," the unicorn said. "Have you seen them, magician? They are wild and sea-white, like me."

Schmendrik shook his head gravely. "I have never see anyone like you, not while I was awake. There were supposed to be a few unicorns left when I was a

48

boy, but I knew only one man who had ever seen one. They are surely gone, lady, all but you. When you walk, you make an echo where they used to be."

"No," she said. "for others have seen them." It gladdened her to hear that there had still been unicorns as recently as the magician's childhood. She said "A butterfly told me of the Red Bull, and the Witch spoke of King Haggard. So I am going wherever they are to learn whatever they know. Can you tell me where Haggard is king?"

The magician's face almost got away, but he caught it and began to smile very slowly, as though his mouth had turned to iron. He bent it into the proper shape in time, but it was an iron smile. "I can tell you a poem," he said.

> "Where all the hills are lean as knives,
> And nothing grows, not leaves nor lives;
> Where hearts are sour as boiled beer—
> Haggard is the ruler here."

"I will know when I get there, then," she said, thinking that he was mocking her. "Do you know any poems about the Red Bull?"

"There are none," Schmendrick answered. He rose to his feet, pale and smiling. "About King Haggard I know only what I have heard," he said. "He is an old man, stingy as late November, who rules over a barren country by the sea. Some say that the land was green and soft once, before Haggard came, but he touched it and it withered. There is a saying among farmers, when they look on a field lost to fire or locusts or the wind: As 'blighted as Haggard's heart.' They say also that there

Direct reference to T.S. Eliot's wasteland

are no lights in his castle and no fires, and that he sends his men out to steal chickens, and bedsheets, and pies from windowsills. The story has it that the last time King Haggard laughed—"

The unicorn stamped her foot. Schmendrick said, "As for the Red Bull, I know less than I have heard, for I have heard too many tales and each argues with another. The Bull is real, the Bull is a ghost, the Bull is Haggard himself when the sun goes down. The Bull was in the land before Haggard, or it came with him, or it came to him. It protects him from raids and revolutions, and saves him the expense of arming his men. It keeps him a prisoner in his own castle. It is the devil, to whom Haggard has sold his soul. It is the thing he sold his soul to possess. The Bull belongs to Haggard. Haggard belongs to the bull."

The unicorn felt a shiver of sureness spreading through her, widening from the center, like a ripple. In her mind the butterfly piped again, "They passed down all the roads long ago, and the Red Bull ran close behind them and covered their footprints." She saw white forms blowing away in a bellowing wind, and yellow horns shaking. "I will go there," she said. "Magician, I owe you a boon, for you set me free. What would you have of me before I leave you?"

Schmendrick's long eyes were glinting like leaves in the sun. "Take me with you."

She moved away, cool and dancing, and she did not answer. The magician said, "I might be useful. I know the way into Haggard's country, and the languages of the lands between here and there." The unicorn seemed very near to vanishing into the sticky mist, and Schmendrick hurried on. "Besides, no wanderer was ever the worse for a wizard's company, even a unicorn. Remember the tale of the great wizard Nikos. Once, in the woods, he beheld a unicorn sleeping with his head in the lap of a giggling virgin, while three hunters advanced with drawn bows to slay him for his horn. Nikos had only a moment to act. With a word and a wave, he changed the unicorn into a handsome young man, who woke, and seeing the astonished bowmen gaping there, charged upon them and killed them all. His sword was of a twisted, tapering design, and he trampled the bodies when the men were dead."

"And the girl?" the unicorn asked. "Did he kill the girl too?"

"No, he married her. He said she was only an aimless child, angry at her family, and that all she really needed was a good man. Which he was, then and always, for even Nikos could never give him back his first form. He died old and respected—of a surfeit of violets, some say—he never could get enough violets. There were no children."

The story lodged itself somewhere in the unicorn's breath. "The magician did him no service, but great ill," she said softly. "How terrible it would be if all my people had been turned human by well-meaning wizards —exiled, trapped in burning houses. I would sooner find that the Red Bull had killed them all."

"Where you are going now," Schmendrick answered, "few will mean you anything but evil, and a friendly heart—however foolish—may be as welcome as water one day. Take me with you, for laughs, for luck, for the unknown. Take me with you."

The rain faded as he spoke, the sky began to clear, and the wet grass glowed like the inside of a seashell. The unicorn looked away, searching through a fog of kings for one king, and through a snowy glitter of castles and palaces for one built on the shoulders of a bull. "No one has ever traveled with me," she said, "but then no one ever caged me before, or took me for a white mare, or disguised me as myself. Many things seem determined to happen to me for the first time, and your company will surely not be the strangest of them, nor the last. So you may come with me if you like, though I wish you had asked me for some other reward."

Schmendrick smiled sadly. "I thought about it." He looked at his fingers, and the unicorn saw the halfmoon marks where the bars had bitten him. "But you could never have granted my true wish."

There it is, the unicorn thought, feeling the first spidery touch of sorrow on the inside of her skin. That is how it will be to travel with a mortal, all the time. "No," she replied. "I cannot turn you into something you are not, no more than the witch could. I cannot turn you into a true magician."

"I didn't think so," Schmendrick said. "It's all right. Don't worry about it."

"I'm not worrying about it," the unicorn said.

A blue jay swooped low over them on that first day of their journey, said, "Well, I'll be a squab under glass," and flapped straight home to tell his wife about it. She was sitting on the nest, singing to their children in a dreary drone.

*Blue jays?*

"Spiders and sowbugs and beetles and crickets,
  Slugs from the roses and ticks from the thickets,
  Grasshoppers, snails, and a quail's egg or two—
  All to be regurgitated for you.
  Lullaby, lullaby, swindles and schemes,
  Flying's not near as much fun as it seems."

"Saw a unicorn today," the blue jay said as he lit.

"You didn't see any supper, I notice," his wife replied coldly. "I hate a man who talks with his mouth empty."

"Baby, a unicorn!" The jay abandoned his casual air and hopped up and down on the branch. "I haven't seen one of those since the time—"

"You've never seen one," she said. "This is me, remember? I know what you've seen in your life, and what you haven't."

The jay paid no attention. "There was a strange-looking party in black with her," he rattled. "They were going over Cat Mountain. I wonder if they were heading for Haggard's country." He cocked his head to the artistic angle that had first won his wife. "What a vision for old Haggard's breakfast," he marveled. "A unicorn coming to call, bold as you please, rat-tat-tat on his dismal door. I'd give anything to see—"

"I suppose the two of you didn't spend the *whole* day watching unicorns," his wife interrupted with a click of her beak. "At least, I understand that *she* used to be considered quite imaginative in matters of spare time." She advanced on him, her neck feathers ruffling.

"Honey, I haven't even seen her—" the blue jay began, and his wife knew that he hadn't, and wouldn't dare, but she batted him one anyway. She was one woman who knew what to do with a slight moral edge.

The unicorn and the magician walked through the spring, over soft Cat Mountain and down into a violet valley where apple trees grew. Beyond the valley were low hills, as fat and docile as sheep, lowering their heads to sniff at the unicorn in wonder as she moved among them. After these came the slower heights of summer, and the baked plains where the air hung shiny as candy. Together she and Schmendrick forded rivers, scrambled up and down brambly banks and bluffs, and wandered in woods that reminded the unicorn of her home, though they could never resemble it, having known time. So has my forest, now, she thought, but she told herself that it did not matter, that all would be as before when she returned.

At night, while Schmendrick slept the sleep of a hungry, footsore magician, the unicorn crouched awake waiting to see the vast form of the Red Bull come charging out of the moon. At times she caught what she was sure was his smell—a dark, sly reek easing through the night, reaching out to find her. Then she would spring to her feet with a cold cry of readiness, only to find two or three deer gazing at her from a respectful distance. Deer love and envy unicorns. Once, a buck in his second summer, prodded forward by his giggling friends, came quite close to her and mumbled without meeting her eyes, "You are very beautiful. You are just as beautiful as our mothers said."

The unicorn looked silently back at him, knowing that he expected no answer from her. The other deer snickered and whispered, "Go on, go on." Then the buck raised his head and cried out swiftly and joyously, "But I know someone more beautiful than you!" He wheeled and dashed away in the moonlight, and his friends followed him. The unicorn lay down again.

Now and then in their journey they came to a village, and there Schmendrick would introduce himself as a wandering wizard, offering, as he cried in the streets, "to sing for my supper, to bother you just a little bit, to trouble your sleep ever so slightly, and pass on." Few were the towns where he was not invited to stable his beautiful white mare and stay the night, and before the children went to bed he would perform in the market square by lantern light. He never actually attempted any greater magic than making dolls talk and turning soap into sweets, and even this trifling sorcery sometimes slipped from his hands. But the children liked him, and their parents were kindly with supper, and the summer evenings were lithe and soft. Ages after, the unicorn still remembered the strange, chocolate stable smell, and Schmendrick's shadow dancing on walls and doors and chimneys in the leaping light.

In the mornings they went on their way, Schmendrick's pockets full of bread and cheese and oranges, and the unicorn pacing beside him: sea white in the sun, sea green in the dark of the trees. His tricks were forgotten before he was out of sight, but his white mare troubled the nights of many a villager, and there were women who woke weeping from dreams of her.

One evening, they stopped in a plump, comfortable town where even the beggars had double chins and the mice waddled. Schmendrick was immediately asked to

*character - princess on a quest*
*appears 2 B human*
*(mortality)/ | \ (sorrow)*
*laughter*
*quest for King Haggard & the Red Bull*

dinner with the Mayor and several of the rounder Councilmen; and the unicorn, unrecognized as always, was turned loose in a pasture where the grass grew sweet as milk. Dinner was served out of doors, at a table in the square, for the night was warm and the Mayor was pleased to show off his guest. It was an excellent dinner.

During the meal Schmendrick told stories of his life as an errant enchanter, filling it with kings and dragons and noble ladies. He was not lying, merely organizing events more sensibly, and so his tales had a taste of truth even to the canny Councilmen. Not only they, but all manner of folk passing in the street leaned forward to understand the nature of the spell that opened all locks, if properly applied. And there was not a one but lost a breath at sight of the marks on the magician's fingers. "Souvenir of my encounter with a harpy," Schmendrick explained calmly. "They bite."

"And were you never afraid?" a young girl wondered softly. The Mayor made a shooing noise at her, but Schmendrick lit a cigar and smiled at her through the smoke. "Fear and hunger have kept me young," he replied. He looked around the circle of dozing, rumbling Councilmen and winked widely at the girl.

The Mayor was not offended. "It's true," he sighed, caressing his dinner with linked fingers. "We do lead a good life here, or if we don't, I don't know anything about it. I sometimes think that a little fear, a little hunger, might be good for us—sharpen our souls, so to speak. That's why we always welcome strangers with tales to tell and songs to sing. They broaden our out-

*she's seeking what it means to be human*

Schmendrick wants 2 B w/her bcuz he's
attracted to the true magic. He can see
what normal mortals can not see.

### THE LAST UNICORN

The unicorn is the dream of the 60's.

look ... set us to looking inward ..." He yawned and
stretched himself, gurgling.

One of the Councilmen suddenly remarked, "My
word, look at the pasture!" Heavy heads turned on
nodding necks, and all saw the village's cows and sheep
and horses clustered at the far end of the field, staring
at the magician's white mare, who was placidly crop-
ping the cool grass. No animal made a noise. Even the
pigs and geese were as silent as ghosts. A crow called
once, far away, and his cry drifted through the sunset
like a single cinder.

"Remarkable," the Mayor murmured. "Most remarkable."

"Yes, isn't she?" the magician agreed. "If I were to
tell you some of the offers I've had for her—"

"The interesting thing," said the Councilman who
had spoken first, "is that they don't seem to be afraid of
her. They have an air of awe, as though they were
doing her some sort of reverence."

"They see what you have forgotten how to see."
Schmendrick had drunk his share of red wine, and the
young girl was staring at him with eyes both sweeter
and shallower than the unicorn's eyes. He thumped his
glass on the table and told the smiling Mayor, "She is a
rarer creature than you dare to dream. She is a myth, a
memory, a will-o'-the-wish. Wail-o'-the-wisp. If you
remembered, if you hungered—"

His voice was lost in a gust of hoofbeats and the
clamor of children. A dozen horsemen, dressed in autumn rags, came galloping into the square, howling and
laughing, scattering the townsfolk like marbles. They
formed a line and clattered around the square, knocking

The "Robin and his merry men."

over whatever came in their way and shrieking incomprehensible brags and challenges to no one in particular. One rider rose up in his saddle, bent his bow, and shot the weathercock off the church spire; another snatched up Schmendrick's hat, jammed it on his own head, and rode on roaring. Some swung screaming children to their saddlebows, and others contented themselves with wineskins and sandwiches. Their eyes gleamed madly in their shaggy faces, and their laughter was like drums.

The round Mayor stood fast until he caught the eye of the raiders' leader. Then he raised one eyebrow; the man snapped his fingers, and immediately the horses were still and the ragged men as silent as the village animals before the unicorn. They put the children gently on the ground, and gave back most of the wineskins.

"Jack Jingly, if you `please," the Mayor said calmly.

The leader of the horsemen dismounted and walked slowly toward the table where the Councilmen and their guest had dined. He was a huge man, nearly seven feet tall, and at every step he rang and jangled because of the rings and bells and bracelets that were sewn to his patched jerkin. "Evenin', Yer Honor," he said in a gruff chuckle.

"Let's get the business over with," the Mayor told him. "I don't see why you can't come riding in quietly, like civilized people."

"Ah, the boys don't mean no harm, Yer Honor," the giant grumbled good-naturedly. "Cooped up in the greenwood all day, they need a little relaxing, a little

Jack Jingly a parody trick of Robin Head
steals from poor to pay rich for
permission to stay around.

THE LAST UNICORN

catharsis, like. Well, well, to it, eh?" With a sigh, he took a wizened bag of coins from his waist and placed it in the Mayor's open hand. "There you be, Yer Honor," said Jack Jingly. "It ben't much, but we can't spare no more than that."

The Mayor poured the coins into his palm and pushed at them with a fat finger, grunting. "It certainly isn't much," he complained. "It isn't even as much as last month's take, and that was shriveled enough. You're a woeful lot of freebooters, you are."

"It's hard times," Jack Jingly answered sullenly. "We ben't to blame if travelers have no more gold than we. You can't squeeze blood out of a turnip, you know."

"I can," the Mayor said. He scowled savagely and shook his fist at the giant outlaw. "And if you're holding out on me," he shouted, "if you're feathering your own pockets at my expense, I'll squeeze you, my friend, I'll squeeze you to pulp and peel and let the wind take you. Be off now, and tell it to your tattered captain. Away, villains!"

As Jack Jingly turned away, muttering, Schmendrick cleared his throat and said hesitantly, "I'll have my hat, if you don't mind."

The giant stared at him out of bloodshot buffalo eyes, saying nothing. "My hat," Schmendrick requested in a firmer voice. "One of your men took my hat, and it would be wise for him to return it."

"Wise, is it?" grunted Jack Jingly at last. "And who be you, pray, that knows what wisdom is?"

The wine was still leaping in Schmendrick's own eyes. "I am Schmendrick the Magician, and I make a

59

bad enemy," he declared. "I am older than I look, and less amiable. My hat."

Jack Jingly regarded him a few moments longer; then he walked back to his horse, stepped over it, and sat down in the saddle. He rode forward until he was hardly a beard's thickness from the waiting Schmendrick. "Na, then," he boomed, "if you be a magician, do summat tricksy. Turn ma nose green, fill ma saddlebags with snow, disappear ma beard. Show me some magic, or show me your heels." He pulled a rusty dagger from his belt and dangled it by the point, whistling maliciously.

"The magician is my guest," the Mayor warned, but Schmendrick said solemnly, "Very well. On your head be it." Making sure with the edge of his eye that the young girl was watching him, he pointed at the scarecrow crew grinning behind their leader and said something that rhymed. Instantly, his black hat snatched itself from the fingers of the man who held it and floated slowly through the darkening air, silent as an owl. Two women fainted, and the Mayor sat down. The outlaws cried out in children's voices.

Down the length of the square sailed the black hat, as far as a horse trough where it dipped low and scooped itself full of water. Then, almost invisible in the shadows, it came drifting back, apparently aiming straight for the unwashed head of Jack Jingly. He covered himself with his hands, muttering, "Na, na, call it off," and even his own men snickered in anticipation. Schmendrick smiled triumphantly and snapped his fingers to hasten the hat.

But as it neared the outlaw leader the hat's flight

began to curve, gradually at first, and then much more sharply as it bent toward the Councilmen's table. The Mayor had just time to lunge to his feet before the hat settled itself comfortably on his head. Schmendrick ducked in time, but a couple of the closer Councilmen were slightly splattered.

In the roar of laughter—varyingly voluntary—that went up, Jack Jingly leaned from his horse and swept up Schmendrick the Magician, who was trying to dry the spluttering Mayor with the tablecloth. "I misdoubt ye'll be asked for encores," the giant bellowed in his ear. "You'd best come with us." He threw Schmendrick face down across his saddlebow and galloped away, followed by his shabby cohorts. Their snorts and belches and guffaws lingered in the square long after the sound of hooves had died away.

Men came running to ask the Mayor if they should pursue to rescue the magician, but he shook his wet head, saying, "I hardly think it will be necessary. If our guest is the man he claims to be, he should be able to take care of himself quite well. And if he isn't—why then, an imposter taking advantage of our hospitality has no claim on us for assistance. No, no, never mind about him."

Creeks were running down his jowls to join the brooks of his neck and the river of his shirt front, but he turned his placid gaze toward the pasture where the magician's white mare glimmered in the darkness. She was trotting back and forth before the fence, making no sound. The Mayor said softly, "I think it might be well to take good care of our departed friend's mount, since he evidently prized her so highly." He sent two men to

## THE LAST UNICORN

the pasture with instructions to rope the mare and put her in the strongest stall of his own stable.

But the men had not yet reached the pasture gate when the white mare jumped the fence and was gone into the night like a falling star. The two men stood where they were for a time, not heeding the Mayor's commands to come back; and neither ever said, even to the other, why he stared after the magician's mare so long. But now and then after that, they laughed with wonder in the middle of very serious events, and so came to be considered frivolous sorts.

frivolous sorts because they saw (for a moment) the unicorn.

# V

**A**LL THAT SCHMENDRICK REMEMBERED later of
his wild ride with the outlaws was the wind, the
saddle's edge, and the laughter of the jingling
giant. He was too busy brooding over the ending of his
hat trick to notice much else. Too much english, he
suggested to himself. Overcompensation. But he shook
his head, which was difficult in his position. The magic
knows what it wants to do, he thought, bouncing as the
horse dashed across a creek. But I never know what it
knows. Not at the right time, anyway. I'd write it a
letter, if I knew where it lived.

Brush and branches raked his face, and owls hooted
in his ears. The horses had slowed to a trot, then to a
walk. A high, trembling voice called out, "Halt and
give the password!"

"Damme, here we go," Jack Jingly muttered. He
scratched his head with a sound like sawing, raised his
voice, and answered, "A short life and a merry one,
here in the sweet greenwood; jolly comrades united, to
victory plighted—"

"Liberty," the thin voice corrected. "To liberty plighted. The _I_ sound makes all the difference."

63

"Thank 'ee. To liberty plighted. Comrades united— na, na, I said that. A short life and a merry one, jolly comrades—na, that's not it." Jack Jingly scratched his head again and groaned. "To liberty plighted—gi'me a little help, will ye?"

"All for one and one for all," the voice said obligingly. "Can you get the rest yourself?"

"All for one and one for all—I haven't!" the giant shouted. "All for one and one for all, united we stand, divided we fall." He kicked his horse and started on again.

An arrow squealed out of the dark, sliced a wedge from his ear, nicked the horse of the man riding behind him, and skittered away like a bat. The outlaws scattered to the safety of the trees, and Jack Jingly yelled with rage, "Damn your eyes, I gave the password ten times over! Let me only get my hands on 'ee—"

"We changed the password while you were gone, Jack," came the voice of the sentry. "It was too hard to remember."

"Ah, you changed the password, did ye?" Jack Jingly dabbed at his bleeding ear with a fold of Schmendrick's cloak. "And how was I to know that, ye brainless, tripeless, liverless get?"

"Don't get mad, Jack," the sentry answered soothingly. "You see, it doesn't really matter if you don't know the new password, because it's so simple. You just call like a giraffe. The captain thought of it himself."

"Call like a giraffe." The giant swore till even the horses fidgeted with embarrassment. "Ye ninny, a giraffe makes no sound at all. The captain might as well have us call like a fish or a butterfly."

64

"I know. That way, nobody can forget the password, even you. Isn't the captain clever?"

"There's no limit to the man," Jack Jingly said wonderingly. "But see here, what's to keep a ranger or one of the king's men from calling like a giraffe when ye hail him?"

"Aha," the sentry chuckled. "That's where the cleverness of it is. You have to give the call three times. Two long and one short."

Jack Jingly sat silent on his horse, rubbing his ear. "Two long and one short," he sighed presently. "Awell, 'tis no more foolish than the time he'd have no password at all, and shot any who answered the challenge. Two long and one short, right." He rode on through the trees, and his men trailed after him.

Voices murmured somewhere ahead, sullen as robbed bees. As they drew nearer Schmendrick thought he could make out a woman's tone among them. Then his cheek felt firelight, and he looked up. They had halted in a small clearing where another ten or twelve men sat around a campfire, fretting and grumbling. The air smelled of burned beans.

A freckled, red-haired man, dressed in somewhat richer rags than the rest, strode forward to greet them. "Well, Jack," he cried. "Who is't you bring us, comrade or captive?" Over his shoulder he called to someone, "Add some more water to the soup, love; there's company."

"I don't know what he is maself," Jack Jingly rumbled. He began to tell the story of the Mayor and the hat, but he had hardly reached the roaring descent upon the town when he was interrupted by a thin thorn of a woman who came pushing through the ring of men to shrill, "I'll not have it, Cully, the soup's no thicker than sweat as it is!" She had a pale, bony face with fierce, tawny eyes, and hair the color of dead grass.

"And who's this long lout?" she asked, inspecting Schmendrick as though he were something she had found sticking to the sole of her shoes. "He's no townsman. I don't like the look of him. Slit his wizard."

She had meant to say either "weasand" or "gizzard," and had said both, but the coincidence trailed down Schmendrick's spine like wet seaweed. He slid off Jack Jingly's horse and stood before the outlaw captain. "I am Schmendrick the Magician," he announced, swirling his cloak with both hands until it billowed feebly. "And are you truly the famous Captain Cully of the greenwood, boldest of the bold and freest of the free?"

A few of the outlaws snickered, and the woman groaned. "I knew it," she declared. "Gut him, Cully, from gills to guilt, before he does you the way the last one did." But the captain bowed proudly, showing an eddy of baldness on his crown, and answered, "That am I. He who hunts me for my head shall find a fearful foe, but he who seeks me as a friend may find me friend enow. How do you come here, sir?"

"On my stomach," said Schmendrick, "and unintentionally, but in friendship nonetheless. Though your leman doubts it," he added nodding at the thin woman. She spat on the ground.

Captain Cully grinned and laid his arm warily along the woman's sharp shoulders. "Ah, that's only Molly Grue's way," he explained. "She guards me better than I do myself. I am generous and easy; to the point of extravagance, perhaps—an open hand to all fugitives from tyranny, that's my motto. It is only natural that Molly should become suspicious, pinched, dour, prematurely old, even a touch tyrannical. The bright balloon needs the knot at one end, eh, Molly? But she's a good heart, a good heart." The woman shrugged herself away from him, but the captain did not turn his head. "You are welcome here, sir sorcerer," he told Schmendrick. "Come to the fire and tell us your tale. How do they speak of me in your country? What have you heard of dashing Captain Cully and his band of freemen? Have a taco."

Schmendrick accepted the place by the fire, graciously declined the gelid morsel, and replied, "I have heard that you are the friend of the helpless and the enemy of the mighty, and that you and your merry men lead a joyous life in the forest, stealing from the rich and giving to the poor. I know the tale of how you and Jack Jingly cracked one another's crowns with quarterstaves and became blood brothers thereby; and how you saved your Molly from marriage to the rich old man her father had chosen for her." In fact, Schmendrick had never heard of Captain Cully before that very evening, but he had a good grounding in Anglo-Saxon folklore and knew the type. "And of course," he hazarded, "there was a certain wicked king—"

"Haggard, rot and ruin him!" Cully cried. "Aye, there's not one here but's been done wrong by old King Haggard—driven from his rightful land, robbed of his rank and rents, skinned out of his patrimony. They live only for revenge—mark you, magician—and one day Haggard will pay such a reckoning—"

A score of shaggy shadows hissed assent, but Molly Grue's laughter fell like hail, rattling and stinging. "Mayhap he will," she mocked, "but it won't be to such chattering cravens he'll pay it. His castle rots and totters more each day, and his men are too old to stand up in armor, but he'll rule forever, for all Captain Cully dares."

Schmendrick raised an eyebrow, and Cully flushed radish-red. "You must understand," he mumbled. "King Haggard has this Bull—"

"Ah, the Red Bull, the Red Bull!" Molly hooted. "I tell you what, Cully, after all these years in the wood with you I've come to think the Bull's nought but the pet name you give your cowardice. If I hear that fable once more, I'll go and down old Haggard myself, and know you for a—"

"Enough!" Cully roared. "Not before strangers!" He tugged at his sword and Molly opened her arms to it, still laughing. Around the fire, greasy hands twiddled dagger hilts and longbows seemed to string themselves, but Schmendrick spoke up then, seeking to salvage Cully's sinking vanity. He hated family scenes.

"They sing a ballad of you in my country," he began. "I forget just how it goes—"

Captain Cully spun like a cat ambushing its own tail. "Which one?" he demanded.

"I don't know," Schmendrick answered, taken aback. "Is there more than one?"

"Aye, indeed!" Cully cried, glowing and growing, as though pregnant with his pride. "Willie Gentle! Willie Gentle! Where is the lad?"

A lank-haired youth with a lute and pimples sham-

bled up. "Sing one of my exploits for the gentleman,"
Captain Cully ordered him. "Sing the one about how
you joined my band. I've not heard it since Tuesday
last."

The minstrel sighed, struck a chord, and began to
sing in a wobbly countertenor:

"Oh, it was Captain Cully came riding home
  From slaying of the king's gay deer,
  When whom should he spy but a pale young man,
  Came drooping o'er the lea?

" 'What news, what news, my pretty young man?
  What ails ye, that ye sigh so deep?
  Is it for the loss of your lady fair?
  Or are ye but scabbit in your greep?'

" 'I am nae scabbit, whatever that means,
  And my greep is as well as a greep may be,
  But I do sigh for my lady fair
  Whom my three brothers ha' riven from me.'

" 'I am Captain Cully of the sweet greenwood,
  And the men at my call are fierce and free.
  If I do rescue your lady fair,
  What service will ye render me?'

" 'If ye do rescue my lady fair,
  I will break your nose, ye silly auld gowk.
  But she wore an emerald at her throat,
  Which my three brothers also took.'

"Then the captain has gone to the three bold thieves,
  And he's made his sword baith to shiver and sing.
  'Ye may keep the lass, but I'll hae the stane,
  For it's fit for the crown of a royal king.' "

"Now comes the best part," Cully whispered to Schmendrick. He was bouncing eagerly on his toes, hugging himself.

"Then it's three cloaks off, and it's three swords out,
And it's three swords whistling like the tea.
'By the faith of my body,' says Captain Cully,
'Now ye shall have neither the stane nor she.'

"And he's driven them up, and he's driven them down,
And he's driven them to and fro like sheep—"

"Like sheep," Cully breathed. He rocked and hummed and parried three swords with his forearm for the remaining seventeen stanzas of the song, rapturously oblivious to Molly's mockery and the restlessness of his men. The ballad ended at last, and Schmendrick applauded loudly and earnestly, complimenting Willie Gentle on his right-hand technique.

"I call it Alan-a-Dale picking," the minstrel answered.

He would have expounded further, but Cully interrupted him, saying, "Good, Willie, good boy, now play the others." He beamed at what Schmendrick hoped was an expression of pleased surprise. "I said that there were several songs about me. There are thirty-one, to be exact, though none are in the Child collection just at present—" His eyes widened suddenly, and he grasped the magician's shoulders. "You wouldn't be Mr. Child himself, now would you?" he demanded. "He often goes seeking ballads, so I've heard, disguised as a plain man—"

Schmendrick shook his head. "No, I'm very sorry, really."

The captain sighed and released him. "It doesn't matter," he murmured. "One always hopes, of course, even now—to be collected, to be verified, annotated, to have variant versions, even to have one's authenticity doubted ... well, well, never mind. Sing the other songs, Willie lad. You'll need the practice one day, when you're field-recorded."

The outlaws grumbled and scuffed, kicking at stones. A hoarse voice bawled from a safe shadow, "Na, Willie, sing us a true song. Sing us one about Robin Hood."

"Who said that?" Cully's loosened sword clacked in its sheath as he turned from side to side. His face suddenly seemed as pale and weary as a used lemon drop.

"I did," said Molly Grue, who hadn't. "The men are bored with ballads of your bravery, captain darling. Even if you did write them all yourself."

Cully winced and stole a side glance at Schmendrick. "They can still be folk songs, can't they, Mr. Child?" he asked in a low, worried voice. "After all—"

"I'm not Mr. Child," Schmendrick said. "Really I'm not."

"I mean, you can't leave epic events to the people. They get everything wrong."

An aging rogue in tattered velvet now slunk forward. "Captain, if we're to have folk songs, and I suppose we must, then we feel they ought to be true songs about real outlaws, not this lying life we live. No

71

offense, captain, but we're really not very merry, when all's said—"

"I'm merry twenty-four hours a day, Dick Fancy," Cully said coldly. "That is a fact."

"And we don't steal from the rich and give to the poor," Dick Fancy hurried on. "We steal from the poor because they can't fight back—most of them—and the rich take from us because they could wipe us out in a day. We don't rob the fat, greedy Mayor on the highway; we pay him tribute every month to leave us alone. We never carry off proud bishops and keep them prisoner in the wood, feasting and entertaining them, because Molly hasn't any good dishes, and besides, we just wouldn't be very stimulating company for a bishop. When we go to the fair in disguise, we never win at the archery or at singlestick. We do get some nice compliments on our disguises, but no more than that."

"I sent a tapestry to the judging once," Molly remembered. "It came in fourth. Fifth. A knight at vigil—everyone was doing vigils that year." Suddenly she was scrubbing her eyes with horny knuckles. "Damn you, Cully."

"What, what?" he yelled in exasperation. "Is it my fault you didn't keep up with your weaving? Once you had your man, you let all your accomplishments go. You don't sew or sing any more, you haven't illuminated a manuscript in years—and what happened to that viola da gamba I got you?" He turned to Schmendrick. "We might as well be married, the way she's gone to seed." The magician nodded fractionally, and looked away.

"And as for righting wrongs and fighting for civil

72

liberties, that sort of thing," Dick Fancy said, "it wouldn't be so bad—I mean, I'm not the crusader type myself, some are and some aren't—but then we have to sing those songs about wearing Lincoln green and aiding the oppressed. We don't, Cully, we turn them in for the reward, and those songs are just embarrassing, that's all, and there's the truth of it."

Captain Cully folded his arms, ignoring the outlaws' snarls of agreement. "Sing the songs, Willie."

"I'll not." The minstrel would not raise a hand to touch his lute. "And you never fought my brothers for any stone, Cully! You wrote them a letter, which you didn't sign—"

Cully drew back his arm, and blades blinked among the men as though someone had blown on a heap of coals. At this point Schmendrick stepped forward again, smiling urgently. "If I may offer an alternative," he suggested, "why not let your guest earn his night's lodging by amusing you? I can neither sing nor play, but I have my own accomplishments, and you may not have seen their like."

Jack Jingly agreed immediately, saying, "Aye, Cully, a magician! 'Twould be a rare treat for the lads." Molly Grue grumbled some savage generalization about wizards as a class, but the men shouted with quick delight, throwing one another into the air. The only reluctance was shown by Captain Cully himself, who protested sadly, "Yes, but the songs. Mr. Child must hear the songs."

"And so I will," Schmendrick assured him. "Later." Cully brightened then and cried to his men to give way and make room. They sprawled and squatted in the shadows, watching with sprung grins as Schmendrick began to run through the old flummeries with which he had entertained the country folk at the Midnight Carnival. It was paltry magic, but he thought it diverting enough for such a crew as Cully's.

But he had judged them too easily. They applauded his rings and scarves, his ears full of goldfish and aces, with a proper politeness but without wonder. Offering no true magic, he drew no magic back from them; and when a spell failed—as when, promising to turn a duck into a duke for them to rob, he produced a handful of duke cherries—he was clapped just as kindly and vacantly as though he had succeeded. They were a perfect audience.

Cully smiled impatiently, and Jack Jingly dozed, but it startled the magician to see the disappointment in Molly Grue's restless eyes. Sudden anger made him laugh. He dropped seven spinning balls that had been glowing brighter and brighter as he juggled them (on a good evening, he could make them catch fire), let go all his hated skills, and closed his eyes. "Do as you will," he whispered to the magic. "Do as you will."

It sighed through him, beginning somewhere secret—in his shoulderblade, perhaps, or in the marrow of his shinbone. His heart filled and tautened like a sail, and something moved more surely in his body than he ever had. It spoke with his voice, commanding. Weak with power, he sank to his knees and waited to be Schmendrick again.

I wonder what I did. I did something.

He opened his eyes. Most of the outlaws were chuckling and tapping their temples, glad of the chance to

mock him. Captain Cully had risen, anxious to pro-
nounce that part of the entertainment ended. Then
Molly Grue cried out in a soft, shaking voice, and all
turned to see what she saw. A man came walking into
the clearing.

He was dressed in green, but for a brown jerkin and
a slanting brown cap with a woodcock's feather in it.
He was very tall, too tall for a living man: the great
bow slung over his shoulder looked as long as Jack
Jingly, and his arrows would have made spears or staves
for Captain Cully. Taking no notice at all of the still,
shabby forms by the fire, he strode through the night
and vanished, with no sound of breath or footfall.

After him came others, one at a time or two together,
some conversing, many laughing, but none making any
sound. All carried longbows and all wore green, save
one who came clad in scarlet to his toes, and another
gowned in a friar's brown habit, his feet in sandals and
his enormous belly contained by a rope belt. One
played a lute and sang silently as he walked.

"Alan-a-Dale." It was raw Willie Gentle. "*Look* at
those changes." His voice was as naked as a baby
bird.

Effortlessly proud, graceful as giraffes (even the tallest among them, a kind-eyed Blunderbore), the bowmen moved across the clearing. Last, hand in hand,
came a man and a woman. Their faces were as beautiful as though they had never known fear. The woman's
heavy hair shone with a secret, like a cloud that hides
the moon.

"Oh," said Molly Grue. "Marian."

"Robin Hood is a myth," Captain Cully said nervously, "a classic example of the heroic folk-figures synthe-sized out of need. John Henry is another. Men have to have heroes, but no man can ever be as big as the need, and so a legend grows around a grain of truth, like a pearl. Not that it isn't a remarkable trick, of course."

It was the seedy dandy Dick Fancy who moved first. All the figures but the last two had passed into the darkness when he rushed after them, calling, hoarsely, "Robin, Robin, Mr. Hood sir, wait for me!" Neither the man nor the woman turned, but every man of Cully's band—saving only Jack Jingly and the captain himself—ran to the clearing's edge, tripping and trampling one another, kicking the fire so that the clearing churned with shadows. "Robin!" they shouted; and "Marian, Scarlet, Little John—come back! Come back!" Schmen-drick began to laugh, tenderly and helplessly.

Over their voices, Captain Cully screamed, "Fools, fools and children! It was a lie, like all magic! There is no such person as Robin Hood!" But the outlaws, wild with loss, went crashing into the woods after the shining archers, stumbling over logs, falling through thorn bushes, wailing hungrily as they ran.

Only Molly Grue stopped and looked back. Her face was burning white.

"Nay, Cully, you have it backward," she called to him. "There's no such a person as you, or me, or any of us. Robin and Marian are real, and we are the legend!" Then she ran on, crying, "Wait, wait!" like the others, leaving Captain Cully and Jack Jingly to stand in the trampled firelight and listen to the magician's laugh-ter.

Schmendrick hardly noticed when they sprang on

him and seized his arms; nor did he flinch when Cully pricked his ribs with a dagger, hissing, "That was a dangerous diversion, Mr. Child, and rude as well. You could have said you didn't want to hear the songs." The dagger twitched deeper.

Far away, he heard Jack Jingly growl, "He's na Child, Cully, nor is he any journeyman wizard, neither. I know him now. He's Haggard's son, the prince Lír, as foul as his father and doubtless handy with the black arts. Hold your hand, captain—he's no good to us dead." accused of being Haggard's son

Cully's voice drooped. "Are you sure, Jack? He seemed such a pleasant fellow."

"Pleasant fool, ye mean. Aye, Lír has that air, I've heard tell. He plays the gormless innocent, but he's the devil for deception. The way he gave out to be this Child cove, just to get you off your guard."

"I wan't off my guard, Jack," Cully protested. "Not for a moment. I may have seemed to be, but I'm very deceptive myself."

"And the way he called up Robin Hood to fill the lads with longing and turn them against you. Ah, but he gave himself away that time, and now he'll bide with us though his father send the Red Bull to free him." Cully caught his breath at that, but the giant stretched around it. Schmendrick giggled gently all time that night and bore him to a great tree, where he bound him with his face to the trunk and his arms stretched around it. Schmendrick giggled gently all through the operation, and made matters easier by hugging the tree as fondly as a new bride.

"There," Jack Jingly said at last. "Do ye guard him

the night, Cully, whiles I sleep, and in the morning it's me to old Haggard to see what his boy's worth to him. Happen we'll all be gentlemen of leisure in a month's time."

"What of the men?" Cully asked worriedly. "Will they come back, do you think?"

The giant yawned and turned away. "They'll be back by morning, sad and sneezing, and ye'll have to be easy with them for a bit. They'll be back, for they'm not the sort to trade something for nothing, and no more am I. Robin Hood might have stayed for us if we were. Good night to ye, captain."

There was no sound when he was gone but crickets, and Schmendrick's soft chuckling to the tree. The fire faded, and Cully turned in circles, sighing as each ember went out. Finally he sat down on a stump and addressed the captive magician.

"Haggard's son you may be," he mused, "and not the collector Child, as you claim. But whoever you are, you know very well that Robin Hood is the fable and I am the reality. No ballads will accumulate around my name unless I write them myself; no children will read of my adventures in their schoolbooks and play at being me after school. And when the professors prowl through the old tales, and scholars sift the old songs to learn if Robin Hood ever truly lived, they will never, never find my name, not till they crack the world for the grain of its heart. But you know, and therefore I am going to sing you the songs of Captain Cully. He was a good, gay rascal who stole from the rich and gave to the poor. In their gratitude, the people made up these simple verses about him."

Whereupon he sang them all, including the one that Willie Gentle had sung for Schmendrick. He paused often to comment on the varying rhyhm patterns, the assonantal rhymes, and the modal melodies. STOP

# VI

APTAIN CULLY fell asleep thirteen stanzas into
the nineteenth song, and Schmendrick—who had
stopped laughing somewhat sooner—promptly
set about trying to free himself. He strained against his
bonds with all his strength, but they held fast. Jack
Jingly had wrapped him in enough rope to rig a small
schooner, and tied knots the size of skulls.

"Gently, gently," he counseled himself. "No man
with the power to summon Robin Hood—indeed, to
create him—can be bound for long. A word, a wish,
and this tree must be an acorn on a branch again, this
rope be green in a marsh." But he knew before he
called on it that whatever had visited him for a moment
was gone again, leaving only an ache where it had
been. He felt like an abandoned chrysalis.

"Do as you will," he said softly. Captain Cully
roused at his voice, and sang the fourteenth stanza.

> " 'There are fifty swords without the house, and
>        fifty more within,
>    And I do fear me, captain, they are like to do
>        us in.'

'Ha' done, ha' done,' says Captain Cully, 'and
     never fear again,
For they may be a hundred swords, but we are
     seven men.'"

"I hope you get slaughtered," the magician told him,
but Cully was asleep again. Schmendrick attempted a
few simple spells for escaping, but he could not use his
hands, and he had no more heart for tricks. What
happened instead was that the tree fell in love with him
and began to murmur fondly of the joy to be found in
the eternal embrace of a red oak. "Always, always," it
sighed, "faithfulness beyond any man's deserving. I will
keep the color of your eyes when no other in the world
remembers your name. There is no immortality but a
tree's love."

"I'm engaged," Schmendrick excused himself. "To a
western larch. Since childhood. Marriage by contract, no
choice in the matter. Hopeless. Our story is never to
be."

A gust of fury shook the oak, as though a storm were
coming to it alone. "Galls and fireblight on her!" it
whispered savagely. "Damned softwood, cursed conifer,
deceitful evergreen, she'll never have you! We will
perish together, and all trees shall treasure our trag-
edy!"

Along his length Schmendrick could feel the tree
heaving like a heart, and he feared that it might actually split in two with rage. The ropes were growing
steadily tighter around him, and the night was beginning to turn red and yellow. He tried to explain to the
oak that love was generous precisely because it could

never be immortal, and then he tried to yell for Captain Cully; but he could only make a small, creaking sound, like a tree. "She means well," he thought, and gave himself up for loved.

Then the ropes went slack as he lunged against them, and he fell to the ground on his back, wriggling for air. The unicorn stood over him, dark as blood in his darkened vision. She touched him with her horn.

When he could rise she turned away, and the magician followed her, wary of the oak, though it was once again as still as any tree that had never loved. The sky was still black, but it was a watery darkness through which Schmendrick could see the violet dawn swimming. Hard silver clouds were melting as the sky grew warm; shadows dulled, sounds lost their shape, and shapes had not yet decided what they were going to be that day. Even the wind wondered about itself.

"Did you see me?" he asked the unicorn. "Were you watching, did you see what I made?"

"Yes," she answered. "It was true magic."

The loss came back, cold and bitter as a sword. "It's gone now," he said. "I had it—it had me—but it's gone now. I couldn't hold it." The unicorn floated on before him, silent as a feather.

Close by, a familiar voice said, "Leaving us so early, magician? The men will be sorry they missed you." He turned and saw Molly Grue leaning against a tree. Dress and dirty hair tattered alike, bare feet bleeding and beslimed, she gave him a bat's grin. "Surprise," she said. "It's Maid Marian."

Then she saw the unicorn. She neither moved nor spoke, but her tawny eyes were suddenly big with tears.

*Molly knows the unicorn - she has called*
*for her before.*
*Molly is a realist - not a victim of illusions*

For a long moment she did not move; then each fist seized a handful of her hem, and she warped her knees into a kind of trembling crouch. Her ankles were crossed and her eyes were lowered, but for all that it took Schmendrick another moment to realize that Molly Grue was curtsying.

He burst out laughing, and Molly sprang up, red from hairline to throat-hollow. "Where have you been?" she cried. "Damn you, where have you been?" She took a few steps toward Schmendrick, but she was looking beyond him, at the unicorn.

When she tried to get by, the magician stood in her way. "You don't talk like that," he told her, still uncertain that Molly had recognized the unicorn. "Don't you know how to behave, woman? You don't curtsy, either."

But Molly pushed him aside and went up to the unicorn, scolding her as though she were a strayed milk cow. *"Where have you been?"* Before the whiteness and the shining horn, Molly shrank to a shrilling beetle, but this time it was the unicorn's old dark eyes that looked down.

"I am here now," she said at last.

Molly laughed with her lips flat. "And what good is it to me that you're here now? Where were you twenty years ago, ten years ago? How dare you, how dare you come to me now, when I am *this?*" With a flap of her hand she summed herself up: barren face, desert eyes, and yellowing heart. "I wish you had never come, why do you come now?" The tears began to slide down the sides of her nose.

The unicorn made no reply, and Schmendrick said, "She is the last. She is the last unicorn in the world."

"She would be." Molly sniffed. "It would be the last unicorn in the world that came to Molly Grue." She reached up then to lay her hand on the unicorn's cheek; but both of them flinched a little, and the touch came to rest on the swift, shivering place under the jaw. Molly said, "It's all right. I forgive you."

"Unicorns are not to be forgiven." The magician felt himself growing giddy with jealousy, not only of the touch but of something like a secret that was moving between Molly and the unicorn. "Unicorns are for beginnings," he said, "for innocence and purity, for newness. Unicorns are for young girls."

Molly was stroking the unicorn's throat as timidly as though she were blind. She dried her grimy tears on the white mane. "You don't know much about unicorns," she said.

The sky was jade-gray now, and the trees that had been drawn on the dark a moment ago were real trees again, hissing in the dawn wind. Schmendrick said coldly, looking at the unicorn. "We must go."

Molly agreed promptly. "Aye, before the men stumble on us and slit your throat for cheating them, the poor lads." She looked over her shoulder. "I had some things I wanted to take, but they don't matter now. I'm ready."

Schmendrick barred her way again as he stepped forward. "You can't come with us. We are on a quest." His voice and eyes were as stern as he could make them, but he could feel his nose being bewildered. He had never been able to discipline his nose.

84

Molly has a knowledge of unicorns and she explains to Schmendrick that the unicorn does not need her or him.

Molly's own face closed like a castle against him, trundling out the guns and slings and caldrons of boiling lead. "And who are you to say *'we'?*"

"I'm her guide," the magician said importantly. The unicorn made a soft, wondering sound, like a cat calling her kittens. Molly laughed aloud, and made it back.

"You don't know much about unicorns," she repeated. "She's letting you travel with her, though I can't think why, but she has no need of you. She doesn't need me either, heaven knows, but she'll take me too. Ask her." The unicorn made the soft sound again, and the castle of Molly's face lowered the drawbridge and threw wide even its deepest keep. "Ask her," she said.

Schmendrick knew the unicorn's answer by the sinking in his heart. He meant to be wise, but then his envy and emptiness hurt him, and he heard himself cry out sadly, "Never! I forbid it—I, Schmendrick the Magician!" His voice darkened, and even his nose grew menacing. "Be wary of wousing a wizard's wrath! Rousing. If I chose to turn you into a frog—"

"I should laugh myself sick," said Molly Grue pleasantly. "You're handy with fairy tales, but you can't turn cream into butter." Her eyes gleamed with a sudden mean understanding. "Have sense, man," she said. "What were you going to do with the last unicorn in the world—keep her in a cage?"

The magician turned away to keep Molly from seeing his face. He did not look directly at the unicorn, but stole small sights of her as stealthily as though he could be made to put them back. White and secret, morning-horned, she regarded him with piercing gentleness, but he could not touch her. He said to the

85

thin woman, "You don't even know where we are bound."

"Do you think it matters to me?" Molly asked. She made the cat sound once more.

Schmendrick said, "We are journeying to King Haggard's country, to find the Red Bull."

Molly's skin was frightened for a moment, whatever her bones believed or her heart knew; but then the unicorn breathed softly into her cupped hand, and Molly smiled as she closed her fingers on the warmth.

"Well, you're going the wrong way," she said.

The sun was rising as she led them back the way they had come, past Cully, still slumped asleep on his stump, across the clearing, and away. The men were returning: dead branches cracked close at hand, and brush broke with a splashing sound. Once they had to crouch among thorns while two of Cully's weary rogues limped by, wondering bitterly whether the vision of Robin Hood had been real or not.

"I smelled them," the first man was saying. "Eyes are easy to deceive, and cheats by nature, but surely no shadow has a smell?"

"The eyes are perjurors, right enough," grunted the second man, who seemed to be wearing a swamp. "But do you truly trust the testimony of your ears, of your nose, of the root of your tongue? Not I, my friend. The universe lies to our senses, and they lie to us, and how can we ourselves be anything but liars? For myself, I trust neither message nor messenger; neither what I am told, nor what I see. There may be truth somewhere, but it never gets down to me."

"Ah," said the first man with a black grin. "But you

86

came running with the rest of us to go with Robin Hood, and you hunted for him all night, crying and calling like the rest of us. Why not save yourself the trouble, if you know better?"

"Well, you never know," the other answered thickly, spitting mud. "I could be wrong."

There were a prince and a princess sitting by a stream in a wooded valley. Their seven servants had set up a scarlet canopy beneath a tree, and the royal young couple ate a box lunch to the accompaniment of lutes and theorbos. They hardly spoke a word to one another until they had finished the meal, and then the princess sighed and said, "Well, I suppose I'd best get the silly business over with." The prince began to read a magazine. reference to the future

"You might at least—" said the princess, but the prince kept on reading. The princess made a sign to two of the servants, who began to play an older music on their lutes. Then she took a few steps on the grass, held up a bridle bright as butter, and called, "Here, unicorn, here! Here, my pretty, here to me! Comecomecome-comecome!"

The prince snickered. "It's not your chickens you're calling, you know," he remarked without looking up. "Why don't you sing something, instead of clucking like that?"

"Well, I'm doing the best I can," the princess cried. "I've never called one of these things before." But after a little silence, she began to sing.

> "I am a king's daughter,
> And if I cared to care,

The moon that has no mistress
Would flutter in my hair.
No one dares to cherish
What I choose to crave.
Never have I hungered,
That I did not have.

"I am a king's daughter,
And I grow old within
The prison of my person,
The shackles of my skin.
And I would run away
And beg from door to door,
Just to see your shadow
Once, and never more."

So she sang, and sang again, and then she called, "Nice unicorn, pretty, pretty, pretty," for a little longer, and then she said angrily, "Well, I've done as much as I'll do. I'm going home."

The prince yawned and folded his magazine. "You satisfied custom well enough," he told her, "and no one expected more than that. It was just a formality. Now we can be married."

"Yes," the princess said, "now we can be married." The servants began to pack everything away again, while the two with the lutes played joyous wedding music. The princess's voice was a little sad and defiant as she said, "If there really were such things as unicorns, one would have come to me. I called as sweetly as anyone could, and I had the golden bridle. And of course I am pure and untouched."

"For all of me, you are," the prince answered indifferently. "As I say, you satisfy custom. You don't satisfy my father, but then neither do I. That would take a unicorn." He was tall, and his face was as soft and pleasant as a marshmallow.

When they and their retinue were gone, the unicorn came out of the wood, followed by Molly and the magician, and took up her journey again. A long time later, wandering in another country where there were no streams and nothing green, Molly asked her why she had not gone to the princess's song. Schmendrick drew near to listen to the answer, though he stayed on his side of the unicorn. He never walked on Molly's side.

The unicorn said, "That king's daughter would never have run away to see my shadow. If I had shown myself, and she had known me, she would have been more frightened than if she had seen a dragon, for no one makes promises to a dragon. I remember that once it never mattered to me whether or not princesses meant what they sang. I went to them all and laid my head in their laps, and a few of them rode on my back, though most were afraid. But I have no time for them now, princesses or kitchenmaids. I have no time."

Molly said something strange then, for a woman who never slept a night through without waking many times to see if the unicorn was still there, and whose dreams were all of golden bridles and gentle young thieves. "It's the princesses who have no time," she said. "The sky spins and drags everything along with it, princesses and magicians and poor Cully and all, but you stand still. You never see anything just once. I wish you could be a princess for a little while, or a flower, or a duck. Something that can't wait."

Molly has joined the journey.

She sang a verse of a doleful, limping song, halting after each line as she tried to recall the next.

"Who has choices need not choose.
We must, who have none.
We can love but what we lose—
What is gone is gone."

Schmendrick peered over the unicorn's back into Molly's territory. "Where did you hear that song?" he demanded. It was the first he had spoken to her since the dawn when she joined the journey. Molly shook her head.

"I don't remember. I've known it a long time."

The land had grown leaner day by day as they traveled on, and the faces of the folk they met had grown bitter with the brown grass; but to the unicorn's eyes Molly was becoming a softer country, full of pools and caves, where old flowers came burning out of the ground. Under the dirt and indifference, she appeared only thirty-seven or thirty-eight years old—no older than Schmendrick, surely, despite the magician's birthdayless face. Her rough hair bloomed, her skin quickened, and her voice was nearly as gentle to all things as it was when she spoke to the unicorn. The eyes would never be joyous, any more than they could ever turn green or blue, but they too had wakened in the earth. She walked eagerly into King Haggard's realm on bare, blistered feet, and she sang often.

And far away on the other side of the unicorn, Schmendrick the Magician stalked in silence. His black cloak was sprouting holes, coming undone, and so was he. The rain that renewed Molly did not fall on him, and he seemed ever more parched and deserted, like the land itself. The unicorn could not heal him. A touch of her horn could have brought him back from death, but over despair she had no power, nor over magic that had come and gone.

So they journeyed together, following the fleeing darkness into a wind that tasted like nails. The rind of the country cracked, and the flesh of it peeled back into gullies and ravines or shriveled into scabby hills. The sky was so high and pale that it disappeared during the day, and the unicorn sometimes thought that the three of them must look as blind and helpless as slugs in the sunlight, with their log or their dank rock tumbled away. But she was a unicorn still, with a unicorn's way of growing more beautiful in evil times and places. Even the breath of the toads that grumbled in the ditches and dead trees stopped when they saw her.

Toads would have been more hospitable than the sullen folk of Haggard's country. Their villages lay bald as bones between knifelike hills where nothing grew, and they themselves had hearts unmistakably as sour as boiled beer. Their children stoned strangers into town, and their dogs chased them out again. Several of the dogs never returned, for Schmendrick had developed a quick hand and a taste for mongrel. This infuriated the townsmen as no mere theft would have done. They gave nothing away, and they knew that their enemies were those who did.

The unicorn was weary of human beings. Watching her companions as they slept, seeing the shadows of their dreams scurry over their faces, she would feel herself bending under the heaviness of knowing their names. Then she would run until morning to ease the ache; swifter than rain, swift as loss, racing to catch up with the time when she had known nothing at all but the sweetness of being herself. Often then, between the rush of one breath and the reach of another, it came to her that Schmendrick and Molly were long dead, and King Haggard as well, and the Red Bull met and mastered—so long ago that the grandchildren of the stars that had seen it all happen were withering now, turning to coal—and that she was still the only unicorn left in the world.

Then, one owl-less autumn evening, they rounded a ridge and saw the castle. It crept into the sky from the far side of a long, deep valley—thin and twisted, bristling with thorny turrets, dark and jagged as a giant's grin. Molly laughed outright, but the unicorn shivered, for to her the rooked towers seemed to be groping toward her through the dusk. Beyond the castle, the sea glimmered like iron.

"Haggard's fortress," Schmendrick murmured, shaking his head in wonderment. "Haggard's dire keep. A witch built it for him, they say, but he wouldn't pay her for her work, so she put a curse on the castle. She swore that one day it would sink into the sea with Haggard, when his greed caused the sea to overflow. Then she gave a fearful shriek, the way they do, and vanished in a sulphurous puff. Haggard moved in right away. He said no tyrant's castle was complete without a curse."

"I don't blame him for not paying her," Molly Grue said scornfully. "I could jump on that place myself and scatter it like a pile of leaves. Anyway, I hope the witch

has something interesting to do while she waits for that
curse to come home. The sea is greater than anyone's
greed."

Bony birds struggled across the sky, screeling,
"*Help*me, *help*me, *help*me!" and small black shapes
bobbled at the lightless windows of King Haggard's
castle. A wet, slow smell found the unicorn. "Where is
the Bull?" she asked. "Where does Haggard keep the
Bull?"

"No one keeps the Red Bull," the magician replied
quietly. "I have heard that he roams at night, and lies
up by day in a great cavern beneath the castle. We'll
know soon enough, but that's not our problem now. The
nearer danger lies *there*." He pointed down into the
valley, where a few lights had begun to shiver.

"That is Hagsgate," he said.

Molly made no answer, but she touched the unicorn
with a hand as cold as a cloud. She often put her hands
on the unicorn when she was sad, or tired, or afraid.

"This is King Haggard's town," Schmendrick said,
"the first one he took when he came over the sea, the
one that has lain longest under his hand. It has a wicked
name, though none I ever met could say exactly why.
No one goes into Hagsgate, and nothing comes out of it
but tales to make children behave—monsters, were-
beasts, witch covens, demons in broad daylight, and the
like. But there is something evil in Hagsgate, I think.
Mommy Fortuna would never go there, and once she
said that even Haggard was not safe while Hagsgate
stood. There is something there."

He peered closely at Molly as he spoke, for it was his
one bitter pleasure these days to see her frightened in

spite of the white presence of the unicorn. But she answered him quite calmly, with her hands at her sides. "I have heard Hagsgate called '*the town that no man knows.*' Maybe its secret was waiting for a woman to find it out—a woman and a unicorn. But what's to be done with you?"

Schmendrick smiled then. "I'm no man," he said. "I'm a magician with no magic, and that's no one at all."

The foxfire lights of Hagsgate grew brighter as the unicorn watched them, but not even a flint flared in King Haggard's castle. It was too dark to see men moving on the walls, but across the valley she could hear the soft boom of armor and the clatter of pikes on stone. Sentinels had met, and marched away again. The smell of the Red Bull sported all around the unicorn as she started down the thin, brambly path that led to Hagsgate.

# VII

HE TOWN of Hagsgate was shaped like a footprint: long toes splaying from a broad paw and ending in the dark claws of a digger. And indeed, where the other towns of King Haggard's realm seemed to scratch like sparrows at the mean land, Hagsgate was well and deeply dug in. Its streets were smoothly paved, its gardens glowed, and its proud houses might have grown up out of the earth, like trees. Lights shone in every window, and the three travelers could hear voices, and dogs barking, and dishes being scrubbed until they squeaked. They halted by a high hedge, wondering.

"Do you suppose we took a wrong turn somewhere, and this isn't Hagsgate at all?" Molly whispered. She brushed foolishly at her hopeless rags and tatters. "I knew I should have brought my good dress." She sighed.

Schmendrick rubbed the back of his neck wearily. "It's Hagsgate," he answered her. "It must be Hagsgate, and yet there's no smell of sorcery, no air of black magic. But why the legends, then, why the fables and fairy tales? Very confusing, especially when you've had half a turnip for dinner."

95

The unicorn said nothing. Beyond the town, darker than dark, King Haggard's castle teetered like a lunatic on stilts, and beyond the castle the sea slid. The scent of the Red Bull moved in the night, cold among the town smells of cooking and living. Schmendrick said, "The good people must all be indoors, counting their blessings. I'll hail them."

He stepped forward and threw back his cloak, but he had not yet opened his mouth when a hard voice said out of the air, "Save your breath, stranger, while you have it." Four men sprang from behind the hedge. Two of them set their swords at Schmendrick's throat, while another guarded Molly with a pair of pistols. The fourth approached the unicorn to seize her mane; but she reared up, shining fiercely, and he jumped away.

"Your name!" the man who had first spoken demanded of Schmendrick. He was middle-aged or more, as were they all, dressed in fine, dull clothing.

"Gick," said the magician, because of the swords.

"Gick," mused the man with the pistols. "An alien name."

"Naturally," the first man said. "All names are alien in Hagsgate. Well, Mr. Gick," he went on, lowering his sword slightly to the point where Schmendrick's collarbones converged, "if you and Mrs. Gick would kindly tell us what brings you skulking here—"

Schmendrick found his voice at that. "I hardly know the woman!" he roared. "My name is Schmendrick, Schmendrick the Magician, and I am hungry and tired and unpleasant. Put those things away, or you'll each have a scorpion by the wrong end."

*the human animal leaves on the level of*
*the heart — to the unicorn that's dangerous*

The four men looked at one another. "A magician," said the first man. "The very thing."

Two of the others nodded, but the man who had tried to capture the unicorn grumbled, "<u>Anyone can say he's a magician</u> these days. <u>The old standards are gone, the old values have been</u> abandoned. Besides, a real magician has a beard."

"Well, if he isn't a magician," the first man said lightly, "he'll wish he were, soon enough." He sheathed his sword and bowed to Schmendrick and Molly. "I am Drinn," he said, "and it is possibly a pleasure to welcome you to Hagsgate. You spoke of being hungry, I believe. That's easily remedied—and then perhaps you will do us a good turn in your professional capacity. Come with me."

Grown suddenly gracious and apologetic, he led them toward a lighted inn, while the three other men followed close behind. More townsfolk came running up now, streaming eagerly from their houses with their own dinners half-eaten and their tea left steaming; so that by the time Schmendrick and Molly were seated, there were nearly a hundred people wedged together on the inn's long benches, jamming into the doorway and falling through the windows. The unicorn, unnoticed, paced slowly after: a white mare with strange eyes.

The man named Drinn sat at the same table with Schmendrick and Molly, chattering as they ate, and filling their glasses with a furry black wine. Molly Grue drank very little. She sat quietly looking at the faces around her and noting that none seemed any younger than Drinn's face, though a few were much older.

There was a way in which all the Hagsgate faces were very much alike, but she could not find it.

"And now," Drinn said when the meal was over, "now you must permit me to explain why we greeted you so uncivilly."

"Pish, no need." Schmendrick chuckled. The wine had made him chuckly and easy, and had brightened his green eyes to gold. "What I want to know is the reason for the rumors that have Hagsgate full of ghouls and werewolves. Most absurd thing I ever heard of."

Drinn smiled. He was a knotty man with a turtle's hard, empty jaws. "It's the same thing," he said. "Listen. The town of Hagsgate is under a curse."

The room was suddenly very still, and in the beery light the faces of the townsfolk looked as tight and pale as cheese. Schmendrick laughed again. "A blessing, you mean. In this bony kingdom of old Haggard's, you are like another land altogether—a spring, an oasis. I agree with you that there's enchantment here, but I drink to it."

Drinn stopped him as he raised his glass. "Not that toast, my friend. Will you drink to a woe fifty years old? It is that long since our sorrow fell, when King Haggard built his castle by the sea."

"When the witch built it, I think." Schmendrick wagged a finger at him. "Credit where it's due, after all."

"Ah, you know that story," Drinn said. "Then you must also know that Haggard refused to pay the witch when her task was completed."

The magician nodded. "Aye," and she cursed him for his greed—cursed the castle, rather. But what had that to do with Hagsgate? The town had done the witch no wrong."

"No," Drinn replied. "But neither had it done her any good. She could not unmake the castle—or would not, for she fancied herself an artistic sort and boasted that her work was years ahead of its time. Anyway, she came to the elders of Hagsgate and demanded that they force Haggard to pay what was due her. 'Look at me and see yourselves,' she rasped. 'That's the true test of a town, or of a king. A lord who cheats an ugly old witch will cheat his own folk by and by. Stop him while you can, before you grow used to him.'" Drinn sipped his wine and thoughtfully filled Schmendrick's glass once more.

"Haggard paid her no money," he went on, "and Hagsgate, alas, paid her no heed. She was treated politely and referred to the proper authorities, whereupon she flew into a fury and screamed that in our eagerness to make no enemies at all, we had now made two." He paused, covering his eyes with lids so thin that Molly was sure he could see through them, like a bird. With his eyes closed, he said, "It was then that she cursed Haggard's castle, and cursed our town as well. Thus his greed brought ruin upon us all."

In the sighing silence, Molly Grue's voice came down like a hammer on a horseshoe, as though she were again berating poor Captain Cully. "Haggard's less at fault than you yourselves," she mocked the folk of Hagsgate, "for he was only one thief, and you were many. You earned your trouble by your own avarice, not your king's."

Drinn opened his eyes and gave her an angry look.

"*We* earned nothing," he protested. "It was our parents and grandparents whom the witch asked for help, and I'll grant you that they were as much to blame as Haggard, in their way. We would have handled the matter quite differently." And every middle-aged face in the room scowled at every older face.

One of the old men spoke up in a voice that wheezed and miaowed. "You would have done just as we did. There were crops to harvest and stock to tend, as there still is. There was Haggard to live with, as there still is. We know very well how you would have behaved. You are our children."

Drinn glowered him down, and other men began to shout spitefully, but the magician quieted them all by asking, "What was the curse? Could it have anything to do with the Red Bull?"

The name rang coldly, even in the bright room, and Molly felt suddenly lonely. On an impulse, she added her own question, though it had nothing to do with the conversation. "Have any of you ever seen a unicorn?"

It was then that she learned two things: the difference between silence and utter silence; and that she had been quite right to ask that question. The Hagsgate faces tried not to move, but they did move. Drinn said carefully, "We never see the Bull, and we never speak of him. Nothing that concerns him can be any business of ours. As for unicorns, there are none. There never were." He poured the black wine again. "I will tell you the words of the curse," he said. He folded his hands before him, and began to chant.

*The curse of Hagsgate*

## THE LAST UNICORN

"You whom Haggard holds in thrall,
Share his feast and share his fall.
You shall see your fortune flower
Till the torrent takes the tower.
Yet none but one of Hagsgate town
May bring the castle swirling down."

A few others joined in as he recited the old malediction. Their voices were sad and far, as though they were not in the room at all but were tumbling in the wind high over the inn's chimney, helpless as dead leaves.

What is it about their faces? Molly wondered. I almost know. The magician sat silently by her, rolling his wine glass in his long hands.

"When those words were first spoken," Drinn said, "Haggard had not been long in the country, and all of it was still soft and blooming—all but the town of Hagsgate. Hagsgate was then as this land has become: a scrabbly, bare place where men put great stones on the roofs of their huts to keep them from blowing away." He grinned bitterly at the older men. "Crops to harvest, stock to tend! You grew cabbages and rutabagas and a few pale potatoes, and in all of Hagsgate there was but one weary cow. Strangers thought the town accursed, having offended some vindictive witch or other."

Molly felt the unicorn go by in the street, then turn and come back, restless as the torches on the walls, that bowed and wriggled. She wanted to run out to her, but instead she asked quietly, "And afterward, when that had come true?"

Drinn answered, "From that moment, we have known nothing but bounty. Our grim earth has grown so kind that gardens and orchards spring up by them-

101

selves—we need neither to plant nor to tend them. Our flocks multiply; our craftsmen become more clever in their sleep; the air we breathe and the water we drink keep us from ever knowing illness. All sorrow parts to go around us—and this has come about while the rest of the realm, once so green, has shriveled to cinders under Haggard's hand. For fifty years, none but he and we have prospered. It is as though all others had been cursed."

"'Share his feast and share his fall.'" Schmendrick murmured. "I see, I see." He gulped another glass of the black wine, and laughed. "But old King Haggard still rules, and will until the sea overflows. You don't know what a real curse is. Let me tell you *my* troubles." Easy tears suddenly glittered in his eyes. "To begin with, my mother never liked me. She pretended, but I knew—"

Drinn interrupted him, and just then Molly realized what was strange about the folk of Hagsgate. Every one of them was well and warmly dressed, but the faces that peered out of their fine clothes were the faces of poor people, cold as ghosts and too hungry to eat. Drinn said, "'Yet none but one of Hagsgate town may bring the castle swirling down.' How can we delight in our good fortune when we know that it must end, and that one of us will end it? Every day makes us richer, and brings us one day nearer to our doom. Magician, for fifty years we have lived leanly, avoided attachments, untied all habits, readying ourselves for the sea. We have taken not a moment's joy in our wealth—or in anything else—for joy is just one more thing to lose. Pity Hagsgate, strangers, for in all the wretched world there can be no town more unhappy."

"Lost, lost, lost," the townsfolk whimpered. "Misery, misery we." Molly Grue stared wordlessly at them, but Schmendrick said respectfully, "That's a *good* curse, that's a professional job. I always say, whatever you're having done, go to an expert. It pays in the long run."

Drinn frowned, and Molly nudged Schmendrick. The magician blinked. "Oh. Well, what is it you wish of me? I must warn you that I am not a very skillful sorcerer, but I will be glad to lift this curse from you, if I can."

"I had not taken you for any more than you are," Drinn answered, "but such as you are, you should do as well as any. I think we will leave the curse the way it is. If it were lifted we might not become poor again, but we would no longer grow steadily richer, and that would be just as bad. No, our real task is to keep Haggard's tower from falling, and since the hero who will destroy it can only come from Hagsgate, this should not be impossible. For one thing, we allow no strangers to settle here. We keep them away, by force if we must, but more often by guile. Those dark tales of Hagsgate that you spoke of—we invented them ourselves, and spread them as widely as we could to make certain that we would have few visitors." He smiled proudly with his hollow jaws.

Schmendrick propped his chin on his knuckles and regarded Drinn with a sagging smile. "What about your own children?" he asked. "How can you keep one of them from growing up to fulfill the curse?" He looked around the inn, sleepily studying every wrinkled face that looked back at him. "Come to think of it," he said slowly, "are there no young people in this town? How early do you send children to bed in Hagsgate?"

No one answered him. Molly could hear blood creaking in ears and eyes, and skin twitching like water plucked by the wind. Then Drinn said, "We have no children. We have had none since the day that the curse was laid upon us." He coughed into his fist and added, "It seemed the most obvious way of foiling the witch."

Schmendrick threw back his head and laughed without making a sound, laughed to make the torches dance. Molly realized that the magician was quite drunk. Drinn's mouth disappeared, and his eyes hardened into cracked porcelain. "I see no humor in our plight," he said softly. "None at all."

"None," Schmendrick gurgled, bowing over the table and spilling his wine. "None, pardon me, none, none at all." Under the angry gaze of two hundred eyes, he managed to recover himself and reply seriously to Drinn. "Then it would seem to me that you have no worries. None that would worry you, anyway." A small whee of laughter sneaked out between his lips, like steam from a teakettle.

"So it would seem," Drinn leaned forward and touched Schmendrick's wrist with two fingers. "But I have not told you all the truth. Twenty-one years ago, a child was born in Hagsgate. Whose child it was, we never knew. I found it myself, as I was crossing the marketplace one winter's night. It was lying on a butcher's block, not crying, although there was snow, but warm and chuckling under a comforter of stray cats. They were all purring together, and the sound was heavy with knowledge. I stood by the strange cradle for a long time, pondering while the snow fell and the cats purred prophecy."

He stopped, and Molly Grue said eagerly, "You took the child home with you, of course, and raised it as your own." Drinn laid his hands palm up on the table.

"I chased the cats away," he said, "and went home alone." Molly's face turned the color of mist. Drinn shrugged slightly. "I know the birth of a hero when I see it," he said. "Omens and portents, snakes in the nursery. Had it not been for the cats, I might have chanced the child, but they made it so obvious, so mythological. What was I to do—knowingly harbor Hagsgate's doom?" His lip twitched, as though a hook had set in it. "As it happens, I erred, but it was on the side of tenderness. When I returned at sunrise, the baby had vanished."

Schmendrick was drawing pictures with his finger in a puddle of wine, and might have heard nothing at all. Drinn went on. "Naturally, no one ever admitted to leaving the child in the marketplace, and though we searched every house from cellar to dovecote, we never found it again. I might have concluded that wolves had taken the brat, or even that I had dreamed the whole encounter, cats and all—but for the fact that on the very next day a herald of King Haggard's came riding into town, ordering us to rejoice. After thirty years of waiting, the king had a son at last." He looked away from the look on Molly's face. "Our fondling, incidentally, was a boy."

Schmendrick licked the tip of his finger and looked up. "Lír," he said thoughtfully. "Prince Lír. But there was no other way to account for his appearance?"

"Not likely," Drinn snorted. "Any woman that would marry Haggard, even Haggard would refuse. He gave out the tale that the boy was a nephew, whom he graciously adopted on the death of his parents. But Haggard has no relatives, no family. There are those who say that he was born of an overcast, as Venus was born out of the sea. No one would give King Haggard a child to raise."

The magician calmly held out his glass, and filled it himself when Drinn refused. "Well, he got one somewhere, and good for him. But how could he have come by your little cat-baby?"

Drinn said, "He walks in Hagsgate at night, not often, but now and then. Many of us have seen him— tall Haggard, gray as driftwood, prowling alone under an iron moon, picking up dropped coins, broken dishes, spoons, stones, handkerchiefs, rings, stepped-on apples; anything, everything, no reason to it. It was Haggard who took the child. I am as certain of it as I am certain that Prince Lír is the one who will topple the tower and sink Haggard and Hagsgate together."

"I hope he is," Molly broke in. "I hope Prince Lír is that baby you left to die, and I hope he drowns your town, and I hope the fish nibble you bare as corn-cobs—"

Schmendrick kicked her ankle as hard as he could, for the listeners were beginning to hiss like embers, and a few were rising to their feet. He asked again, "What is it you wish of me?"

"You are on your way to Haggard's castle, I believe." Schmendrick nodded. "Ah," Drinn said. "Now, a clever magician would find it simple to become friendly with Prince Lír, who is reputed to be a young man of eagerness and curiosity. A clever magician might be acquainted with all manner of odd potions and powders, poppets and philters, herbs and banes and unguents. A clever magician—mind you, I said 'clever,' no more—a clever magician might be able, under the proper circumstances ..." He let the rest drift away unspoken, but no less said.

"For a meal?" Schmendrick stood up, knocking his chair over. He leaned on the table with both hands, breathing harshly. "Is that the going rate these days? Dinner and wind the price of a poisoned prince? You'll have to do better than that, friend Drinn. I wouldn't do in a chimneysweep for such a fee."

Moly Grue gripped his arm, crying, "What are you saying?" The magician shook her hand away, but at the same time he lowered one eyelid in a slow wink. Drinn leaned back in his chair, smiling. "I never haggle with a professional," he said. "Twenty-five pieces of gold."

They haggled for half an hour, Schmendrick demanding a hundred gold pieces, and Drinn refusing to offer more than forty. At last they settled at seventy, half to be paid then and half upon Schmendrick's successful return. Drinn counted out the money on the spot from a leather pouch at his belt. "You'll spend the night in Hagsgate, of course," he said. "I would be pleased to put you up myself."

But the magician shook his head. "I think not. We will go on to the castle, since we're so near it now. The sooner there, the sooner back, eh?" And he grinned a crafty and conspiratorial grin.

"Haggard's castle is always dangerous," Drinn warned. "But it is never more dangerous than at night."

"They say that about Hagsgate too," Schmendrick replied. "You mustn't believe everything you hear, Drinn." He walked to the door of the inn, and Molly followed him. There he turned and beamed at the folk of Hagsgate, hunched in their finery. "I would like to leave you with this last thought," he told them. "The most professional curse ever snarled or croaked or thundered can have no effect on a pure heart. Good night."

Outside, the night lay coiled in the street, cobra-cold and scaled with stars. There was no moon. Schmendrick stepped out boldly, chuckling to himself and jingling his gold coins. Without looking at Molly, he said, "Suckers. To assume so lightly that all magicians dabble in death. Now if they had wanted me to lift the curse— ah, I might have done that for no more than the meal. I might have done it for a single glass of wine."

"I'm glad you didn't," Molly said savagely. "They deserve their fate, they deserve worse. To leave a child out in the snow—"

"Well, if they hadn't, he couldn't have grown up to be a prince. Haven't you ever been in a fairy tale before?" The magician's voice was kind and drunken, and his eyes were as bright as his new money. "The hero has to make a prophecy come true, and the villain is the one who has to stop him—though in another kind of story, it's more often the other way around. And a hero has to be in trouble from the moment of his birth, or he's not a real hero. It's a great relief to find out about Prince Lír. I've been waiting for this tale to turn up a leading man."

The unicorn was there as a star is suddenly there, moving a little way ahead of them, a sail in the dark. Molly said, "If Lír is the hero, what is she?"

"That's different. Haggard and Lír and Drinn and you and I—we are in a fairy tale, and must go where it goes. But she is real. She is real." Schmendrick yawned and hiccupped and shivered all at once. "We'd better hurry," he said. "Perhaps we should have stayed the night, but old Drinn makes me nervous. I'm sure I deceived him completely, but all the same."

It seemed to Molly, dreaming and waking as she walked, that Hagsgate was stretching itself like a paw to hold the three of them back, curling around them and batting them gently back and forth, so that they trod in their own tracks over and over. In a hundred years they reached the last house and the end of the town; in another fifty years they had blundered through the damp fields, the vineyards, and the crouching orchards. Molly dreamed that sheep leered at them from treetops, and that cold cows stepped on their feet and shoved them off the withering path. But the light of the unicorn sailed on ahead, and Molly followed it, awake or asleep.

King Haggard's castle was stalking in the sky, a blind black bird that fished the valley by night. Molly could hear the breathing of its wings. Then the unicorn's breath stirred in her hair, and she heard Schmendrick asking, "How many men?"

"Three men," the unicorn said. "They have been behind us since we left Hagsgate, but now they are coming swiftly. Listen."

Steps too soft for their quickness; voices too muffled to mean any good. The magician rubbed his eyes. "Perhaps Drinn has started to feel guilty about underpaying his poisoner," he murmured. "Perhaps his conscience is keeping him awake. Anything is possible. Perhaps I have feathers." He took Molly by the arm and pulled her down into a hard hollow by the side of the road. The unicorn lay nearby, still as moonlight.

Daggers gleaming like fishtrails on a dark sea. A voice, suddenly loud and angry. "I tell you, we've lost them. We passed them a mile back, where I heard that rustling. I'm damned if I'll run any farther."

"Be still!" a second voice whispered fiercely. "Do you want them to escape and betray us? You're afraid of the magician, but you'd do better to be afraid of the Red Bull. If Haggard finds out about our half of the curse, he'll send the Bull to trample us all into crumbs."

The first man answered in a softer tone. "It isn't that I'm afraid. A magician without a beard is no magician at all. But we're wasting our time. They left the road and cut across country as soon as they knew we were following. We could chase along here all night and never come up with them."

Another voice, wearier than the first two. "We have chased them all night. Look over there. Dawn is coming."

Molly found that she had wriggled halfway under Schmendrick's back cloak and buried her face in a clump of spiny dead grass. She dared not raise her head, but she opened her eyes and saw that the air was growing strangely light. The second man said, "You're a fool. It's a good two hours to morning, and besides, we're heading west."

"In that case," the third voice replied, "I'm going home."

Footsteps started briskly back up the road. The first man called, "Wait, don't go! Wait, I'll go with you!" To the second man, he muttered hastily, "I'm not going home, I just want to retrace our trail a little way. I still think I heard them, and I've dropped my tinderbox somewhere ..." Molly could hear him edging off as he spoke.

"Damn you for cowards!" the second man swore. "Wait a moment then, will you wait till I try what Drinn told me?" The retreating footsteps hesitated, and he chanted loudly: " 'Warmer than summer, more filling than food, sweeter than woman and dearer than blood—' "

"Hurry," the third voice said. "Hurry. Look at the sky. What is this nonsense?"

Even the second man's voice was growing nervous. "It isn't nonsense. Drinn treats his money so well that it cannot bear to be parted from him. Most touching relationship you ever saw. This is the way he calls to it." He went on rapidly, quavering a little. " 'Stronger than water and kinder than drove, Say the name of the one you love.' "

"Drinn," rang the gold coins in Schmendrick's purse, "drinndrinndrinndrinn." Then everything happened.

The ragged black cloak whipped against Molly's

111

cheek as Schmendrick rolled to his knees, groping desperately for the purse. It buzzed like a rattlesnake in his hand. He hurled it far into the brush, but the three men were running at them together, daggers as red as though they had already been struck. Beyond King Haggard's castle, a burning brightness was rising, breaking into the night like a great shoulder. The magician stood erect, menacing the attackers with demons, metamorphoses, paralyzing ailments, and secret judo holds. Molly picked up a rock.

With an old, gay, terrible cry of ruin, the unicorn reared out of her hiding place. Her hoofs came slashing down like a rain of razors, her mane raged, and on her forehead she wore a plume of lightning. The three assassins dropped their daggers and hid their faces, and even Molly Grue and Schmendrick cowered before her. But the unicorn saw none of them. Mad, dancing, sea-white, she belled her challenge again.

And the brightness answered her with a bellow like the sound of ice breaking up in the spring. Drinn's men fled, stumbling and shrieking.

Haggard's castle was on fire, tossing wildly in a sudden cold wind. Molly said aloud, "But it has to be the sea, it's supposed to be." She thought that she could see a window, as far away as it was, and a gray face. Then the Red Bull came.

King Haggard - looking for joy but
couldn't possess it when he wanted
it and now that he has it, he
has it all and it's locked away.

Schmendrick is a maker

# VIII

E WAS THE COLOR of blood, not the springing blood of the heart but the blood that
stirs under an old wound that never really
healed. A terrible light poured from him like sweat,
and his roar started landslides flowing into one another.
His horns were as pale as scars.

For one moment the unicorn faced him, frozen as a
wave about to break. Then the light of her horn went
out, and she turned and fled. The Red Bull bellowed
again, and leaped down after her.

The unicorn had never been afraid of anything.
She was immortal, but she could be killed: by a
harpy, by a dragon or a chimera, by a stray arrow
loosed at a squirrel. But dragons could only kill her—
they could never make her forget what she was, or
themselves forget that even dead she would still be
more beautiful than they. The Red Bull did not know
her, and yet she could feel that it was herself he sought,
and no white mare. Fear blew her dark then, and she
ran away, while the Bull's raging ignorance filled the
sky and spilled over into the valley.

The trees lunged at her, and she veered wildly among
them; she who slipped so softly through eternity without bumping into anything. Behind her they were

breaking like glass in the rush of the Red Bull. He roared once again, and a great branch clubbed her on the shoulder so hard that she staggered and fell. She was up immediately, but now roots humped under her feet as she ran, and others burrowed as busily as moles to cut across the path. Vines struck at her like strangling snakes, creepers wove webs between the trees, dead boughs crashed all around her. She fell a second time. The Bull's hoofs on the earth boomed through her bones, and she cried out.

She must have found some way out of the trees, for she was running on the hard, bald plain that lay beyond the prosperous pasture lands of Hagsgate. Now she had room to race, and a unicorn is only loping when she leaves the hunter kicking his burst and sinking horse. She moved with the speed of life, winking from one body to another or running down a sword; swifter than anything burdened with legs or wings. Yet without looking back, she knew that the Red Bull was gaining on her, coming like the moon, the sullen, swollen hunter's moon. She could feel the shock of the livid horns in her side, as though he had already struck.

Ripe, sharp cornstalks leaned together to make a hedge at her breast, but she trampled them down. Silver wheatfields turned cold and gummy when the Bull breathed on them; they dragged at her legs like snow. Still she ran, bleating and defeated, hearing the butterfly's icy chiming: "They passed down all the roads long ago, and the Red Bull ran close behind them." He had killed them all.

Suddenly the Bull was facing her, as though he had been lifted like a chess piece, swooped through the air, and set down again to bar her way. He did not charge immediately, and she did not run. He had been huge when she first fled him, but in the pursuit he had grown so vast that she could not imagine all of him. Now he seemed to curve with the curve of the bloodshot sky, his legs like great whirlwinds, his head rolling like the northern lights. His nostrils wrinkled and rumbled as he searched for her, and the unicorn realized that the Red Bull was blind.

If he had rushed her then, she would have met him, tiny and despairing with her darkened horn, even though he stamped her to pieces. He was swifter than she; better to face him now than to be caught running. But the Bull advanced slowly, with a kind of sinister daintiness, as though he were trying not to frighten her, and again she broke before him. With low, sad cry, she whirled and ran back the way she had come: back through the tattered fields and over the plain, toward King Haggard's castle, dark and hunched as ever. And the Red Bull went after her, following her fear.

Schmendrick and Molly had been spun away like chips when the Bull went by—Molly slammed breathless and witless against the ground, and the magician hurled into a tangle of thorns that cost him half his cloak and an eighth of his skin. They got up when they could, and went limping in pursuit, leaning on one another. Neither one said a word.

The way through the trees was easier for them than the unicorn had found it, for the Red Bull had been there since. Molly and the magician scrambled over great treetrunks not only smashed but trodden halfway into the ground, and dropped to hands and knees to crawl around crevasses they could not fathom in the dark. No hoofs could have made these, Molly thought dazedly; the earth had torn itself shrinking from the burden of the Bull. She thought of the unicorn, and her heart paled.

When they came out on the plain, they saw her—far and faint, a tuft of white water on the wind, almost invisible in the glare of the Red Bull. Molly Grue, a little crazy with weariness and fear, saw them moving the way stars and stones move through space: forever falling, forever following, forever alone. The Red Bull would never catch the unicorn, not until Now caught up with New, Bygone with Begin. Molly smiled serenely.

But the blazing shadow loomed over the unicorn until the Bull seemed to be all around her. She reared, swerved, and sprang away in another direction, only to meet the Bull there, his head lowered and his jaws drooling thunder. Again she turned, and again, backing and sidling, making crafty little dashes to this side or that; and each time the Red Bull headed her off by standing still. He did not attack, but he left her no way to go, save one.

"He's driving her," Schmendrick said quietly. "If he wanted to kill her, he could have done it by now. He's driving her the way he drove the others—to the castle, to Haggard. I wonder why."

Molly said, "Do something." Her voice was strangely calm and casual, and the magician answered her in the same tone.

"There is nothing I can do."

The unicorn fled once more, pitifully tireless, and the Red Bull let her have room to run, but none to turn.

When she faced him for a third time, she was close enough for Molly to see her hind legs shivering like those of a frightened dog. Now she set herself to stand, pawing the ground wickedly and laying back her small, lean ears. But she could make no sound, and her horn did not grow bright again. She cowered when the Red Bull's bellow made the sky ripple and crack, and yet she did not back away.

"Please," Molly Grue said. "Please do something."

Schmendrick turned on her, and his face was wild with helplessness. "What can I do? What can I do, with my magic? Hat tricks, penny tricks, or the one where I scramble stones to make an omelet? Would that entertain the Red Bull, do you think, or shall I try the trick with the singing oranges? I'll try whatever you suggest, for I would certainly be happy to be of some practical use."

Molly did not answer him. The Bull came on, and the unicorn crouched lower and lower, until she seemed about to snap in two. Schmendrick said, "I know what to do. If I could, I'd change her into some other creature, some beast too humble for the Bull to be concerned with. But only a great magician, a wizard like Nikos, who was my teacher, would have that kind of power. To transform a unicorn—anyone who could do that could juggle the seasons and shuffle years like playing cards. And I have no more power than you have; less, for you can touch her, and I cannot." Then he said suddenly, "Look. It is over."

The unicorn was standing very still before the Red Bull, her head down and her whiteness drabbled to a soapy gray. She looked gaunt and small; and even

117

Molly, who loved her, could not keep from seeing that a unicorn is an absurd animal when the shining has gone out of her. Tail like a lion's tail, deerlegs, goatfeet, the mane cold and fine as foam over my hand, the charred horn, the eyes—oh the eyes! Molly took hold of Schmendrick's arm and dug her nails into it as hard as she could.

"You have magic," she said. She heard her own voice, as deep and clear as a sibyl's. "Maybe you can't find it, but it's there. You called up Robin Hood, and there is no Robin Hood, but he came, and he was real. And that is magic. You have all the power you need, if you dare to look for it."

Schmendrick regarded her in silence, staring as hard as though his green eyes were beginning the search for his magic in Molly Grue's eyes. The Bull stepped lightly toward the unicorn, no longer pursuing, but commanding her with the weight of his presence, and she moved ahead of him, docile, obedient. He followed like a sheepdog, guiding her in the direction of King Haggard's jagged tower and the sea.

"Oh, please!" Molly's voice was crumbling now. "Please, it's not fair, it can't be happening. He'll drive her to Haggard, and no one will ever see her again, no one. Please, you're a magician, you won't let him." Her fingers struck even deeper into Schmendrick's arm. "Do something!" She wept. "Don't let him, do something!"

Schmendrick was prying futilely at her clenched fingers. "I'm not going to do a damn thing," he said through his teeth, "until you let go of my arm."

"Oh," Molly said. "I'm sorry."

"You can cut off the circulation like that, you know," the magician said severely. He rubbed his arm and took a few steps forward, into the path of the Red Bull. There he stood with his arms folded and his head high, though it dropped now and then, because he was very tired.

"Maybe this time," Molly heard him mutter, "maybe this time. Nikos said—what was it that Nikos said? I don't remember. It has been so long." There was an odd, old sorrow in his voice that Molly had never heard before. Then a gaiety leaped up like a flame as he said, "Well, who knows, who knows? If this is not the time, perhaps I can make it so. There's this much of comfort, friend Schmendrick. For once, I don't see how you can possibly make things any worse than they already are," and he laughed softly.

The Red Bull, being blind, took no notice of the tall figure in the road until he was almost upon it. Then he halted, sniffing the air; storm stirring in his throat, but a certain confusion showing in the swing of his great head. The unicorn stopped when he stopped, and Schmendrick's breath broke to see her so tractable. "Run!" he called to her. "Run now!" but she never looked at him, or back at the Bull, or at anything but the ground.

At the sound of Schmendrick's voice, the Bull's rumble grew louder and more menacing. He seemed eager to be out of the valley with the unicorn, and the magician thought he knew why. Beyond the towering brightness of the Red Bull, he could see two or three sallow stars and a cautious hint of a warmer light. Dawn was near.

"He doesn't care for daylight," Schmendrick said to

himself. "That's worth knowing." Once more he shouted to the unicorn to fly, but his only answer came in the form of a roar like a drumroll. The unicorn bolted forward, and Schmendrick had to spring out of her way, or she would have run him down. Close behind her came the bull, driving her swiftly now, as the wind drives the thin, torn mist. The power of his passage picked Schmendrick up and dropped him elsewhere, tumbling and rolling to keep from being trampled, his eyes jarred blind and his head full of flames. He thought he heard Molly Grue scream.

Scrabbling to one knee, he saw that the Red Bull had herded the unicorn almost to the beginning of the trees. If she would only try one more time to escape—but she was the Bull's and not her own. The magician had one glimpse of her, pale and lost between the pale horns, before the wild red shoulders surged across his sight. Then, swaying and sick and beaten, he closed his eyes and let his hopelessness march through him, until something woke somewhere that had wakened in him once before. He cried aloud, for fear and joy.

What words the magic spoke this second time, he never knew surely. They left him like eagles, and he let them go; and when the last one was away, the emptiness rushed back with a thunderclap that threw him on his face. It happened as quickly as that. This time he knew before he picked himself up that the power had been and gone.

Ahead, the Red Bull was standing still, nosing at something on the ground. Schmendrick could not see the unicorn. He went forward as fast as he could, but it was Molly who first drew near enough to see what the

Bull was sniffing. She put her fingers in her mouth, like a child.

At the feet of the Red Bull there lay a young girl, spilled into a very small heap of light and shadow. She was naked, and her skin was the color of snow by moonlight. Fine tangled hair, white as a waterfall, came down almost to the small of her back. Her face was hidden in her arms.

"Oh," Molly said. "Oh, what have you done?" and, heedless of any danger, she ran to the girl and knelt beside her. The Red Bull raised his huge, blind head and swung it slowly in Schmendrick's direction. He seemed to be waning and fading as the gray sky grew light, though he still smoldered as savagely bright as crawling lava. The magician wondered what his true size was, and his color, when he was alone.

Once more the Red Bull sniffled at the still form, stirring it with his freezing breath. Then, without a sound, he bounded away into the trees and was gone from sight in three gigantic strides. Schmendrick had a last vision of him as he gained the rim of the valley: no shape at all, but a swirling darkness, the red darkness you see when you close your eyes in pain. The horns had become the two sharpest towers of old King Haggard's crazy castle.

Molly Grue had taken the white girl's head onto her lap, and was whispering over and over, "What have you done?" The girl's face, quiet in sleep and close to smiling, was the most beautiful that Schmendrick had ever seen. It hurt him and warmed him at the same time. Molly smoothed the strange hair, and Schmendrick noticed on the forehead, above and between the closed eyes, a small, raised mark, darker than the rest of the skin. It was neither a scar nor a bruise. It looked like a flower.

"What do you mean, what have I done?" he demanded of the moaning Molly. "Only saved her from the Bull by magic, that's what I've done. By magic, woman, by my own true magic!" Now he was helpless with delight, for he wanted to dance and he wanted to be still; he shook with shouting and speeches, and yet there was nothing that he wanted to say. He ended by laughing foolishly, hugging himself until he gasped, and sprawling down beside Molly as his legs let go.

"Give me your cloak," Molly said. The magician beamed at her, blinking. She reached over and ungently pulled the shredded cloak from his shoulders. Then she wrapped it around the sleeping girl, as much as it would wrap. The girl shone through it like the sun through leaves.

"Doubtless you are wondering how I plan to return her to her proper shape," Schmendrick offered. "Wonder not. The power will come to me when I need it—I know that much now. One day it will come when I call, but that time is not yet." Impulsively he seized Molly Grue, hugging her head in his long arms. "But you were right," he cried, "you were right! It is there, and it is mine!"

Molly pulled away from him, one cheek roughed red and both ears mashed. The girl sighed in her lap, ceased to smile, turned her face from the sunrise. Molly said, "Schmendrick, you poor man, you magician, don't you see—"

"See what? There's nothing to see." But his voice was

suddenly hard and wary, and the green eyes were beginning to be frightened. "The Red Bull came for a unicorn, so she had to become something else. You begged me to change her—what is it frets you now?"

Molly shook her head in the wavering way of an old woman. She said, "I didn't know you meant to turn her into a human girl. You would have done better—" She did not finish, but looked away from him. One hand continued to stroke the white girl's hair.

"The magic chose the shape, not I," Schmendrick answered. "A mountebank may select this cheat or that, but a magician is a porter, a donkey carrying his master where he must. The magician calls, but the magic chooses. If it changes a unicorn to a human being, then that was the only thing to do." His face was fevered with an ardent delirium which made him look even younger. "I am a bearer," he sang. "I am a dwelling, I am a messenger—"

"You are an idiot," Molly Grue said fiercely. "Do you hear me? You're a magician, all right, but you're a stupid magician." But the girl was trying to wake, her hands opening and closing, and her eyelids beating like birds' breasts. As Molly and Schmendrick looked on, the girl made a soft sound and opened her eyes.

They were farther apart than common, and somewhat deeper set, and they were as dark as the deep sea; and illuminated, like the sea, by strange, glimmering creatures that never rise to the surface. The unicorn could have been transformed into a lizard, Molly thought, or into a shark, a snail, a goose, and somehow still her eyes would have given the change away. To me, anyway. I would know.

The girl lay without moving, her eyes finding herself in Molly's eyes, and in Schmendrick's. Then, in one motion, she was on her feet, the black cloak falling back across Molly's lap. For a moment she turned in a circle, staring at her hands, which she held high and useless, close to her breast. She bobbed and shambled like an ape doing a trick, and her face was the silly, bewildered face of a joker's victim. And yet she could make no move that was not beautiful. Her trapped terror was more lovely than any joy that Molly had ever seen, and that was the most terrible thing about it.

"Donkey," Molly said. "Messenger."

"I can change her back," the magician answered hoarsely. "Don't worry about it. I can change her back."

Shining in the sun, the white girl hobbled to and fro on her strong young legs. She stumbled suddenly and fell, and it was a bad fall because she did not know how to catch herself with her hands. Molly flew to her, but the girl crouched on the ground staring at her, and spoke in a low voice. "*What have you done to me?*" Molly Grue began to cry.

Schmendrick came forward, his face cold and wet, but his voice level. "I turned you into a human being to save you from the Red Bull. There was nothing else I could do. I will turn you to yourself again, as soon as I can."

"The Red Bull," the girl whispered. "Ah!" She was trembling wildly, as though something were shaking and hammering at her skin from within. "He was too strong," she said, "too strong. There was no end to his strength, and no beginning. He is older than I."

Her eyes widened, and it seemed to Molly that the Bull moved in them, crossing their depths like a flaming fish, and vanishing. The girl began to touch her face timidly, recoiling from the feel of her own features. Her curled fingers brushed the mark on her forehead, and she closed her eyes and gave a thin, stabbing howl of loss and weariness and utter despair.

"What have you done to me?" she cried. "I will die here!" She tore at the smooth body, and blood followed her fingers. "I will die here! I will die!" Yet there was no fear in her face, though it ramped in her voice, in her hands and feet, in the white hair that fell down over her new body. Her face remained quiet and un-troubled.

Molly huddled over her, as near as she dared, begging her not to hurt herself. But Schmendrick said, "Be still," and the two words cracked like autumn branches. He said, "The magic knew what it was doing. Be still and listen."

"Why did you not let the Bull kill me?" The white girl moaned. "Why did you not leave me to the harpy? That would have been kinder than closing me in this cage." The magician winced, remembering Molly Grue's mocking accusation, but he spoke with a desperate calmness.

"In the first place, it's quite an attractive shape," he said. "You couldn't have done much better and still remained human."

She looked at herself: sideways at her shoulders and along her arms, then down her scratched and welting body. She stood on one foot to inspect the sole of the other; cocked her eyes up to see the silver brows, squinted down her cheeks to catch a flash of her nose; and even peered closely at the sea-green veins inside her wrists, themselves as gaily made as young otters. At last she turned her face to the magician, and again he caught his breath. I have made magic, he thought, but sorrow winked sharp in his throat, like a fishhook setting fast.

"All right," he said. "It would make no difference to you if I had changed you into a rhinoceros, which is where the whole silly myth got started. But in this guise you have some chance of reaching King Haggard and finding out what has become of your people. As a unicorn, you would only suffer their fate—unless you think you could defeat the Bull if you met him a second time."

The white girl shook her head. "No," she answered, "never. Another time, I would not stand so long." Her voice was too soft, as though its bones had been broken. She said, "My people are gone, and I will follow them soon, whatever shape you trap me in. But I would have chosen any other than this for my prison. A rhinoceros is as ugly as a human being, and it too is going to die, but at least it never thinks that it is beautiful."

"No, it never thinks that," the magician agreed. "That's why it goes on being a rhinoceros and will never be welcome even at Haggard's court. But a young girl, a girl to whom it can never mean anything that she is not a rhinoceros—such a girl, while the king and his son seek to solve her, might unravel her own riddle until she comes to its end. Rhinoceri are not questing beasts, but young girls are."

The sky was hot and curdled; the sun had already

melted into a lion-colored puddle; and on the plain of Hagsgate nothing stirred but the stale, heavy wind. The naked girl with the flower-mark on her forehead stared silently at the green-eyed man, and the woman watched them both. In the tawny morning, King Haggard's castle seemed neither dark nor accursed, but merely grimy, rundown, and poorly designed. Its skinny spires looked nothing like a bull's horns, but rather like those on a jester's cap. Or like the horns of a dilemma, Schmendrick thought. They never have just two.

The white girl said, "I am myself still. This body is dying. I can feel it rotting all around me. How can anything that is going to die be real? How can it be truly beautiful?" Molly Grue put the magician's cloak around her shoulders again, not for modesty or seemliness, but out of a strange pity, as though to keep her from seeing herself.

"I will tell you a story," Schmendrick said. "As a child I was apprenticed to the mightiest magician of all, the great Nikos, whom I have spoken of before. But even Nikos, who could turn cats into cattle, snowflakes into snowdrops, and unicorns into men, could not change me into so much as a carnival cardsharp. At last he said to me, 'My son, your ineptitude is so vast, your incompetence so profound, that I am certain you are inhabited by greater power than I have ever known. Unfortunately, it seems to be working backward at the moment, and even I can find no way to set it right. It must be that you are meant to find your own way to reach your power in time; but frankly, you should live so long as that will take you. Therefore I grant it that you shall not age from this day forth, but will travel the world round and round, eternally inefficient, until at last you come to yourself and know what you are. Don't thank me. I tremble at your doom.' "

The white girl regarded him out of the unicorn's clear, amaranthine eyes—gentle and frightening in the unused face—but she said nothing. It was Molly Grue who asked, "And if you should find your magic—what then?"

"Then the spell will be broken and I will begin to die, as I began at my birth. Even the greatest wizards grow old, like other men, and die." He swayed and nodded, and then snapped awake again: a tall, thin, shabby man, smelling of dust and drink. "I told you that I was older than I look," he said. "I was born mortal, and I have been immortal for a long, foolish time, and one day I will be mortal again; so I know something that a unicorn cannot know. Whatever can die is beautiful—more beautiful than a unicorn, who lives forever, and who is the most beautiful creature in the world. Do you understand me?"

"No," she said.

The magician smiled wearily. "You will. You're in the story with the rest of us now, and you must go with it, whether you will or no. If you want to find your people, if you want to become a unicorn again, then you must follow the fairy tale to King Haggard's castle, and wherever else it chooses to take you. The story cannot end without the princess."

The white girl said, "I will not go." She stepped away, her body wary and the cold hair falling down. She said, "I am no princess, no mortal, and I will not go. Nothing but evil has happened to me since I left my *what is truly beautiful can die.*

forest, and nothing but evil can have become of unicorns in this country. Give me my true shape again, and I will return to my trees, to my pool, to my own place. Your tale has no power over me. I am a unicorn. I am the last unicorn."

Had she said that once before, long ago, in the blue-green silence of the trees? Schmendrick continued to smile, but Molly Grue said, "Change her back. You said you could change her. Let her go home."

"I cannot," the magician answered. "I told you, the magic is not mine to command, not yet. That is why I too must go on to the castle, and the fate or fortune that waits there. If I tried to undo the transformation now, I might actually turn her into a rhinoceros. That would be the best thing that could happen. As for the worst—" He shivered and fell silent.

The girl turned from them and looked away at the castle that stooped over the valley. She could see no movement at any window or among the tottering turrets, or any sign of the Red Bull. Yet she knew that he was there, brooding at the castle's roots till night should fall again: strong beyond strength, invincible as the night itself. For a second time she touched the place on her forehead where her horn had been.

When she turned again, they were asleep where they sat, the man and the woman. Their heads were pillowed on air, and their mouths hung open. She stood by them, watching them breathe, one hand holding the black cloak closed at her throat. Very faintly, for the first time, the smell of the sea came to her. STOP

# IX

HE SENTINELS saw them coming a little before sunset, when the sea was flat and blinding. The sentinels were pacing the second tallest of the many awry towers that sprouted up from the castle and made it resemble one of those odd trees that grow with their roots in the air. From where they stood, the two men could survey the entire valley of Hagsgate as far as the town and the sharp hills beyond, as well as the road that ran from the rim of the valley to the great, though sagging, front gate of King Haggard's castle.

"A man and two women," said the first sentinel. He hurried to the far side of the tower; a stomach-startling motion, since the tower tilted so that half of the sentinels' sky was sea. The castle sat on the edge of a cliff which dropped like a knife blade to a thin yellow shore, frayed bare over green and black rocks. Soft, baggy birds squatted on the rocks, snickering, "Saidso, saidso."

The second man followed his comrade across the tower at an easier pace. He said, "A man and a woman. The third one, in the cloak—I am not certain of the third." Both men were clad in homemade mail—rings, bottlecaps, and links of chain sewn onto half-cured hides—and their faces were invisible behind rusted visors, but the second sentinel's voice and gait alike marked him as the elder. "The one in the black cloak," he said again. "Do not be too sure of that one too soon."

But the first sentinel leaned out into the orange glare of the tipped-up sea, scraping a few studs loose from his poor armor on the parapet. "It is a woman," he declared. "I would doubt my own sex before hers."

"And well you may," the other observed sardonically, "since you do nothing that becomes a man but ride astraddle. I warn you again: be slow to call that third male or female. Wait a little, and see what you see."

The first sentinel answered him without turning. "If I had grown up never dreaming that there were two separate secrets to the world, if I had taken every woman I met to be exactly like myself, still I would know that this creature was different from anything I had ever seen before. I have always been sorry that I have never pleased you; but now, when I look at her I am sorry that I have never pleased myself. Oh, I am sorry."

He bent still further over the wall, straining his eyes toward the three slow figures on the road. A chuckle clattered behind his visor. "The other woman looks sore-footed and bad-tempered," he reported. "The man appears an amiable sort, though plainly of the strolling life. A minstrel, like enough, or a player." He said nothing more for a long while, watching them draw near.

"And the third?" the older man inquired presently.

"Your sundown fancy with the interesting hair? Have you outworn her in a quarter of an hour—already seen her closer than love dares?" His voice rustled in his helmet like small, clawed feet.

"I don't think I could ever see her closely," the sentinel replied, "however close she came." His own voice was hushed and regretful, echoing with lost chances. "She has a newness," he said. "Everything is for the first time. See how she moves, how she walks, how she turns her head—all for the first time, the first time anyone has ever done these things. See how she draws her breath and lets it go again, as though no one else in the world knew that air was good. It is all for her. If I learned that she had been born this very morning, I would only be surprised that she was so old."

The second sentinel stared down from his tower at the three wanderers. The tall man saw him first, and next the dour woman. Their eyes reflected nothing but his armor, grim and cankered and empty. But then the girl in the ruined black cloak raised her head, and he stepped back from the parapet, putting out one tin glove against her glance. In a moment she passed into the shadow of the castle with her companions, and he lowered his hand.

"She may be mad," he said calmly. "No grown girl looks like that unless she is mad. That would be annoying, but far preferable to the remaining possibility."

"Which is?" the younger man prompted after a silence.

"Which is that she was indeed born this morning. I

would rather that she were mad. Let us go down now."

When the man and the women reached the castle, the two sentries were standing on either side of the gate, their blunt, bent halberds crossed and their falchions hitched round in front of them. The sun had gone down, and their absurd armor grew steadily more menacing as the sea faded. The travelers hesitated, looking at one another. They had no dark castle at their backs, and their eyes were not hidden.

"Give your names," said the parched voice of the second sentinel.

The tall man stepped a pace foward. "I am Schmendrick the Magician," he said. "This is Molly Grue, my helper—and this is the Lady Amalthea." He stumbled over the name of the white girl, as though he had never before spoken it. "We seek audience with King Haggard," he continued. "We have come a long way to see him."

The second sentinel waited for the first to speak, but the younger man was looking only at the Lady Amalthea. Impatiently he said, "State your business with King Haggard."

"I will," the magician replied, "to Haggard himself. What kind of royal matter could it be that I might confide to doormen and porters? Take us to the king."

"What kind of royal matter could a wandering wizard with a foolish tongue have to discuss with King Haggard?" the second sentinel asked somberly. But he turned and strode through the castle gate, and the king's visitors straggled after him. Last wandered the younger

sentinel, his step grown as tender as that of the Lady
Amalthea, whose every movement he imitated unaware.
She stayed a moment before the gate, looking out to
sea, and the sentinel did the same.

His former comrade called angrily to him, but the
young sentry was on a different duty, answerable to a
new captain for his derelictions. He entered at the gate
only after the Lady Amalthea had chosen to go in.
Then he followed, singing to himself in a dreamy
drone.

> "What is it that is happening to me?
> What is it that is happening to me?
> I cannot tell whether to be glad or be afraid.
> What is it that is happening to me?"

They crossed a cobbled courtyard where cold laundry
groped their faces, and passed through a smaller door
into a hall so vast that they could not see the walls or
the ceiling in the darkness. Great stone pillars rushed up
to them as they trudged across the hall, and then leaned
away without ever really letting themselves be seen.
Breath echoed in that huge place, and the footsteps of
other, smaller creatures sounded just as clearly as their
own. Molly Grue stayed quite close to Schmendrick.

After the great hall, there came another door and
then a thin stair. There were few windows, and no
lights. The stair coiled tighter and tighter as it ascended,
until it seemed that every step turned round on itself,
and that the tower was closing on them all like a sweaty

fist. The darkness looked at them and touched them. It had a rainy, doggy smell.

Something rumbled somewhere deep and near. The tower trembled like a ship run aground, and answered with a low, stone wail. The three travelers cried out, scrambling to keep their feet on the shuddering stairs, but their guide pressed on without faltering or speaking. The younger man whispered earnestly to the Lady Amalthea, "It's all right, don't be afraid. It's just the Bull." The sound was not repeated.

The second sentinel halted abruptly, produced a key from a secret place, and jabbed it—apparently—straight into the blank wall. A section of the wall swung inward, and the small procession filed into a low, narrow chamber with one window and a chair at the far end. There was nothing else: no other furnishings, no rug, no draperies, no tapestries. In the room were five people, the tall chair, and the mealy light of the rising new moon.

"This is King Haggard's throne room," said the sentinel.

The magician gripped him by his mailed elbow and turned him until they faced each other. "This is a cell. This is a tomb. No living king sits here. Take us to Haggard, if he is alive."

"You must judge that for yourself," replied the scurrying voice of the sentinel. He unlaced his helmet and lifted it from his gray head. "I am King Haggard," he said.

His eyes were the same color as the horns of the Red Bull. He was taller than Schmendrick, and though his face was bitterly lined there was nothing fond or foolish in it. It was a pike's face: the jaws long and cold, the cheeks hard, the lean neck alive with power. He might have been seventy years old, or eighty, or more.

The first sentinel came forward now with his own helmet under his arm. Molly Grue gaped when she saw his face, for it was the friendly, rumpled face of the young prince who had read a magazine while his princess tried to call a unicorn. King Haggard said, "This is Lír."

"Hi," said Prince Lír. "Glad to meet you." His smile wriggled at their feet like a hopeful puppy, but his eyes—a deep, shadowy blue behind stubby lashes—rested quietly on the eyes of the Lady Amalthea. She looked back at him, silent as a jewel, seeing him no more truly than men see unicorns. But the prince felt strangely, happily certain that she had looked him round and through, and down into caverns that he had never known were there, where her glance echoed and sang. Prodigies began to waken somewhere southwest of his twelfth rib, and he himself—still mirroring the Lady Amalthea—began to shine.

"What is your concern with me?"

Schmendrick the Magician cleared his throat and bowed to the pale-eyed old man. "We seek to enter your service. Far and wide has the fabled court of King Haggard—"

"I need no servants." The king turned away, his face and body suddenly slack with indifference. Yet Schmendrick sensed a curiosity lingering in the stone-colored skin and at the roots of the gray hair. He said cautiously, "But surely you keep some suite, some following.

Simplicity is the richest adornment of a king, I grant you, but for such a king as Haggard—"

"You are losing my interest," the rustling voice interrupted him again, "and that is very dangerous. In a moment I will have forgotten you quite entirely, and will never be able to remember just what I did with you. What I forget not only ceases to exist, but never really existed in the first place." As he said this, his eyes, like those of his son, turned to meet the Lady Amalthea's eyes.

"My court," he continued, "since you choose to call it that, consists of four men-at-arms. I would do without them if I could, for they cost more than they are worth, like everything else. But they take their turns as sentries, and as cooks, and they give the appearance of an army, from a distance. What other attendants should I need?"

"But the pleasures of court," the magician cried, "the music, the talk, the women and the fountains, the hunts and the masques and the great feasts—"

"They are nothing to me," King Haggard said. "I have known them all, and they have not made me happy. I will keep nothing near me that does not make me happy."

The Lady Amalthea moved quietly past him to the window, and looked out at the night sea.

Schmendrick came about to catch the wind again, and declared, "I understand you perfectly! How weary, stale, flat and unprofitable seem to you all the uses of this world! You are bored with bliss, satiated with sensation, jaded with dejune joys. It is a king's affliction, and therefore no one wants the services of a magician more than a king does. For only to a magician is the world forever fluid, infinitely mutable and eternally new. Only he knows the secret of change, only he knows truly that all things are crouched in eagerness to become something else, and it is from this universal tension that he draws his power. To a magician, March is May, snow is green, and grass is gray; this is that, or whatever you say. Get a magician today!"

He finished on one knee with both arms flung wide. King Haggard stepped nervously away from him, muttering, "Get up, get up, you make my head hurt. Besides, I already have a royal magician."

Schmendrick rose heavily to his feet, his face red and empty. "You never said. What is his name?"

"He is called Mabruk," King Haggard replied. "I do not often speak of him. Even my men-at-arms do not know that he lives here in the castle. Mabruk is all that you have said a wizard should be, and much more that I doubt you dream of. He is known in his trade as 'the magician's magician.' I can see no reason to replace him with some vagrant, nameless, clownish—"

"Ah, but I can!" Schmendrick broke in desperately. "I can think of one reason, uttered by you yourself not a minute since. This marvelous Mabruk does not make you happy."

Over the king's fierce face there fell a slow shadow of disappointment and betrayal. For a breath, he looked like a bewildered young man. "Why no, that is true," King Haggard murmured. "Mabruk's magic has not delighted me for a long time. How long has it been, I wonder?" He clapped his hands briskly, crying out, "Mabruk! Mabruk! Appear, Mabruk!"

"I am here," said a deep voice from a far corner of the room. An old man in a dark, spangled gown and a pointed, spangled hat was standing there, and no one could say surely that he had not been standing there in plain sight since they entered the throne room. His beard and brows were white, and the cast of his face was mild and wise, but his eyes were as hard as hailstones. "What does Your Majesty wish of me?"

"Mabruk," King Haggard said, "this gentleman is of your fraternity. His name is Schmendrick."

The old wizard's icy eyes widened slightly, and he peered at the shabby man. "Why, so it is!" he exclaimed in seeming pleasure. "Schmendrick, my dear boy, how nice to see you! You won't remember me, but I was a dear, dear friend of your tutor, dear old Nikos. He had such high hopes for you, the poor man. Well, well, this is a surprise! And are you really still in the profession? My, you're a determined fellow! I always say perseverance is nine-tenths of any art—not that it's much help to be nine-tenths an artist, of course. But what can it be that brings you here?"

"He has come to take your place." King Haggard's voice was flat and final. "He is now my royal magician."

Schmendrick's start of amazement was not lost on old Mabruk, though the wizard himself seemed little surprised by the king's decision. For a moment he obviously considered the worth of wrath, but instead he chose a tone of genial amusement. "As your Majesty wills it, now and always," he purred. "But perhaps Your Majesty might be interested in learning a bit of the history of his new magician. I'm sure dear Schmendrick won't mind my mentioning that he is already something of a legend in the trade. Indeed, among adepts, he is best remembered as 'Nikos's Folly.' His charming and complete inability to master the simplest rune; his creative way with the most childish rhyme of theurgy, let alone—"

King Haggard made a thin motion with the edge of one hand, and Mabruk was suddenly silent. Prince Lír giggled. The king said, "I do not need to be persuaded of his unfitness for the position. A single glance at him tells me that, as a glance makes it plain that you are one of the great wizards of the world." Mabruk swelled gently, fondling his glorious beard and wrinkling his benign brow.

"But that also is nothing to me," King Haggard went on. "In the past, you have performed whatever miracle I required of you, and all it has done has been to spoil my taste for miracles. No task is too vast for your powers—and yet, when the wonder is achieved, nothing has changed. It must be that great power cannot give me whatever it is that I really want. A master magician has not made me happy. I will see what an incompetent one can do. You may go, Mabruk." He nodded his head to dismiss the old wizard.

Mabruk's semblance of affability vanished like a spark on snow, and with the same sound. His whole face became like his eyes. "I am not packed off as easily as that," he said very softly. "Not on a whim, even a king's whim, and not in favor of a fool. Beware, Haggard! Mabruk is no one to anger lightly."

A wind began to rise in the dark chamber. It came as much from one place as another—through the window, through the half-open door—but its true source was the clenched figure of the wizard. The wind was cold and rank, a wet, hooty marsh wind, and it leaped here and there in the room like a gleeful animal discovering the flimsiness of human beings. Molly Grue shrank against Schmendrick, who looked uncomfortable. Prince Lír fidgeted his sword in and out of its sheath.

Even King Haggard gave back a step before the triumphant grin of old Mabruk. The walls of the room seemed to thaw and run away, and the wizard's starry gown became the huge, howling night. Mabruk spoke no word himself, but the wind was beginning to make a wicked, grunting sound as it gained strength. In another moment it would become visible, burst into shape. Schmendrick opened his mouth, but if he were shouting a counterspell it could not be heard, and it did not work.

In the darkness, Molly Grue saw the Lady Amalthea turning far away, stretching out a hand on which the ring and middle fingers were of equal length. The strange place on her forehead was glowing as bright as a flower.

Then the wind was gone as though it had never been, and the stone walls were around them once more, the dull chamber as gay as noon after Mabruk's night. The wizard was crouched almost to the floor, staring at the Lady Amalthea. His wise, benevolent face looked like the face of a drowned man, and his beard dripped thinly from his chin, like stagnant water. Prince Lír took him by the arm.

"Come on, old man," he said, not unkindly. "This way out, granddad. I'll write you a reference."

"I am going," Mabruk said. "Not from fear of you—you lump of stale dough—nor of your mad, ungrateful father; nor of your new magician, much happiness may you have of him." His eyes met King Haggard's hungry eyes, and he laughed like a goat.

"Haggard, I would not be you for all the world," he declared. "You have let your doom in by the front door, though it will not depart that way. I would explain myself more fully, but I am no longer in your service. That is a pity, for there will come a time when none but a master will be able to save you—and in that hour, you will have Schmendrick to call upon! Farewell, poor Haggard, farewell!"

Still laughing, he disappeared; but his mirth dwelled forever in the corners of that chamber, like the smell of smoke, or of old, cold dust.

"Well," said King Haggard in the gray moonlight. "Well." He came slowly toward Schmendrick and Molly, his feet silent, his head weaving almost playfully. "Stand still," he commanded when they moved. "I want to see your faces."

His breath rasped like a knife on a grindstone as he peered from one of them to the other. "Closer!" he grumbled, squinting through the dark. "Come closer—closer! I want to see you."

"Light a light then," said Molly Grue. The calmness of her own voice frightened her more than the fury of the old wizard had. It is easy to be brave for *her* sake, she thought, but if I begin being brave on my own account, where will it end?

"I never light lights," the king replied. "What is the good of light?"

He turned from them, muttering to himself, "One face is almost guileless, almost foolish, but not quite foolish enough. The other is a face like my face, and that must mean danger. Yet I saw all that at the gate—why did I let them enter, then? Mabruk was right; I have grown old and daft and easy. Still, I see only Haggard when I look in their eyes."

Prince Lír stirred nervously as the king paced across the throne room toward the Lady Amalthea. She was again gazing out of the window, and King Haggard had drawn very near before she wheeled swiftly, lowering her head in a curious manner. "I will not touch you," he said, and she stood still.

"Why do you linger at the window?" he demanded. "What are you looking at?"

"I am looking at the sea," said the Lady Amalthea. Her voice was low and tremorous; not with fear, but with life, as a new butterfly shivers in the sun.

"Ah," said the king. "Yes, the sea is always good. There is nothing that I can look at for very long, except the sea." Yet he stared at the Lady Amalthea's face for a long time, his own face giving back none of her light—as Prince Lír's had—but taking it in and keeping it somewhere. His breath was as musty as the wizard's wind, but the Lady Amalthea never moved.

Suddenly he shouted, "What is the matter with your eyes? They are full of green leaves, crowded with trees and streams and small animals. Where am I? Why can I not see myself in your eyes?"

The Lady Amalthea did not answer him. King Haggard swung around to face Schmendrick and Molly. His scimitar smile laid its cold edge along their throats. "Who is she?" he demanded.

Schmendrick coughed several times. "The Lady Amalthea is my niece," he offered. "I am her only living relative, and so her guardian. No doubt the state of her attire puzzles you, but it is easily explained. On our journey, we were attacked by bandits and robbed of all our—"

"What nonsense are you jabbering? What about her attire?" The king turned again to regard the white girl, and Schmendrick suddenly understood that neither King Haggard nor his son had noticed that she was naked under the rags of his cloak. The Lady Almathea held herself so gracefully that she made shreds and tatters seem the only fitting dress for a princess; and besides, she did not know that she was naked. It was the armored king who seemed bare before her.

King Haggard said, "What she wears, what may have befallen you, what you all are to one another—these things are fortunately no concern of mine. In such matters you may lie to me as much as you dare. I want to know who she is. I want to know how she broke Mabruk's magic without saying a word. I want to know why there are green leaves and fox cubs in her eyes. Speak quickly, and avoid the temptation to lie, especially about the green leaves. Answer me."

Schmendrick did not reply quickly. He made a few small sounds of an earnest nature, but not a sensible word was among them. Molly Grue gathered her courage to answer, even though she suspected that it was impossible to speak the truth to King Haggard. Something in his winter presence blighted all words, tangled meanings, and bent honest intentions into shapes as tormented as the towers of his castle. Still she would have spoken, but another voice was heard in the gloomy chamber: the light, kind, silly voice of the young Prince Lír.

"Father, what difference does it make? She is here now."

King Haggard sighed. It was not a gentle sound, but low and scraping; not a sound of surrender, but the rumbling meditation of a tiger taut to spring. "Of course you are right," he said. "She is here, they are all here, and whether they mean my doom or not, I will look at them for a while. A pleasant air of disaster attends them. Perhaps that is what I want."

To Schmendrick he said curtly, "As my magician, you will entertain me when I wish to be entertained, in manners variously profound and frivolous. You will be expected to know when you are required, and in what guise, for I cannot be forever identifying my moods and desires for your benefit. You will receive no wages, since that is certainly not what you came here for. As for your drab, your assistant, whatever you choose to call her, she will serve me also if she wishes to remain in my castle. From this evening, she is cook and maid-servant together, scrubwoman and scullery maid as well."

He paused, seemingly waiting for Molly to protest, but she only nodded. The moon had moved away from the window, but Prince Lír could see that the dark room was no darker for that. The cool brightness of the Lady Amalthea grew more slowly than had Mabruk's wind, but the prince understood quite well that it was far more dangerous. He wanted to write poems by that light, and he had never wanted to write poems before.

"You may come and go as you please," said King Haggard to the Lady Amalthea. "It may have been foolish of me to admit you, but I am not so foolish as to forbid you this door or that. My secrets guard themselves—will yours do the same? What are you looking at?"

"I am looking at the sea," the Lady Amalthea replied again.

"Yes, the sea is always good," said the king. "We will look at it together one day." He walked slowly to the door. "It will be curious," he said, "to have a creature in the castle whose presence causes Lír to call me 'father' for the first time since he was five years old."

"Six," said Prince Lír. "I was six."

"Five or six," the king said, "it had stopped making me happy long before, and it does not make me happy now. Nothing has yet changed because she is here." He was gone almost as silently as Mabruk, and they heard his tin boots ticking on the stairs.

Molly Grue went softly to the Lady Amalthea and stood by her at the window. "What is it?" she asked. "What do you see?" Schmendrick leaned on the throne, regarding Prince Lír with his long green eyes. Away in the valley of Hagsgate, the cold roar sounded again.

"I will find quarters for you," said Prince Lír. "Are you hungry? I will get you something to eat. I know where there is some cloth, fine satin. You could make a dress."

146

No one answered him. The heavy night swallowed his words, and it seemed to him that the Lady Amalthea neither heard nor saw him. She did not move, and yet he was certain that she was going away from him as he stood there, like the moon. "Let me help you," Prince Lír said. "What can I do for you? Let me help you."

# X

"WHAT CAN I DO for you?" Prince Lír asked. "Nothing very much just now," Molly Grue said. "The water was all I needed. Unless you want to peel the potatoes, which woud be all right with me."

"No, I didn't mean that. I mean yes, I will if you want me to, but I was talking to her. I mean, when I talk to her, that's what I keep asking."

"Sit down and peel me a few potatoes," Molly said. "It'll give you something to do with your hands."

They were in the scullery, a dank little room smelling strongly of rotting turnips and fermenting beets. A dozen earthenware dishes were piled in one corner, and a very small fire was shivering under a tripod, trying to boil a large pot of gray water. Molly sat at a rude table which was covered with potatoes, leeks, onions, peppers, carrots, and other vegetables, most of them limp and spotty. Prince Lír stood before her, rocking slowly along his feet and twisting his big, soft fingers together.

"I killed another dragon this morning," he said presently.

"That's nice," Molly answered. "That's fine. How many does that make now?"

"Five. This one was smaller than the others, but it really gave me more trouble. I couldn't get near it on foot, so I had to go in with the lance, and my horse got pretty badly burned. It was funny about the horse—"

Molly interrupted him. "Sit down, Your Highness, and stop doing that. I start to twitch all over just watching you." Prince Lír sat down opposite her. He drew a dagger from his belt and moodily began peeling potatoes. Molly regarded him with a slight, slow smile.

"I brought her the head," he said. "She was in her chamber, as she usually is. I dragged that head all the way up the stairs to lay it at her feet." He sighed, and nicked his finger with the dagger. "Damn. I didn't mind that. All the way up the stairs it was a dragon's head, the proudest gift anyone can give anyone. But when she looked at it, suddenly it became a sad, battered mess of scales and horns, gristly tongue, bloody eyes. I felt like some country butcher who had brought his lass a nice chunk of fresh meat as a token of his love. And then she looked at me, and I was sorry I had killed the thing. Sorry for killing a dragon!" He slashed at a rubbery potato and wounded himself again.

"Cut away from yourself, not toward," Molly advised him. "You know, I really think you could stop slaying dragons for the Lady Amalthea. If five of them haven't moved her, one more isn't likely to do it. Try something else."

"But what's left on earth that I haven't tried?" Prince Lír demanded. "I have swum four rivers, each in full flood and none less than a mile wide. I have climbed seven mountains never before climbed, slept three nights in the Marsh of the Hanged Men, and walked alive out of that forest where the flowers burn your eyes and the nightingales sing poison. I have ended my betrothal to the princess I had agreed to marry— and if you don't think that was a heroic deed, you don't know her mother. I have vanquished exactly fifteen black knights waiting by fifteen fords in their black pavilions, challenging all who come to cross. And I've long since lost count of the witches in the thorny woods, the giants, the demons disguised as damsels; the glass hills, fatal riddles, and terrible tasks; the magic apples, rings, lamps, potions, swords, cloaks, boots, neckties, and nightcaps. Not to mention the winged horses, the basilisks and sea serpents, and all the rest of the livestock." He raised his head, and the dark blue eyes were confused and sad.

"And all for nothing," he said. "I cannot touch her, whatever I do. For her sake, I have become a hero—I, sleepy Lír, my father's sport and shame—but I might just as well have remained the dull fool I was. My great deeds mean nothing to her."

Molly took up her own knife and began to slice the peppers. "Then perhaps the Lady Amalthea is not to be won by great deeds." The prince stared at her, frowning in puzzlement.

"Is there another way to win a maiden?" he asked earnestly. "Molly, do you know another way? Will you tell it to me?" He leaned across the table to seize her hand. "I like being brave well enough, but I will be a lazy coward again if you think that would be better.

The sight of her makes me want to do battle with all evil and ugliness, but it also makes me want to sit still and be unhappy. What should I do, Molly?"

"I don't know," she said, suddenly embarrassed. "Kindness, courtesy, good works, that sort of thing. A good sense of humor." A small copper-and-ashes cat with a crooked ear jumped into her lap, purring thunderously and leaning against her hand. Hoping to change the subject, she asked, "What about your horse? What was funny?"

But Prince Lír was staring at the little cat with the crooked ear. "Where did he come from? Is he yours?"

"No," Molly said. "I just feed him, and hold him sometimes." She stroked the cat's thin throat, and it closed its eyes. "I thought he lived here."

The prince shook his head. "My father hates cats. He says that there is no such thing as a cat—it is just a shape that all manner of imps, hobs, and devilkins like to put on, to gain easy entrance into the homes of men. He would kill it if he knew you had it here."

"What about the horse?" Molly asked.

Prince Lír's face grew glum again. "That was strange. When she took no delight in the gift itself, I thought she might be interested to hear how it was won. So I told her about the view and the charge—you know—about the hissing and the naked wings and the way dragons smell, especially on a rainy morning; and the way the black blood jumped at the point of my lance. But she heard none of it, not a word, until I spoke of the rush of fire that nearly burned my poor horse's legs from under him. Then—ah, then she came back from wherever she goes when I talk to her, and she said that she must go and see my horse. So I led her to the stable where the poor brute stood crying with the pain, and she put her hand on him, on his legs. And he stopped moaning. That's a terrible sound they make when they're really hurt. When they stop, it's like a song."

The prince's dagger lay glittering among the potatoes. Outside, great gusts of rain growled round and round the castle walls, but those in the scullery could only hear it, for there was not a single window in the cold room. Nor was there any light, except for the meager glow of the cooking fire. It made the cat dozing in Molly's lap look like a heap of autumn leaves.

"And what happened then?" she asked. "When the Lady Amalthea touched your horse."

"Nothing happened. Nothing at all." Prince Lír suddenly seemed to become angry. He slammed his hand down on the table, and leeks and lentils leaped in all directions. "Did you expect something to happen? She did. Did you expect the beast's burns to heal on the instant—the crackling skin to knit, the black flesh to be whole again? She did—by my hope of her I swear it! And when his legs didn't grow well under her hand, then she ran away. I don't know where she is now."

His voice softened as he spoke, and the hand on the table curled sadly on its side. He rose and went to look into the pot over the fire. "It's boiling," he said, "if you want to put the vegetables in. She wept when my horse's legs did not heal—I heard her weeping—and yet there were no tears in her eyes when she ran away. Everything else was there, but no tears."

Molly put the cat gently on the floor and began

gathering the venerable vegetables for the pot. Prince Lír watched her as she moved back and forth, around the table and across the dewy floor. She was singing.

> "If I danced with my feet
> As I dance in my dreaming,
> As graceful and gleaming
> As Death in disguise—
> Oh, that would be sweet,
> But then would I hunger
> To be ten years younger,
> Or wedded, or wise?"

The prince said, "Who is she, Molly? What kind of woman is it who believes—who *knows,* for I saw her face—that she can cure wounds with a touch, and who weeps without tears?" Molly went on about her work, still humming to herself.

"Any woman can weep without tears," she answered over her shoulder, "and most can heal with their hands. It depends on the wound. She is a woman, Your Highness, and that's riddle enough."

But the prince stood up to bar her way, and she stopped, her apron full of herbs and her hair trailing into her eyes. Prince Lír's face bent toward her: older by five dragons, but handsome and silly still. He said, "You sing. My father sets you to the weariest work there is to do, and still you sing. There has never been singing in this castle, or cats, or the smell of good cooking. It is the Lady Amalthea who causes this, as she causes me to ride out in the morning, seeking danger."

"I was always a fair cook," Molly said mildly. "Living in the greenwood with Cully and his men for seventeen years—"

Prince Lír continued as though she had not spoken. "I want to serve her, as you do, to help her find whatever she has come here to find. I wish to be whatever she has most need of. Tell her so. Will you tell her so?"

Even as he spoke, a soundless step sounded in his eyes, and the sigh of a satin gown troubled his face. The Lady Amalthea stood in the doorway.

A season in King Haggard's chill domain had not dimmed or darkened her. Rather, the winter had sharpened her beauty until it invaded the beholder like a barbed arrow that could not be withdrawn. Her white hair was caught up with a blue ribbon, and her gown was lilac. It did not fit her well. Molly Grue was an indifferent seamstress, and satin made her nervous. But the Lady Amalthea seemed more lovely for the poor work, for the cold stones and the smell of turnips. There was rain in her hair.

Prince Lír bowed to her; a quick, crooked bow, as though someone had hit him in the stomach. "My lady," he mumbled. "You really should cover your head when you go out, this weather."

The Lady Amalthea sat down at the table, and the little autumn-colored cat immediately sprang up before her, purring swiftly and very softly. She put out her hand, but the cat slid away, still purring. He did not appear frightened, but he would not let her touch his rusty fur. The Lady Amalthea beckoned, and the cat wriggled all over, like a dog, but he would not come near.

Prince Lír said hoarsely, "I must go. There is an ogre of some sort devouring village maidens two days' ride from here. It is said that he can be slain only by one who wields the Great Ax of Duke Alban. Unfortunately, Duke Alban himself was one of the first consumed—he was dressed as a village maiden at the time, to deceive the monster—and there is little doubt who holds the Great Ax now. If I do not return, think of me. Farewell."

"Farewell, Your Highness," Molly said. The prince bowed again, and left the scullery on his noble errand. He looked back only once.

"You are cruel to him," Molly said. The Lady Amalthea did not look up. She was offering her open palm to the crook-eared cat, but he stayed where he was, shivering with the desire to go to her.

"Cruel?" she asked. "How can I be cruel? That is for mortals." But then she did raise her eyes, and they were great with sorrow, and with something very near to mockery. She said, "So is kindness."

Molly Grue busied herself with the cooking pot, stirring the soup and seasoning it, bustling numbly. In a low voice, she remarked, "You might give him a gentle word, at the very least. He has undergone mighty trials for you."

"But what word shall I speak?" asked the Lady Amalthea. "I have said nothing to him, yet every day he comes to me with more heads, more horns and hides and tails, more enchanted jewels and bewitched weapons. What will he do if I speak?"

Molly said, "He wishes you to think of him. Knights and princes know only one way to be remembered. It's not his fault. I think he does very well." The Lady Amalthea turned her eyes to the cat again. Her long fingers twisted at a seam of the satin gown.

"No, he does not want my thoughts," she said softly. "He wants me, as much as the Red Bull did, and with no more understanding. But he frightens me even more than the Red Bull, because he has a kind heart. No, I will never speak a promising word to him."

The pale mark on her brow was invisible in the gloom of the scullery. She touched it and then drew her hand away quickly, as though the mark hurt her. "The horse died," she said to the little cat. "I could do nothing."

Molly turned quickly and put her hands on the Lady Amalthea's shoulders. Beneath the sleek cloth, the flesh was cold and hard as any stone of King Haggard's castle. "Oh, my lady," she whispered, "that is because you are out of your true form. When you regain yourself, it will all return—all your power, all your strength, all your sureness. It will come back to you." Had she dared, she would have taken the white girl in her arms and lulled her like a child. She had never dreamed of such a thing before.

But the Lady Amalthea answered, "The magician gave me only the semblance of a human being—the seeming, but not the spirit. If I had died then, I would still have been a unicorn. The old man knew, the wizard. He said nothing, to spite Haggard, but he knew."

Of itself, her hair escaped the blue ribbon and came hurrying down her neck and over her shoulders. The cat was all but won by this eagerness; he lifted a paw to play with it, but then he drew back once more and sat on his haunches, tail curled around his front feet, queer head to the side. His eyes were green, speckled with gold.

"But that was long ago," the girl said. "Now I am two—myself, and this other that you call 'my lady.' For she is here as truly as I am now, though once she was only a veil over me. She walks in the castle, she sleeps, she dresses herself, she takes her meals, and she thinks her own thoughts. If she has no power to heal, or to quiet, still she has another magic. Men speak to her, saying 'Lady Amalthea,' and she answers them, or she does not answer. The king is always watching her out of his pale eyes, wondering what she is, and the king's son wounds himself with loving her and wonders who she is. And every day she searches the sea and the sky, the castle and the courtyard, the keep and the king's face, for something she cannot always remember. What is it, what is it that she is seeking in this strange place? She knew a moment ago, but she has forgotten."

She turned her face to Molly Grue, and her eyes were not the unicorn's eyes. They were lovely still, but in a way that had a name, as a human woman is beautiful. Their depth could be sounded and learned, and their degree of darkness was quite describable. Molly saw fear and loss and bewilderment when she looked into them, and herself; and nothing more.

"Unicorns," she said. "The Red Bull has driven them all away, all but you. You are the last unicorn. You came here to find the others, and to set them free. And so you will."

Slowly the deep, secret sea returned to the Lady

Amalthea's eyes, filling them until they were as old and dark and unknowable and indescribable as the sea. Molly watched it happen, and was afraid, but she gripped the bowed shoulders even more tightly, as though her hands could draw despair like a lightning rod. And as she did so, there shivered in the scullery floor a sound she had heard before: a sound like great teeth—molars—grinding together. The Red Bull was turning in his sleep. I wonder if he dreams, Molly thought.

The Lady Amalthea said, "I must go to him. There is no other way, and no time to spare. In this form or my own, I must face him again, even if all my people are dead and there is nothing to be saved. I must go to him, before I forget myself forever, but I do not know the way, and I am lonely." The little cat switched his tail and made an odd sound that was neither a miaow nor a purr.

"I will go with you," Molly said. "I don't know the way down to the Bull either, but there must be one. Schmendrick will come too. He'll make the way for us if we can't find it."

"I hope for no help from the magician," the Lady Amalthea replied disdainfully. "I see him every day playing the fool for King Haggard, amusing him by his failures, by blundering at even the most trifling trick. He says that it is all he can do until his power speaks in him again. But it never will. He is no magician now, but the king's clown."

Molly's face suddenly hurt her, and she turned away to inspect the soup again. Answering past a sharpness in her throat, she said, "He is doing it for you. While you brood and mope and become someone else, he jigs and jests for Haggard, diverting him so that you may have time to find your folk, if they are to be found. But it cannot be long before the king tires of him, as he tires of all things, and casts him down to his dungeons, or some place darker. You do wrong to mock him."

Her voice was a child's thin, sad mumble. She said, "But that will never happen to you. Everyone loves you."

They had a moment to look at each other, the two women: the one fair and foreign in the cold, low room; the other appearing quite at home in such surroundings —an angry little beetle with her own kitchen beauty. Then they heard boots scraping, armor clicking, and the gusty voices of old men. King Haggard's four men-at-arms came trooping into the scullery.

They were all at least seventy years old, gaunt and limping, fragile as crusted snow, but all clad from head to foot in King Haggard's miserly mail and bearing his wry weapons. They entered hailing Molly Grue cheerfully and asking what she had made for their supper, but at the sight of the Lady Amalthea all four became very quiet and bowed deep bows that made them gasp.

"My lady," said the oldest of the men, "command your servants. We are used men, spent men—but if you would see miracles, you have only to request the impossible of us. We will become young again, if you wish it so." His three comrades muttered their agreement.

But the Lady Amalthea whispered in answer, "No, no, you will never be young again." Then she fled from them, with her wild, blinding hair hiding her face, and the satin gown hissing.

"How wise she is!" the oldest man-at-arms declared. "She understands that not even her beauty can do battle with time. It is a rare, sad wisdom for one so young. That soup smells delicious, Molly."

"It smells too savory for this place," a second man grumbled as they all sat down around the table. "Haggard hates good food. He says that no meal is good enough to justify all the money and effort wasted in preparing it. 'It is an illusion,' says he, 'and an expense. Live as I do, undeceived.' *Brraaahh!*" He shuddered and grimaced, and the others laughed.

"To live like Haggard," said another man-at-arms as Molly spooned the steaming soup into his bowl. "That will be my fate in the next world, if I don't behave myself in this one."

"Why do you stay in his service, then?" Molly demanded. She sat down with them and rested her chin on her hands. "He pays you no wages," she said, "and he feeds you as little as he dares. He sends you out in the worst weather to steal for him in Hagsgate, for he never spends a penny of the wealth in his strong room. He forbids everything, from lights to lutes, from fires to fairs and singing to sinning; from books and beer and talk of spring to games you play with bits of string. Why not leave him? What in the world is there to keep you here?"

The four old men looked nervously at one another, coughing and sighing. The first said, "It is our age. Where else could we go? We are too old to be wandering the roads, looking for work and shelter."

"It is our age," said the second man-at-arms. "When you are old, anything that does not disturb you is a comfort. Cold and darkness and boredom long ago lost their sharp edges for us, but warmth, singing, spring— no, they would all be disturbances. There are worse things than living like Haggard."

The third man said, "Haggard is older than we are. In time Prince Lír will be king in this country, and I will not leave the world until I have seen that day. I have always been fond of the boy, since he was small."

Molly found that she was not hungry. She looked around at the faces of the old men, and listened to the sounds their seamy lips and shrunken throats made as they drank her soup; and she was suddenly glad that King Haggard always had his meals alone. Molly inevitably came to care for anyone she fed.

Cautiously she asked them, "Have you ever heard a tale that Prince Lír is not Haggard's adopted nephew at all?" The men-at-arms showed no surprise at the question.

"Ay," the eldest replied, "We know that story. It may well be true, for the prince certainly bears no family resemblance to the king. But what of it? Better a stolen stranger ruled the land than a true son of King Haggard."

"But if the prince was stolen from Hagsgate" Molly cried, "then he is the man who will make the curse on this castle come true!" And she repeated the rhyme that the man Drinn had recited in the inn at Hagsgate.

> "Yet none but one of Hagsgate town
> May bring the castle swirling down."

But the old men shook their heads, grinning with teeth as rusty as their casques and corselets. "Not Prince Lír," the third man said. "The prince may slay a thousand dragons, but he will level no castles, overthrow no kings. It is not in his nature. He is a dutiful son who seeks—alas—only to be worthy of the man he calls his father. Not Prince Lír. The rhyme must speak of some other."

"And even if Prince Lír were the one," the second man added, "even if the curse had marked him for its messenger, still he would fail. For between King Haggard and any doom stands the Red Bull."

A silence sprang into the room and stood there, darkening all faces with its savage shadow and chilling the good hot soup with its breath. The little autumn cat stopped purring on Molly's lap, and the thin cooking fire cowered down. The cold scullery walls seemed to draw closer together.

The fourth man-at-arms, who had not spoken before, called across the dark to Molly Grue, "There is the true reason that we stay in Haggard's employ. He does not wish us to leave, and what King Haggard wishes or does not wish is the only concern of the Red Bull. We are Haggard's minions, but we are the Red Bull's prisoners."

Molly's hand was steady as she stroked the cat, but her voice was pinched and dry when she spoke. "What is the Red Bull to King Haggard?"

It was the oldest man-at-arms who answered. "We do not know. The Bull has always been here. It serves Haggard as his army and his bulwark; it is his strength and the source of his strength; and it must be his one companion as well, for I am sure he descends to its lair betimes, down some secret stair. But whether it obeys Haggard from choice or compulsion, and whether the Bull or the king is the master—that we have never known."

The fourth man, who was the youngest, leaned toward Molly Grue, his pink, wet eyes suddenly eager. He said, "The Red Bull is a demon, and its reckoning for attending Haggard will one day be Haggard himself." Another man interrupted him, insisting that the clearest evidence showed that the Bull was King Haggard's enchanted slave, and would be until it broke the bewitchment that held it and destroyed its former lord. They began to shout and spill their soup.

But Molly asked, not loudly, but in a way that made them all be still. "Do you know what a unicorn is? Have you ever seen one?"

Of everything alive in the little room, only the cat and the silence seemed to look back at her with any understanding. The four men blinked and belched and rubbed their eyes. Deep, restless, the sleeping Bull stirred again.

The meal being over, the men-at-arms saluted Molly Grue and left the scullery, two for their beds, two to take up their night's vigil in the rain. The oldest of the men waited until the others were gone before he said quietly to Molly, "Be careful of the Lady Amalthea. When she first came here, her beauty was such that even this accursed castle became beautiful too—like the moon, which is only a shining stone. But she has been here too long. Now she is as beautiful as ever, but the rooms and roofs that contain her are somehow meaner for her presence."

He gave a long sigh, which frayed into a whine. "I am familiar with that kind of beauty," he said, "but I had never seen that other sort before. Be careful of her. She should go away from here."

Alone, Molly put her face in the little cat's random fur. The cooking fire fluttered low, but she did not get up to feed it. Small, swift creatures scuttled across the room, making a sound like King Haggard's voice; and the rain rumbled against the castle walls, sounding like the Red Bull. Then, as though in answer, she heard the Bull. His bellow shattered the stones under her feet, and she clutched desperately at the table to keep herself and the cat from plunging down to him. She cried out.

The cat said, "He is going out. He goes out every sundown to hunt for the strange white beast that escaped him. You know that perfectly well. Don't be stupid."

The hungering roar came again, further away. Molly caught her breath and stared at the little cat. She was not as amazed as another might have been; these days she was harder to surprise than most women. "Could you always talk?" she asked the cat. "Or was it the sight of the Lady Amalthea that gave you speech?"

The cat licked a front paw reflectively. "It was the sight of her that made me feel like talking," he said at length, "and let us leave it at that. So that is a unicorn. She is very beautiful."

"How do you know she is a unicorn?" Molly demanded. "And why were you afraid to let her touch you? I saw you. You were afraid of her."

"I doubt that I will feel like talking for very long," the cat replied without rancor. "I would not waste time in foolishness if I were you. As to your first question, no cat out of its first fur can ever be deceived by appearances. Unlike human beings, who enjoy them. As for your second question—" Here he faltered, and suddenly became very interested in washing; nor would he speak until he had licked himself fluffy and then licked himself smooth again. Even then he would not look at Molly, but examined his claws.

"If she had touched me," he said very softly, "I would have been hers and not my own, not ever again. I wanted her to touch me, but I could not let her. No cat will. We let human beings caress us because it is pleasant enough and calms them—but not her. The price is more than a cat can pay."

Molly picked him up then, and he purred into her neck for such a long while that she began to fear that his moment of speech had passed. But presently he said, "You have very little time. Soon she will no longer remember who she is, or why she came to this place, and the Red Bull will no longer roar in the night for her. It may be that she will marry the good prince, who loves her." The cat pushed his head hard into Molly's suddenly still hand. "Do that," he commanded. "The prince is very brave, to love a unicorn. A cat can appreciate valiant absurdity."

"No," Molly Grue said. "No, that cannot be. She is the last."

"Well then, she must do what she came to do," the cat replied. "She must take the king's way down to the Bull."

Constant colors - white, green, gold

Molly held him so fiercely that he gave a mouselike squeak of protest. "Do you know the way?" she asked, as eagerly as Prince Lír had demanded of her. "Tell me the way, tell me where we must go." She put the cat down on the table and took her hands off him.

The cat made no answer for a long time, but his eyes grew brighter and brighter: gold shivering down to cover the green. His crooked ear twitched, and the black tip of his tail, and nothing more.

"When the wine drinks itself," he said, "when the skull speaks, when the clock strikes the right time— only then will you find the tunnel that leads to the Red Bull's lair." He tucked his paws under his chest and added, "There's a trick to it, of course."

"I'll bet," Molly said grimly. "There is a horrible, crumbly old skull stuck up high on a pillar in the great hall, but it hasn't had anything to say for some time. The clock that stands nearby is mad, and strikes when it pleases—midnight every hour, seventeen o'clock at four, or perhaps not a sound for a week. And the wine—oh, cat, wouldn't it be simpler just to show me the tunnel? You know where it is, don't you?"

"Of course I know," answered the cat, with a glinting, curling yawn. "Of course it would be simpler for me to show you. Save a lot of time and trouble."

His voice was becoming a sleepy drawl, and Molly realized that, like King Haggard himself, he was losing interest. Quickly she asked him, "Tell me one thing, then. What became of the unicorns? Where are they?"

The cat yawned again. "Near and far, far and near," he murmured. "They are within sight of your lady's eyes, but almost out of reach of her memory. They are coming closer, and they are going away." He closed his eyes.

Molly's breath came like rope, fretting against her harsh throat. "Damn you, why won't you help me?" she cried. "Why must you always speak in riddles?"

One eye opened slowly, green and gold as sunlight in the woods. The cat said, "I am what I am. I would tell you what you want to know if I could, for you have been kind to me. But I am a cat, and no cat anywhere ever gave anyone a straight answer."

His last few words drowsed away into a deep, regular purr, and he was asleep with the one eye partly open. Molly held him on her lap and stroked him, and he purred in his sleep, but he did not speak again. STOP

# XI

PRINCE LÍR CAME HOME three days after he set out to slay the maiden-fancying ogre, with the Great Axe of Duke Alban slung behind him and the ogre's head bumping at his saddlebow. He offered neither prize to the Lady Amalthea, nor did he rush to find her with the monster's blood still brown on his hands. He had made up his mind, as he explained to Molly Grue in the scullery that evening, nevermore to trouble the Lady Amalthea with his attentions, but to live quietly in the thought of her, serving her ardently until his lonely death, but seeking neither her company, her admiration, nor her love. "I will be as anonymous as the air she breathes," he said, "as invisible as the force that holds her on the earth." Thinking about it for a little, he added, "I may write a poem for her now and then, and slip it under her door, or just leave it somewhere for her to chance upon. But I won't ever sign the poem."

"It's very noble," Molly said. She felt relieved that the prince was giving up his courtship, and amused as well, and somewhat sad. "Girls like poems better than dead dragons and magic swords," she offered. "I always did, anyway, when I was a girl. The reason I ran off with Cully—"

But Prince Lír interrupted her, saying firmly, "No, do not give me hope. I must learn to live without hope, as my father does, and perhaps we will understand each other at last." He dug into his pockets, and Molly heard paper crackling. "Actually, I've already written a few poems about it—hope and her, and so on. You might look them over if you wanted to."

"I'd be very pleased," Molly said. "But will you never go out again, then, to fight with black knights and ride through rings of fire?" The words were meant teasingly, but she found as she spoke that she would have been a little sorry if it were so, for his adventures had made him much handsomer and taken off a lot of weight, and given him, besides, a hint of the musky fragrance of death that clings to all heroes. But the prince shook his head, looking almost embarrassed.

"Oh, I suppose I'll keep my hand in," he muttered. "But it wouldn't be for the show of it, or for her to find out. It was like that at first, but you get into the habit of rescuing people, breaking enchantments, challenging the wicked duke in fair combat—it's hard to give up being a hero, once you get used to it. Do you like the first poem?"

"It certainly has a lot of feeling," she said. "Can you really rhyme 'bloomed' and 'ruined'?"

"It needs a bit of smoothing out," Prince Lír admitted. " 'Miracle' 's the word I'm worried about."

"I was wondering about 'grackle' myself."

"No, the spelling. Is it one *r* and two *l*s, or the other way round?"

"One *r*, anyway, I think," Molly said. "Schmendrick"
—for the magician had just stooped through the doorway—"how many *r*s in 'miracle'?"

"Two," he answered wearily. "It has the same root as
'mirror.'" Molly ladled him out a bowl of broth, and
he sat down at the table. His eyes were hard and cloudy
as jade, and one of the lids was twitching.

"I can't do this very much longer," he said slowly. "It
isn't this horrible place, and it isn't having to be listening for him all the time—I'm getting rather good at
that—it's the wretched cheapjack flummery he has me
perform for him, hours on end—all night last night. I
wouldn't mind if he asked for the real magic, or even
for simple conjuring, but it's always the rings and the
goldfish, the cards and the scarves and the string, exactly
as it was in the Midnight Carnival. I can't do it. Not
much more."

"But that was what he wanted you for," Molly protested. "If he wanted real magic, he'd have kept the old
magician, that Mabruk." Schmendrick raised his head
and gave her a look that was almost amused. "I didn't
mean it like that," she said. "Besides it's only a little
while, until we find the way to the Red Bull that the cat
told me about."

She lowered her voice to a whisper as she spoke this
last, and both of them glanced quickly over at Prince
Lír; but he was sitting on a stool in the corner, evidently writing another poem. "Gazelle," he murmured,
tapping his pen against his lips. "Demoiselle, citadel,
asphodel, philomel, parallel . . ." He chose 'farewell,'
and scribbled rapidly.

"We will never find the way," Schmendrick said very

quietly. "Even if the cat told the truth, which I doubt, Haggard will make sure we never have time to investigate the skull and the clock. Why do you suppose he piles more work on you every day, if not to keep you from prowling and prying in the great hall? Why do you think he keeps me entertaining him with my carnival tricks?—why do you think he took me as his wizard in the first place? Molly, he *knows*, I'm sure of it! He knows what she is, though he doesn't quite believe it yet—but when he does, he'll know what to do. He knows. I see it in his face sometimes."

"The lift of longing, and the crash of loss," Prince Lír said. "The bitterness of tumpty-umpty-oss. Cross, boss, moss. Damn."

Schmendrick leaned across the table. "We can't stay here and wait for him to strike. The only hope we have is to escape at night—by sea, perhaps, if I can lay hold of a boat somewhere. The men-at-arms will look the other way, and the gate—"

"But the others!" she cried softly. "How can we leave, when she has come so far to find the other unicorns, and we know they are here?" Yet one small, tender, treacherous part of her was suddenly eager to be convinced of the quest's failure, and she knew it, and was angry at Schmendrick. "Well, but what about your magic?" she asked, "what about your own little search? Are you going to give that up too? Will she die in human shape, and you live forever? You might as well let the Bull have her then."

The magician sank back, his face gone as pale and crumpled as a washerwoman's fingers. "It doesn't really matter, one way or the other," he said, almost to himself. "She's no unicorn now, but a mortal woman—someone for that lout to sigh over and write poems about. Maybe Haggard won't find her out after all. She'll be his daughter, and he'll never know. That's funny." He put his soup aside untasted and leaned his head into his hands. "I couldn't change her back into a unicorn if we did find the others," he said. "There's no magic in me."

"Schmendrick—" she began; but at that moment he jumped to his feet and rushed out of the scullery, though she had not heard the king summon him. Prince Lír never looked up, but went on drumming meters and sampling rhymes. Molly hung a kettle over the fire for the sentries' tea.

"I've got it all but the final couplet," Lír said presently. "Do you want to hear it now, or would you rather wait?"

"Whichever you like," she said, so he read it then, but she never heard a word of it. Fortunately, the men-at-arms came in before he had finished reading, and he was too shy to ask her opinion in their presence. By the time they left he was working on something else, and it was very late when he bade her good night. Molly was sitting at the table, holding her motley cat.

The new poem was meant to be a sestina, and Prince Lír's head was jangling happily as he juggled the end words on his way up the stairs to his chamber. "I will leave the first one at her door," he thought, "and save the others until tomorrow." He was debating his original decision against signing his work, and playing with such pen names as "The Knight of the Shadows," and

"*Le Chevalier Mal-Aimé*," when he turned a corner and met the Lady Amalthea. She was coming down quickly in the dark, and when she saw him she made a strange, bleating sound and stood still, three steps above him.

She wore a robe that one of the king's men had stolen for her in Hagsgate. Her hair was down and her feet were bare, and the sight of her on the stair sent such sorrow licking along Prince Lír's bones that he dropped his poems and his pretenses together and actually turned to run. But he was a hero in all ways, and he turned bravely back to face her, saying in a calm and courtly manner, "Give you good evening, my lady."

The Lady Amalthea stared at him through the gloom, putting out a hand, but drawing it back before she touched him. "Who are you?" she whispered. "Are you Rukh?"

"I'm Lír," he answered, suddenly frightened. "Don't you know me?" But she backed away, and it seemed to the prince that her steps were as flowing as an animal's, and that she even lowered her head in the way of a goat or a deer. He said, "I'm Lír."

"The old woman," said the Lady Amalthea. "The moon went out. Ah!" She shivered once, and then her eyes recognized him. But all her body was still wild and watchful and she came no nearer to him.

"You were dreaming, my lady," he said, finding knightly speech again. "I would that I might know your dream."

"I have dreamed it before," she answered slowly. "I was in a cage, and there were others—beasts in cages, and an old woman. But I will not trouble you, my lord prince. I have dreamed it many times before."

She would have left him then, but he spoke to her in a voice that only heroes have, as many animals develop a certain call when they become mothers. "A dream that returns so often is like to be a messenger, come to warn you of the future or to remind you of things untimely forgotten. Say more of this, if you will, and I will try to riddle it for you."

Thereupon she halted, looking at him with her head a little turned, still with the air of some slim, furred ceature peering out of a thicket. But her eyes held a human look of loss, as though she had missed something she needed, or suddenly realized that she had never had it. If he had even blinked, she would have been gone; but he did not blink, and he held her, as he had learned to hold griffins and chimeras motionless with his steady gaze. Her bare feet wounded him deeper than any tusk or riving talon ever had, but he was a true hero.

The Lady Amalthea said, "In the dream there are black, barred wagons, and beasts that are and are not, and a winged being that clangs like metal in the moonlight. The tall man has green eyes and bloody hands."

"The tall man must be your uncle, the magician," Prince Lír mused. "That part's clear enough, anyway, and the bloody hands don't surprise me. I never cared much for his looks, if you'll pardon my saying so. Is that all the dream?"

"I cannot tell you all of it," she said. "It is never finished." Fear came back to her eyes like a great stone falling into a pool: all was clouded and swirling, and quick shadows were rushing everywhere. She said, "I am running away from a good place where I was safe, and the night is burning around me. But it is day too, and I am walking under beech trees in the warm, sour rain, and there are butterflies, and a honey sound, and dappled roads, and towns like fishbones, and the flying thing is killing the old woman. I am running and running into the freezing fire, however I turn, and my legs are the legs of a beast—"

"Lady," Prince Lír broke in, "my lady, by your leave, no more." Her dream was darkening into shape between them, and suddenly he did not want to know what it meant. "No more," he said.

"But I must go on," said the Lady Amalthea, "for it is never finished. Even when I wake, I cannot tell what is real, and what I am dreaming as I move and speak and eat my dinner. I remember what cannot have happened, and forget something that is happening to me now. People look at me as though I should know them, and I do know them in the dream, and always the fire draws nearer, though I am awake—"

"No more," he said desperately. "A witch built this castle, and to speak of nightmares here often makes them come true." It was not her dream that chilled him, but that she did not weep as she told it. As a hero, he understood weeping women and knew how to make them stop crying—generally you killed something—but her calm terror confused and unmanned him, while the shape of her face crumbled the distant dignity he had been so pleased at maintaining. When he spoke again, his voice was young and stumbling.

"I would court you with more grace," he said, "if I knew how. My dragons and my feats of arms weary you, but they are all I have to offer. I haven't been a hero for very long, and before I was a hero I was nothing at all, nothing but my father's dull, soft son. Perhaps I am only dull in a new way now, but I am here, and it is wrong of you to let me go to waste. I wish you wanted something of me. It wouldn't have to be a valiant deed—just useful."

Then the Lady Amalthea smiled at him for the first time since she had come to stay in King Haggard's castle. It was a small smile, like the new moon, a slender bend of brightness on the edge of the unseen, but Prince Lír leaned toward it to be warm. He would have cupped his hands around her smile and breathed it brighter, if he had dared.

"Sing to me," she said. "That would be valiant, to raise your voice in this dark, lonely place, and it will be useful as well. Sing to me, sing loudly—drown out my dreams, keep me from remembering whatever wants me to remember it. Sing to me, my lord prince, if it please you. It may not seem a hero's task, but I would be glad of it."

So Prince Lír sang out lustily, there on the cold stairway, and many damp, unseen creatures went flopping and scurrying for cover before the daylight gaiety of his voice. He sang the first words that came to him, and they were these:

"When I was a young man, and very well thought of,
    I couldn't ask aught that the ladies denied.
I nibbled their hearts like a handful of raisins,
    And I never spoke love but I knew that I lied.

"But I said to myself, 'Ah, they none of them know
The secret I shelter and savor and save.
I wait for the one who will see through my seeming,
And I'll know when I love by the way I behave.'

"The years drifted over like clouds in the heavens;
The ladies went by me like snow on the wind.
I charmed and I cheated, deceived and dissembled,
And I sinned, and I sinned, and I sinned, and I sinned.

"But I said to myself, 'Ah, they none of them see
There's part of me pure as the whisk of a wave.
My lady is late, but she'll find I've been faithful,
And I'll know when I love by the way I behave.'

"At last came a lady both knowing and tender,
Saying, 'You're not at all what they take you to be.'
I betrayed her before she had quite finished speaking,
And she swallowed cold poison and jumped in the sea.

"And I say to myself, when there's time for a word,
As I gracefully grow more debauched and depraved,
'Ah, love may be strong, but a habit is stronger,
And I knew when I loved by the way I behaved.'"

The Lady Amalthea laughed when he was done, and
that sound seemed to set the old, old darkness of the
castle hissing back from them both. "That was useful,"
she said. "Thank you, my lord."

"I don't know why I sang that one," Prince Lír said
awkwardly. "One of my father's men used to sing it to
me. I don't really believe it. I think that love is stronger
than habits or circumstances. I think it is possible to
keep yourself for someone for a long time, and still
remember why you were waiting when she comes at

last." The Lady Amalthea smiled again, but she did not answer, and the prince took a single step closer to her.

Marveling at his own boldness, he said softly, "I would enter your sleep if I could, and guard you there, and slay the thing that hounds you, as I would if it had the courage to face me in fair daylight. But I cannot come in unless you dream of me."

Before she could speak, if she meant to, they heard footsteps below them on the winding stair, and King Haggard's veiled voice saying, "I heard him singing. What business had he to be singing?"

Then Schmendrick, the royal wizard, his own voice meek and hurried, "Sire, it was but some heroic lay, some *chanson de geste,* such as he often sings when he rides out to glory, or rides home to renown. Be assured, Your Majesty—"

"He never sings here," the king said. "He sings continuously on his fool's wanderings, I am sure, because that is what heroes do. But he was singing here, and not of battle and gallantry either, but of love. Where is she? I knew he was singing of love before I ever heard him, for the very stones shuddered as they do when the Bull moves in the earth. Where is she?"

The prince and the Lady Amalthea looked at each other in the darkness, and in that moment they were side by side, though neither moved. With this came fear of the king, for whatever had been born between them, it might be something he wanted. A landing above them gave onto a corridor; they turned and ran together, though they could not see beyond their breaths. Her feet were as silent as the promise she had given him, but his own heavy boots rang exactly like boots on the stone floor. King Haggard made no pursuit, but his voice rustled down the hallway after them, whispering under the magician's words, "Mice, my lord, beyond a doubt. Fortunately, I am possessed of a singular spell—"

"Let them run," the king said. "It suits me well that they should run."

When they stopped running, wherever they stopped, they looked at each other again.

So the winter whined and crept along, not toward any spring, but toward the brief, devouring summer of King Haggard's country. Life in the castle went on in the silence that fills a place where no one hopes for anything. Molly Grue cooked and laundered, scrubbed stone, mended armor and sharpened swords; she chopped wood, milled flour, groomed horses and cleaned their stalls, melted down stolen gold and silver for the king's coffers, and made bricks without straw. And in the evenings, before she went to bed, she usually read over Prince Lír's new poems to the Lady Amalthea, and praised them, and corrected the spelling.

Schmendrick fooled and juggled and flimflammed as the king bade him, hating it, and knowing that Haggard knew he hated it and took his pleasure thereby. He never again suggested to Molly that they escape from the castle before Haggard made sure of the truth of the Lady Amalthea; but he no longer sought to discover the secret way down to the Red Bull, even when he was allowed time to himself. He seemed to have surrendered, not to the king but to some far older, crueler enemy that had caught up with him at last, this winter in this place.

The Lady Amalthea grew as much more beautiful every day as that day was grimmer and gloomier than the one before. The old men-at-arms, coming down drenched and shivering from walking their posts in the rain, or in from stealing things for the king, opened as quietly as flowers when they met her on the stairs or in the hallways. She would smile at them, and speak gently; but when she had passed by, the castle always seemed darker than ever, and the wind outside would rattle the thick sky like a sheet on a clothesline. For her beauty was human and doomed, and there was no comfort in it for old men. They could only draw their dripping cloaks tighter and limp on down to the small fire in the scullery.

But the Lady Amalthea and Prince Lír walked and spoke and sang together as blithely as though King Haggard's castle had become a green wood, wild and shadowy with spring. They climbed the crooked towers like hills, picnicked in stone meadows under a stone sky, and splashed up and down stairways that had softened and quickened into streams. He told her everything he knew, and what he thought about all of it, and happily invented a life and opinions for her, which she helped him do by listening. Nor was she deceiving him, for she truly remembered nothing before the castle and him. She began and ended with Prince Lír—except for the dreams, and they soon faded, as he had said they would.

They seldom heard the hunting roar of the Red Bull at night any more, but when the hungering sound came to her ears, then she would be frightened, and the walls and the winter would grow up around them again, as though their spring were all of her making, her joy's gift to the prince. He would have held her at such times, but he had long known her dread of being touched.

One afternoon the Lady Amalthea stood on the highest tower of the castle, watching for Prince Lír's return from an expedition against a brother-in-law of the ogre he had slain; for he still went out on occasional errantries, as he had told Molly he might. The sky was piled up over the valley of Hagsgate, the color of dirty soap, but it was not raining. Far below, the sea slid out toward the smoky horizon in hard bands of silver and green and kelpy brown. The ugly birds were restless: they flew out often, two and three together, circled swiftly over the water, and then returned to strut on the sand, chortling and cocking their heads at King Haggard's castle on the cliff. "Saidso, saidso!" The tide was low, and near to turning.

The Lady Amalthea began to sing, and her voice balanced and hovered in the slow, cold air like another sort of bird.

> "I am a king's daughter,
>   And I grow old within
>   The prison of my person,
>   The shackles of my skin.
>   And I would run away
>   And beg from door to door—"

She did not remember having heard the song before,

but the words pinched and plucked at her like children, trying to drag her back to some place that they wanted to see again. She moved her shoulders to get away from them.

"But I am not old," she said to herself, "and I am no prisoner. I am the Lady Amalthea, beloved of Lír, who has come into my dreams so that I may not doubt myself even while I sleep. Where could I have learned a song of sorrow? I am the Lady Amalthea, and I know only the songs that Prince Lír has taught me."

She lifted a hand to touch the mark on her forehead. The sea wheeled by, calm as the zodiac, and the ugly birds screamed. It troubled her a little that the mark would not go away.

"Your majesty," she said, though there had been no sound. She heard the rustling chuckle at her back, and turned to see the king. He wore a gray cloak over his mail, but his head was bare. The black lines on his face showed where the fingernails of age had skidded down the hard skin, but he looked stronger than his son, and wilder.

"You are quick for what you are," he said, "but slow, I think, for what you were. It is said that love makes men swift and women slow. I will catch you at last if you love much more."

She smiled at him without replying. She never knew what to say to the pale-eyed old man whom she so rarely saw, except as a movement on the edge of the solitude that she shared with Prince Lír. Then armor winked deep in the valley, and she heard the scrape of a weary horse stumbling on stone. "Your son is coming home," she said. "Let us watch him together."

King Haggard came slowly to stand beside her at the parapet, but he gave no more than a glance to the tiny, glinting figure riding home. "Nay, what concern have you or I with Lír, truly?" he asked. "He's none of mine, either by birth or belonging. I picked him up where someone else had set him down, thinking that I had never been happy and never had a son. It was pleasant enough at first, but it died quickly. All things die when I pick them up. I do not know why they die, but it has always been so, save for the one dear possession that has not turned cold and dull as I guarded it—the only thing that has ever belonged to me." His grim face gave the sudden starved leap of a sprung trap. "And Lír will be no help to you in finding it," he said. "He has never even known what it is."

Without warning, the whole castle sang like a plucked string as the beast asleep at its root shifted his dire weight. The Lady Amalthea caught her balance easily, being well used to this, and said lightly, "The Red Bull. But why do you think I have come to steal the Bull? I have no kingdom to keep, and no wish for conquest. What would I do with him? How much does he eat?"

"Do not mock me!" the king answered. "The Red Bull is no more mine than the boy is, and he does not eat, and he cannot be stolen. He serves anyone who has no fear—and I have no more fear than I have rest." Yet the Lady Amalthea saw forebodings sliding over the long, gray face, scuttling in the shadows of brows and bones. "Do not mock me," he said. "Why will you play that you have forgotten your quest, and that I am to remind you of it? I know what you have come for, and you know very well that I have it. Take it, then, take it if you can—but do not dare to surrender now!" The black wrinkles were all on edge, like knives.

Prince Lír was singing as he rode, though the Lady Amalthea could not yet hear the words. She said quietly to the king, "My lord, in all your castle, in all your realm, in all the kingdoms that the Red Bull may bring you, there is only one thing I desire—and you have just told me that he is not yours to give or to keep. Whatever it is you treasure that is not he, I truly wish you joy of it. Good day, Your Majesty."

She moved toward the tower stairway, but he stood in her way and she paused, looking at him with her eyes as dark as hoofprints in snow. The gray king smiled, and a strange kindness for him chilled her for an instant, for she suddenly fancied that they were somehow alike. But then he said, "I know you. I almost knew you as soon as I saw you on the road, coming to my door with your cook and your clown. Since then, there is no movement of yours that has not betrayed you. A pace, a glance, a turn of the head, the flash of your throat as you breathe, even your way of standing perfectly still—they were all my spies. You have made me wonder for a little while, and in my own way I am grateful. But your time is done."

He looked seaward over his shoulder, and suddenly stepped to the parapet with the thoughtless grace of a young man. "The tide is turning," he said. "Come and see it. Come here." He spoke very softly, but his voice suddenly held the crying of the ugly birds on the shore. "Come here," he said fiercely. "Come here, I won't touch you."

Prince Lír sang:

> "I will love you as long as I can,
> However long that may be ..."

The horrible head on his saddle was harmonizing in a kind of bass falsetto. The Lady Amalthea went to stand with the king.

The waves were coming in under the thick, swirling sky, growing as slowly as trees as they bulged across the sea. They crouched as they neared the shore, arching their backs higher and higher, and then sprang up the beach as furiously as trapped animals bounding at a wall and falling back with a sobbing snarl to leap again and again, claws caked and breaking, while the ugly birds yelled mournfully. The waves were gray and green as pigeons until they broke, and then they were the color of the hair that blew across her eyes.

"There," a strange, high voice said close to her. "There they are." King Haggard was grinning at her and pointing down to the white water. "There they are," he said, laughing like a frightened child, "there they are. Say that they are not your people, say that you did not come here searching for them. Say now that you have stayed all winter in my castle for love."

He could not wait for her answer, but turned away to look at the waves. His face was changed beyond believing: delight coloring the somber skin, rounding over the cheekbones, and loosening the bowstring mouth. "They are mine," he said softly, "they belong to me. The Red Bull gathered them for me, one at a time, and I bade him drive each one into the sea. What better place could there be to keep unicorns, and what other cage could hold them? For the Bull keeps guard over them, awake or asleep, and he daunted their hearts long ago. Now they live in the sea, and every tide still carries them within an easy step of the land, but they dare not take that step, they dare not come out of the water. They are afraid of the Red Bull."

Nearby, Prince Lír sang, "Others may offer more than they can give, All that they have for as long as they live . . ." The Lady Amalthea closed her hands on the parapet and wished for him to come to her, for she knew now that King Haggard was mad. Below them lay the thin, sallow beach, and the rocks, and the rising tide, and nothing more.

"I like to watch them. They fill me with joy." The childish voice was all but singing. "I am sure it is joy. The first time I felt it, I thought I was going to die. There were two of them in the early morning shadows. One was drinking from a stream, and the other was resting her head on his back. I thought I was going to die. I said to the Red Bull, 'I must have that. I must have all of it, all there is, for my need is very great.' So the Bull caught them, one by one. It was all the same to the Bull. It would have been the same if I had demanded tumblebugs or crocodiles. He can only tell the difference between what I want and what I do not want."

He had forgotten her for the moment as he leaned over the low wall, and she might have fled the tower then. But she stayed where she was, for an old bad dream was waking all around her, though it was daylight. The tide shattered on the rocks and tumbled together again, and Prince Lír rode along singing,

"But I will love you as long as I can, And never ask if you love me."

"I suppose I was young when I first saw them," King Haggard said. "Now I must be old—at least I have picked many more things up than I had then, and put them all down again. But I always knew that nothing was worth the investment of my heart, because nothing lasts, and I was right, and so I was always old. Yet each time I see my unicorns, it is like that morning in the woods, and I am truly young in spite of myself, and anything can happen in a world that holds such beauty."

In the dream I looked down at four white legs, and felt the earth under split hoofs. There was a burning on my brow, as there is now. But there were no unicorns coming in on the tide. The king is mad. He said, "I wonder what will become of them when I am gone. The Red Bull will forget them immediately, I know, and be off to find a new master, but I wonder if they will take their freedom even then. I hope not, for then they will belong to me forever."

Then he turned to look at her again, and his eyes were as gentle and greedy as Prince Lír's eyes became when he looked at her. "You are the last," he said. "The Bull missed you because you were shaped like a woman, but I always knew. How did you manage the change, by the way? Your magician couldn't have done it. I don't think he could turn cream into butter."

If she had let go of the parapet she would have fallen, but she answered him quite calmly, "My lord, I do not understand. I see nothing at all in the water."

The king's face shivered as though she were looking

at him through fire. "Do you still deny yourself?" he whispered. "Do you dare deny yourself? Nay, that's as false and cowardly as though you were truly human. I'll hurl you down to your folk with my own hands if you deny yourself." He took a step toward her, and she watched him with her eyes open, unable to move.

The tumult of the sea filled her head, together with Prince Lír's singing, and the blubbering death wail of the man named Rukh. King Haggard's gray face hung over her like a hammer, muttering, "It must be so, I cannot be mistaken. Yet her eyes are as stupid as his— as any eyes that never saw unicorns, never saw anything but themselves in a glass. What cheat is this, how can it be? There are no green leaves in her eyes now."

Then she did close her eyes, but she shut in more than she kept out. The bronze-winged creature with a hag's face swung by, laughing and prattling, and the butterfly folded its wings to strike. The Red Bull moved silently through the forest, pushing the bare branches aside with his pale horns. She knew when King Haggard went away, but she did not open her eyes.

It was long after, or only a little while later, that she heard the magician's voice behind her. "Be still, be still, it's over." She had not known that she was making any sound.

"In the sea," he said. "In the sea. Well, don't feel too bad about it. I didn't see them either, not this time or any other that I've stood here and watched the tide coming in. But he saw them—and if Haggard sees something, it's there." He laughed with a sound like an ax falling on wood. "Don't feel bad. This is a witch-castle, and it's hard to look closely at things, living here.

It's not enough to be ready to see—you have to be looking all the time." He laughed again, more gently. "All right," he said. "We'll find them now. Come on. Come with me."

She turned to him, moving her mouth to make words, but no words came out. The magician was studying her face with his green eyes. "Your face is wet," he said worriedly. "I hope that's spray. If you've become human enough to cry, then no magic in the world—oh, it must be spray. Come with me. It had better be spray."

# XII

N THE GREAT HALL of King Haggard's castle, the clock struck six. Actually, it was eleven minutes past midnight, but the hall was little darker than it had been at six o'clock, or at noon. Yet those who lived in the castle told time by the difference in the dark. There were hours when the hall was cold simply for want of warmth and gloomy for lack of light; when the air was stale and still, and the stones stank of old water because there were no windows to let in the scouring wind. That was daytime.

But at night, as some trees hold a living light all day, hold it with the undersides of their leaves until long after sundown—so at night the castle was charged and swarming with darkness, alive with darkness. Then the great hall was cold for a reason; then the small sounds that slept by day woke up to patter and scratch in the corners. It was night when the old smell of the stones seemed to rise from far below the floor.

"Light a light," Molly Grue said. "Please, can you make a light?"

Schmendrick muttered something curt and professional. For a moment nothing happened, but then a strange, sallow brightness began to spread over the floor, scattering itself about the room in a thousand scurrying shards that shone and squeaked. The little night beasts of the castle were glowing like fireflies. They darted here and there in the hall, raising swift shadows with their sickly light and making the darkness even colder than before.

"I wish you hadn't done that," Molly said. "Can you turn them off again? The purple ones, anyway, with the—with the legs, I guess."

"No, I can't," Schmendrick answered crossly. "Be quiet. Where's the skull?"

The Lady Amalthea could see it grinning from a pillar, lemon-small in the shadows and dim as the morning moon, but she said nothing. She had not spoken since she came down from the tower.

"There," the magician said. He strode to the skull and peered into its split and crumbling eyesockets for a long time, nodding slowly and making solemn sounds to himself. Molly Grue stared with equal earnestness, but she glanced often at the Lady Amalthea. At last Schmendrick said, "All right. Don't stand so close."

"Are there really spells to make a skull speak?" Molly asked. The magician stretched out his fingers and gave her a small, competent smile.

"There are spells to make everything speak. The master wizards were great listeners, and they devised ways to charm all things of the world, living and dead, into talking to them. That is most of it, being a wizard— seeing and listening." He drew a long breath, suddenly looking away and rubbing his hands together. "The rest is technique," he said. "Well. Here we go."

Abruptly he turned to face the skull, put one hand

lightly on the pale crown, and addressed it in a deep, commanding voice. The words marched out of his mouth like soldiers, their steps echoing with power as they crossed the dark air, but the skull made no answer at all.

"I just wondered," the magician said softly. He lifted his hand from the skull and spoke to it again. This time the sound of the spell was reasonable and cajoling, almost plaintive. The skull remained silent, but it seemed to Molly that a wakefulness slipped across the faceless front and was gone again.

In the scuttling light of the radiant vermin, the Lady Amalthea's hair shone like a flower. Appearing neither interested nor indifferent, but quiet in the way that a battlefield is sometimes quiet, she watched as Schmendrick recited one incantation after another to a desert-colored knob of bone that spoke not one word more than she did. Each charm was uttered in a more despairing tone than the last, the skull would not speak. And yet Molly Grue was certain that it was aware and listening, and amused. She knew the silence of mockery too well to mistake it for death.

The clock struck twenty-nine—at least, it was at that point that Molly lost count. The rusty strokes were still clanking to the floor when Schmendrick suddenly shook both fists at the skull and shouted, "All right, all right for you, you pretentious kneecap! How would you like a punch in the eye?" On the last words, his voice unraveled completely into a snarl of misery and rage.

"That's right," the skull said. "Yell. Wake up old Haggard." Its own voice sounded like branches creaking and knocking together in the wind. "Yell louder," it said. "The old man's probably around here somewhere. He doesn't sleep much."

Molly gave a small cry of delight, and even the Lady Amalthea moved a step nearer. Schmendrick stood with his fists shut and no triumph in his face. The skull said, "Come on. Ask me how to find the Red Bull. You can't go wrong asking my advice. I'm the king's watchman, set to guard the way to the Bull. Even Prince Lír doesn't know the secret way, but I do."

A little timidly, Molly Grue asked, "If you are truly on guard here, why don't you give the alarm? Why do you offer to help us, instead of summoning the men-at-arms?"

The skull gave a rattling chuckle. "I've been upon this pillar a long time," it said. "I was Haggard's chief henchman once, until he smote off my head for no reason. That was back in the days when he was being wicked to see if that was what he really liked to do. It wasn't, but he thought he might as well get some use out of my head, so he stuck it up here to serve as his sentinel. Under the circumstances, I'm not as loyal to King Haggard as I might be."

Schmendrick spoke in a low voice. "Answer the riddle, then. Tell us the way to the Red Bull."

"No," said the skull. Then it laughed like mad.

"Why not?" Molly cried furiously. "What kind of game—?" The skull's long yellow jaws never moved, but it was some time before the mean laughter chattered to a halt. Even the hurrying night things paused for a moment, stranded in their candy light, until it stopped.

"I'm dead," said the skull. "I'm dead, and I'm hanging in the dark watching over Haggard's property. The only small amusement I have is to irk and exasperate the living, and I don't get much chance of that. It's a sad loss, because in life mine was a particularly exasperating nature. You'll pardon me, I'm sure, if I indulge myself with you a little. Try me tomorrow. Maybe I'll tell you tomorrow."

"But we have no time!" Molly pleaded. Schmendrick nudged her, but she rushed on, stepping close to the skull and appealing directly to its uninhabited eyes. "We have no time. We may be too late now."

"I have time," the skull replied reflectively. "It's really not so good to have time. Rush, scramble, desperation, this missed, that left behind, those others too big to fit into such a small space—that's the way life was meant to be. You're supposed to be too late for some things. Don't worry about it."

Molly would have entreated further, but the magician gripped her arm and pulled her aside. "Be still!" he said in a swift, fierce voice. "Not a word, not another word. The damned thing spoke, didn't it? Maybe that's all the riddle requires."

"It isn't," the skull informed him. "I'll talk as much as you like, but I won't tell you anything. That's pretty rotten, isn't it? You should have seen me when I was alive."

Schmendrick paid no attention. "Where's the wine?" he demanded of Molly. "Let me see what I can do with the wine."

"I couldn't find any," she said nervously. "I looked everywhere, but I don't think there's a drop in the

194

castle." The magician glared at her in vast silence. "I *looked*," she said.

Schmendrick raised both arms slowly and let them fall to his sides. "Well," he said. "Well, that's it, then, if we can't find the wine. I have my illusions, but I can't make wine out of the air."

The skull giggled in a clacking, tocky way. "Matter can neither be created nor destroyed," it remarked. "Not by most magicians anyway."

From a fold of her dress Molly produced a small flask that gleamed faintly in the darkness. She said, "I thought if you had some water to start with . . ." Schmendrick and the skull gave her very much the same look. "Well, it's been done," she said loudly. "It's not as though you'd have to make up something new. I'd never ask that of you."

Hearing herself, she looked sideways at the Lady Amalthea; but Schmendrick took the flask from her hand and studied it thoughtfully, turning it over and murmuring curious, fragile words to himself. Finally he said, "Why not? As you say, it's a standard trick. There was quite a vogue for it at one time, I remember, but it's really a bit dated these days." He moved one hand slowly over the flask, weaving a word into the air.

"What are you doing?" the skull asked eagerly. "Hey, do it closer, do it over here. I can't see a thing." The magician turned away, holding the flask to his breast and bowing over it. He began a whispery chant that made Molly think of the sounds that a dead fire continues to make, long after the last coal has faded.

"You understand," he said, interrupting himself, "it won't be anything special. *Vin ordinaire*, if that." Molly nodded solemnly. Schmendrick said, "And it's usually too sweet; and how I'm supposed to get it to drink itself, I haven't the faintest idea." He took up the incantation again, even more softly, while the skull complained bitterly that it couldn't see or hear *anything.* Molly said something quiet and hopeful to the Lady Amalthea, who neither looked at her nor replied.

The chant stopped abruptly, and Schmendrick raised the flask to his lips. He sniffed at it first, muttering, "Weak, weak, hardly any bouquet at all. Nobody ever made good wine by magic." Then he tilted it to drink— then shook it, then stared at it; and then, with a small, horrible smile, turned it over. Nothing ran out, nothing at all.

"That's done it," Schmendrick said almost cheerfully. He touched a dry tongue to his dry lips and repeated, "That's done it, that has finally done it." Still smiling, he lifted the flask again to hurl it across the hall.

"No, wait—hey, don't!" The skull's clattering voice protested so wildly that Schmendrick halted before the flask left his hand. He and Molly turned together to regard the skull, which—so great was its anguish—had actually begun to wriggle where it hung, cracking its weathered (occiput) hard against the pillar as it strove to free itself. "Don't do that!" it wailed. "You people must be crazy, throwing away wine like that. Give it to me if you don't want it, but don't throw it away!" It rocked and lurched on the pillar, whimpering.

A dreamy, wondering look crossed Schmendrick's face, rather like a raincloud drifting over dry country. Slowly he asked, "And what use have you for wine, with no tongue to taste it, no ribby palate to savor it, no gullet to gulp it down? Fifty years dead, can it be that you still remember, still desire—?"

"Fifty years dead, what else can I do?" The skull had ceased its grotesque twitching, but frustration had made its voice almost human. "I remember," it said. "I remember more than wine. Give me a swallow, that's all—give me a sip—and I'll taste it as you never will, with all your runny flesh, all your buds and organs. I've had time to think. I know what wine is like. Give it to me."

Schmendrick shook his head, grinning. He said, "Eloquent, but I've been feeling a bit spiteful myself lately." For a third time, he lifted the empty flask, and the skull groaned in mortal misery.

Out of pity, Molly Grue began to say, "But it isn't—" but the magician stepped on her foot. "Of course," he mused aloud, "if you should happen to remember the entrance to the Red Bull's cavern as well as you remember wine, we might bargain yet." He twiddled the flask casually between two fingers.

"Done!" the skull cried instantly. "Done, for a dram, but give it to me now! I am more thirsty with thinking of wine than ever I was in life, when I had a throat to be dry. Only give me a single swig now, and I'll tell you anything you want to know." The rusted jaws were beginning to grind sideways on each other. The skull's slaty teeth were trembling and splitting.

"Give it to him," Molly whispered to Schmendrick. She was terrified that the naked eyesockets might start to fill up with tears. But Schmendrick shook his head again.

"I will give it all to you," he said to the skull. "After you tell us how we may find the Bull."

The skull sighed, but never hesitated. "The way is through the clock," it said. "You simply walk through the clock and there you are. Now can I have the wine?"

"Through the clock." The magician turned to peer into a far corner of the great hall, where the clock stood. It was tall and black and thin, the sundown shadow of a clock. The glass over its face was broken, and the hour hand was gone. Behind gray glass, the works could barely be seen, twitching and turning as fretfully as fish. Schmendrick said, "You mean, when the clock strikes the right time it opens, and then there is a tunnel, a hidden stair." His voice was doubtful, for the clock seemed far too lean to conceal any such passageway.

"I don't know anything about that," the skull replied. "If you wait for this clock to strike the hour, you'll be here till you're as bald as I am. Why complicate a simple secret? You walk through the clock, and the Red Bull is on the other side. Gimme."

"But the cat said—" Schmendrick began. Then he turned and walked toward the clock. The darkness made him seem to be going away down a hill, growing small and stooped. When he reached the clock he kept walking without pause, as though it were truly no more than a shadow. But he bumped his nose.

"This is stupid," he said coldly to the skull as he returned. "How do you think to cheat us? The way to the Bull may well lead through the clock, but there is something more to know. Tell me, or I will spill the wine out on the floor, for you to remember the smell and look of it as much as you choose. Be quick!"

But the skull was laughing again; this time making a thoughtful, almost kindly noise. "Remember what I told you about time," it said. "When I was alive, I believed—as you do—that time was at least as real and solid as myself, and probably more so. I said 'one o'clock' as though I could see it, and 'Monday' as though I could find it on the map; and I let myself be hurried along from minute to minute, day to day, year to year, as though I were actually moving from one place to another. Like everyone else, I lived in a house bricked up with seconds and minutes, weekends and New Year's Days, and I never went outside until I died, because there was no other door. Now I know that I could have walked through the walls."

Molly blinked bewilderedly, but Schmendrick was nodding. "Yes," he said. "That's how the real magicians do it. But then the clock—"

"The clock will never strike the right time," the skull said. "Haggard scrambled the works long ago, one day when he was trying to grab hold of time as it swung by. But the important thing is for you to understand that it doesn't matter whether the clock strikes ten next, or seven, or fifteen o'clock. You can strike your own time, and start the count anywhere. When you understand that—then any time at all will be the right time for you."

At that moment, the clock struck four. The last bang had not yet faded when there came an answering sound from beneath the great hall. Neither a bellow nor the savage grumble that the Red Bull often made when he dreamed, it was a low, inquiring sound, as though the Bull had awakened sensing something new in the night. Every flagstone buzzed like a snake, and the darkness itsef seemed to shudder as the glowing night creatures scampered wildly to the edges of the hall. Molly knew, suddenly and surely, that King Haggard was near.

"Give me the wine," the skull said. "I have kept my part of the bargain." Silently Schmendrick tipped the empty flask to the empty mouth, and the skull gurgled and sighed and smacked. "Ah," it said at last, "ah, that was the real stuff, that was *wine!* You're more of a magician than I took you for. Do you understand me now, about time?"

"Yes," Schmendrick answered. "I think so." The Red Bull made his curious sound again, and the skull rattled against the pillar. Schmendrick said, "No. I don't know. Is there no other way?"

"How can there be?" Molly heard footsteps; then nothing; then the thin, cautious ebb and flow of breathing. She could not tell where it came from. Schmendrick turned to her, and his face seemed to be smudged from within, like the inside of a lantern glass, with fear and confusion. There was a light too, but it shook like a lantern in a storm.

"I think I understand," he said, "but I'm sure I don't. I'll try."

"I still think it's a real clock," Molly said. "That's all right, though. I can walk through a real clock." She spoke partly to comfort him, but she felt a brightness in her own body as she realized that what she had said was true. "I know where we have to go," she said, "and that's as good as knowing the time any day."

The skull interrupted her. It said, "I'll give you a bit of advice in the bargain, because the wine was so good." Schmendrick looked guilty. The skull said, "Smash me. Just knock me to the floor and let me break in pieces. Don't ask why, just do it." It was speaking very quickly, almost whispering.

Together Schmendrick and Molly said, "What? Why?" The skull repeated its request. Schmendrick demanded, "What are you saying? Why on earth should we break you?"

"Do it!" the skull insisted. "Do it!" The sound of breath came nearer from all directions, though only on one pair of feet.

"No," Schmendrick said. "You're crazy." He turned his back and started a second time toward the gaunt, dark clock. Molly took the Lady Amalthea by her cold hand and followed him, trailing the white girl like a kite.

"All right," the skull said sadly. "I warned you." In a terrible voice, a voice like hail on iron, it began at once to cry, "Help ho, the king! Guards, to me! Here are burglars, bandits, mosstroopers, kidnapers, housebreakers, murderers, character assassins, plagiarists! King Haggard! Ho, King Haggard!"

Now over their heads and all around them, feet came clattering, and they heard the whistling voices of the aged men-at-arms calling as they ran. No torches flared, for no light could be struck in the castle unless the king himself ordered it, and Haggard was yet silent. The three thieves stood confounded and undone, gaping helplessly at the skull.

"I'm sorry," it said. "I'm just like that, treacherous. But I did try—" Then its vanished eyes suddenly saw the Lady Amalthea, and they went wide and bright, although they could not have. "Oh no," it said softly. "No, you don't. I'm disloyal, but I'm not *that* disloyal."

"Run," Schmendrick said, as he had said it long ago to the wild, sea-white legend that he had just set free. They fled across the great hall while the men-at-arms blundered loudly in the dark, and the skull shrieked, "Unicorn! Unicorn! Haggard, Haggard, there she goes, down to the Red Bull! Mind the clock, Haggard— where are you? Unicorn! Unicorn!"

Then the king's voice, rustling savagely under the uproar. "Fool, traitor, it was you who told her!" His quick, secret footsteps sounded close by, and Schmendrick set himself to turn and fight; but there came a grunt, and a crack, and a scraping noise, and then the bouncing crunch of old bone on old stone. The magician ran on.

When they stood before the clock, there was little grace either for doubting or understanding. The men-at-arms were in the hall now, and their clashing steps sent echoes booming back and forth between the walls, while King Haggard hissed and cursed them on. The Lady Amalthea never hesitated. She entered the clock and vanished as the moon passes behind clouds—hidden by them, but not in them, thousands of miles alone.

As though she were a dryad, Molly thought madly, and time were her tree. Through the dim, speckled glass

Molly could see the weights and the pendulum and the cankered chimes, all swaying and burning as she stared. There was no door beyond, through which the Lady Amalthea might have gone. There was only the rusty avenue of the works, leading her eyes away into rain. The weights drifted from side to side like seaweed.

King Haggard was shouting, "Stop them! Smash the clock!" Molly started to turn her head, meaning to tell Schmendrick that she thought she knew what the skull had meant; but the magician had disappeared, and so had the hall of King Haggard. The clock was gone too, and she was standing beside the Lady Amalthea in a cold place.

The king's voice came to her from very far away, not so much heard as remembered. She went on turning her head, and found herself looking into the face of Prince Lír. Behind him there fell a bright mist, shivering like the sides of a fish, and bearing no resemblance at all to corroded clockwork. Schmendrick was nowhere to be seen.

Prince Lír bent his head gravely to Molly, but it was to the Lady Amalthea that he spoke first. "And you would have gone without me," he said. "You haven't been listening at all."

She answered him then, when she had not spoken to Molly or the magician. In a low, clear voice, she said, "I would have come back. I do not know why I am here, or who I am. But I would have come back."

"No," said the prince, "you would never have come back."

Before he could say anything more, Molly broke in—much to her own surprise—crying, "Never mind all that! Where's Schmendrick?" The two strangers looked at her in courteous wonder that anyone else in the world should be able to speak, and she felt herself shake once from head to heels. "Where is he?" she demanded. "I'll go back myself, if you won't," and she turned round again.

He came out of the mist, walking with his head down, as though he were leaning against a strong wind. He was holding a hand to his temple, and when he took it away the blood came softly down.

"It's all right," he said when he saw that the blood was falling on Molly Grue's hands. "It's all right, it's not deep. I couldn't get through until it happened." He bowed shakily to Prince Lír. "I thought it was you who went by me in the dark," he said. "Tell me, how did you pass through the clock so easily? The skull said you didn't know the way."

The prince looked puzzled. "What way?" he asked. "What was there to know? I saw where she had gone, and I followed."

Schmendrick's sudden laugh rubbed itself raw against the snaggy walls that came swimming in on them as their eyes grew familiar with this new darkness. "Of course," he said. "Some things have their own time by nature." He laughed again, shaking his head, and the blood flew. Molly tore a piece out of her dress.

"Those poor old men," the magician said. "They didn't want to hurt me, and I wouldn't have hurt them if I could. We dodged around and around, apologizing to each other, and Haggard was yelling, and I kept bumping into the clock. I knew that it wasn't a real clock, but it felt real, and I worried about it. Then

Haggard came up with his sword and hit me." He closed his eyes as Molly bound his head. "Haggard," he said. "I was getting to like him. I still do. He looked so frightened." The dim, removed voices of the king and his men seemed to be growing louder.

"I don't understand," Prince Lír said. "Why was he frightened—my father? What did he—?" But just then from the far side of the clock, they heard a wordless squall of triumph and the beginning of a great crash. The shimmering haze vanished immediately, and black silence caved in on them all.

"Haggard has destroyed the clock," Schmendrick said presently. "Now there is no way back, and no way out but the Bull's way." A slow, thick wind began to wake. STOP

# XIII

FINISH

THE WAY was wide enough for all of them to walk abreast, but they went one by one. The Lady Amalthea walked in front, by her own choosing. Prince Lír, Schmendrick, and Molly Grue, following, had only her hair for lantern, but she herself had no light before her at all. Yet she went on as easily as though she had been this way before.

Where they truly were, they never knew. The cold wind seemed real, as did the cold reek that rode it, and the darkness let them pass far more grudgingly than had the clock. The path itself was enough of a fact to bruise feet, and to be partly choked in places by real stones and real earth that had crumbled down the sides of the cave. But its course was the impossible way of a dream: pitched and skewed, rounding on itself; now dropping almost sheer, now seeming to rise a little; now working out and slowly down, and now wandering back to take them, perhaps, once again below the great hall where old King Haggard must still be raging over a toppled clock and a shivered skull. Witchwork, surely, Schmendrick thought, and nothing made by a witch is real, at the last. Then he added, But this must

206

be the last. It will all be real enough if this is not the last.

As they stumbled along, he hurriedly told Prince Lír the tale of their adventures, beginning with his own strange history and stranger doom; recounting the ruin of the Midnight Carnival and his flight with the unicorn, and continuing through their meeting with Molly Grue, the journey to Hagsgate, and Drinn's story of the double curse on the town and the tower. Here he halted, for beyond lay the night of the Red Bull: a night that ended, for good or ill, with magic—and with a naked girl who struggled in her body like a cow in quicksand. He hoped that the prince would be more interested in learning of his heroic birth than in the origins of the Lady Amalthea.

Prince Lír marveled suspiciously, which is an awkward thing to manage. "I have known for a very long time that the king is not my father," he said. "But I tried hard to be his son all the same. I'm the enemy of any who plot against him, and it would take more than a crone's gibbering to make me work his downfall. As for the other, I think there are no unicorns any more, and I know that King Haggard has never seen one. How could any man who had looked upon a unicorn even once—let alone thousands with every tide— possibly be as sad as King Haggard is? Why, if I had only seen *her* once, and never again—" Now he himself paused in some confusion, for he also felt that the talk was going on to some sorrow from which it could never be called back. Molly's neck and shoulders were listening intently, but if the Lady Amalthea could hear what the two men were saying, she gave no sign.

"Yet the king has a joy hidden somewhere about his life," Schmendrick pointed out. "Have you never seen a trace of it, truly—never seen its track in his eyes? I have. Think for a moment, Prince Lír."

The prince was silent, and they wound further into the foul dark. They could not always tell whether they were climbing or descending; nor, sometimes, if the passage were bending once again, until the gnarly nearness of stone at their shoulders suddenly became the bleak rake of a wall against their faces. There was not the smallest sound of the Red Bull, or any glimmer of the wicked light; but when Schmendrick touched his damp face, the smell of the Bull came off on his fingers.

Prince Lír said, "Sometimes, when he has been on the tower, there is something in his face. Not a light, exactly, but a clearness. I remember. I was little, and he never looked like that when he looked at me, or at anything else. And I had a dream." He was walking very slowly now, scuffing his feet. "I used to have a dream," he said, "the same dream over and over, about standing at my window in the middle of the night and seeing the Bull, seeing the Red Bull—" He did not finish.

"Seeing the Bull driving unicorns into the sea," Schmendrick said. "It was no dream. Haggard has them all now drifting in and out on the tides for his delight—all but one." The magician drew a deep breath. "That one is the Lady Amalthea."

"Yes," Prince Lír answered him. "Yes, I know."

Schmendrick stared at him. "What do you mean, you know?" he demanded angrily. "How could you possibly know that the Lady Amalthea is a unicorn? She can't have told you, because she doesn't remember it herself. Since you took her fancy, she has thought only of being a mortal woman." He knew quite well that the truth was the other way around, but it made no difference to him just then. "How do you know?" he asked again.

Prince Lír stopped walking and turned to face him. It was too dark for Schmendrick to see anything but the cool, milky shining where his wide eyes were.

"I did not know what she was until now," he said. "But I knew the first time I saw her that she was something more than I could see. Unicorn, mermaid, lamia, sorceress, Gorgon—no name you give her would surprise me, or frighten me. I love whom I love."

"That's a very nice sentiment," Schmendrick said. "But when I change her back into her true self, so that she may do battle with the Red Bull and free her people—"

"I love whom I love,'" Prince Lír repeated firmly. "You have no power over anything that matters."

Before the magician could reply, the Lady Amalthea was standing between them, though neither man had seen or heard her as she came back along the passage-way. In the darkness she gleamed and trembled like running water. She said, "I will go no farther."

It was to the prince that she spoke, but it was Schmendrick who said, "There is no choice. We can only go on." Molly Grue came nearer; one anxious eye and the pale start of a cheekbone. The magician said again, "We can only go on."

The Lady Amalthea would not look straight at him. "He must not change me," she said to Prince Lír. "Do not let him work his magic on me. Ths Bull has no care for human beings—we may walk out past him and get away. It is a unicorn the Bull wants. Tell him not to change me into a unicorn."

Prince Lír twisted his fingers until they cracked. Schmendrick said, "It is true. We might very well escape the Red Bull that way even now, as we escaped before. But if we do, there will never be another chance. All the unicorns of the world will remain his prisoners forever, except one, and she will die. She will grow old and die."

"Everything dies," she said, still to Prince Lír. "It is good that everything dies. I want to die when you die. Do not let him enchant me, do not let him make me immortal. I am no unicorn, no magical creature. I am human, and I love you."

He answered her, saying gently, "I don't know much about enchantments, except how to break them. But I know that even the very greatest wizards are powerless against two who keep to each other—and this one is only poor Schmendrick, after all. Don't be afraid. Don't be afraid of anything. Whatever you have been, you are mine now. I can hold you."

She turned to look at the magician at last, and even through the darkness he could feel the terror in her eyes. "No," she said. "No, we are not strong enough. He will change me, and whatever happens after that, you and I will lose each other. I will not love you when I am a unicorn, and you will love me only because you cannot help it. I will be more beautiful than anything in the world, and live forever."

Schmendrick began to speak, but the sound of his

voice made her cower like a candle flame. "I will not have it. I will not have it so." She was looking back and forth from the prince to the magician, holding her voice together like the edges of a wound. She said, "If there is left a single moment of love when he changes me, you will know it, for I will let the Red Bull drive me into the sea with the others. Then at least I will be near you."

"There's no need for all that." Schmendrick spoke lightly, making himself laugh. "I doubt I could turn you back if you wished it. Nikos himself never could turn a human being into a unicorn—and you are truly human now. You can love, and fear, and forbid things to be what they are, and overact. Let it end here then, let the quest end. Is the world any the worse for losing the unicorns, and would it be any better if they were running free again? One good woman more in the world is worth every single unicorn gone. Let it end. Marry the prince and live happily ever after."

The passageway seemed to be growing lighter, and Schmendrick imagined the Red Bull stealing toward them, grotesquely cautious, setting his hoofs down as primly as a heron. The thin glimmer of Molly Grue's cheekbone went out as she turned her face away. "Yes," said the Lady Amalthea. "That is my wish."

But at the same moment, Prince Lír said, "No."

The word escaped him as suddenly as a sneeze, emerging in a questioning squeak—the voice of a silly young man mortally embarassed by a rich and terrible gift. "No," he repeated, and this time the word tolled in another voice, a king's voice: not Haggard, but a king

211

whose grief was not for what he did not have, but for what he could not give.

"My lady," he said, "I am a hero. It is a trade, no more, like weaving or brewing, and like them it has its own tricks and knacks and small arts. There are ways of perceiving witches, and of knowing poison streams; there are certain weak spots that all dragons have, and certain riddles that hooded strangers tend to set you. But the true secret of being a hero lies in knowing the order of things. The swineherd cannot already be wed to the princess when he embarks on his adventures, nor can the boy knock at the witch's door when she is away on vacation. The wicked uncle cannot be found out and foiled before he does something wicked. Things must happen when it is time for them to happen. Quests may not simply be abandoned; prophecies may not be left to rot like unpicked fruit; unicorns may go unrescued for a long time, but not forever. The happy ending cannot come in the middle of the story."

The Lady Amalthea did not answer him. Schmendrick asked, "Why not? Who says so?"

"Heroes," Prince Lír replied sadly. "Heroes know about order, about happy endings—heroes know that some things are better than others. Carpenters know grains and shingles, and straight lines." He put his hands out to the Lady Amalthea, and took one step toward her. She did not draw back from him, nor turn her face; indeed, she lifted her head higher, and it was the prince who looked away.

"You were the one who taught me," he said. "I never looked at you without seeing the sweetness of the way the world goes together, or without sorrow for its spoiling. I became a hero to serve you, and all that is like you. Also to find some way of starting a conversation." But the Lady Amalthea spoke no word to him.

Pale as lime, the brightness was rising in the cavern. They could see one another clearly now, each gone tallowy and strange with fear. Even the beauty of the Lady Amalthea drained away under that dull, hungry light. She looked more mortal than any of the other three.

"The Bull is coming," Prince Lír said. He turned and set off down the passageway, taking the bold, eager strides of a hero. The Lady Amalthea followed him, walking as lightly and proudly as princesses are taught to try to walk. Molly Grue stayed close to the magician, taking his hand as she had been used to touch the unicorn when she was lonely. He smiled down at her, looking quite pleased with himself.

Molly said, "Let her stay the way she is. Let her be."

"Tell that to Lír," he replied cheerfully. "Was it I who said that order is all? Was it I who said that she must challenge the Red Bull because it will be more proper and precise that way? I have no concern for regulated rescues and official happy endings. That's Lír."

"But you made him do it," she said. "You know that all he wants in the world is to have her give up her quest and stay with him. And he would have done it, but you reminded him that he is a hero, and now he has to do what heroes do. He loves her, and you tricked him."

"I never," Schmendrick said. "Be quiet, he'll hear

you." Molly felt herself growing light-headed, silly with the nearness of the Bull. The light and the smell had become a sticky sea in which she floundered like the unicorns, hopeless and eternal. The path was beginning to tilt downward, into the deepening light; and far ahead Prince Lír and the Lady Amalthea went marching along to disaster as calmly as candles burning down. Molly Grue snickered.

She went on, "I know why you did it too. You can't become mortal yourself until you change her back again. Isn't that it? You don't care what happens to her, or to the others, just as long as you become a real magician at last. Isn't that it? Well, you'll never be a real magician, even if you change the Bull into a bull-frog, because it's still just a trick when you do it. You don't care about anything but magic, and what kind of magician is that? Schmendrick, I don't feel good. I have to sit down."

Schmendrick must have carried her for a time, because she was definitely not walking and his green eyes were ringing in her head. "That's right. Nothing but magic matters to me. I would round up unicorns for Haggard myself if it would heighten my power by half a hair. It's true. I have no preferences and no loyalties. I have only magic." His voice was hard and sad.

"Really?" she asked, rocking dreamily in her terror, watching the brightness flowing by. "That's awful." She was very impressed. "Are you really like that?"

"No," he said, then or later. "No, it's not true. How could I be like that, and still have all these troubles?" Then he said, "Molly, you have to walk now. He's there. He's there."

Molly saw the horns first. The light made her cover her face, but the pale horns struck bitterly through hands and eyelids to the back of her mind. She saw Prince Lír and the Lady Amalthea standing before the horns, while the fire flourished on the walls of the cavern and soared up into the roofless dark. Prince Lír had drawn his sword, but it blazed up in his hand, and he let it fall, and it broke like ice. The Red Bull stamped his foot, and everyone fell down.

Schmendrick had thought to find the Bull waiting in his lair, or in some wide place with room enough to do battle. But he had come silently up the passageway to meet them; and now he stood across their sight, not only from one burning wall to the other, but somehow in the walls themselves, and beyond them, bending away forever. Yet he was no mirage, but the Red Bull still, steaming and snuffling, shaking his blind head. His jaws champed over his breath with a terrible wallowing sound.

*Now. Now is the time, whether I work ruin or great good. This is the end of it.* The magician rose slowly to his feet, ignoring the Bull, listening only to his cupped self, as to a seashell. But no power stirred or spoke in him; he could hear nothing but the far, thin howling of emptiness against his ear; as old King Haggard must have heard it waking and sleeping, and never another sound. *It will not come to me. Nikos was wrong. I am what I seem.*

The Lady Amalthea had stepped back a pace from the Bull, but no more, and she was regarding him quietly as he pawed with his front feet and snorted great, rumbling, rainy blasts out of his vast nostrils. He seemed

215

puzzled about her, and almost foolish. He did not roar. The Lady Amalthea stood in his freezing light with her head tipped back to see all of him. Without turning her head, she put her hand out to find Prince Lír's hand.

*Good, good. There is nothing I can do, and I am glad of it. The Bull will let her by, and she will go away with Lír. It is as right as anything. I am only sorry about the unicorns.* The prince had not yet noticed her offered hand, but in a moment he would turn and see, and touch her for the first time. *He will never know what she has given him, but neither will she.* The Red Bull lowered his head and charged.

He came without warning, with no sound but the rip of his hoofs; and if he had chosen, he could have crushed all four of them in that one silent onslaught. But he let them scatter before him and flatten themselves into the wrinkled walls; and he went by without harming them, though he might easily have horned them out of their shallow shelters like so many periwinkles. Supple as fire, he turned where there was no room to turn and met them again, his muzzle almost touching the ground, his neck swelling like a wave. It was then that he roared.

They fled and he followed: not as swiftly as he had charged, but quickly enough to keep each one alone, friendless in the wild dark. The ground tore under their feet, and they cried out, but they could not even hear themselves. Every bellow of the Red Bull brought great slides of stones and earth shuddering down on them; and still they scrambled along like broken insects and still he came after them. Through his mad blaring they heard another sound: the deep whine of the castle itself as it strained at its roots, drumming like a flag in the wind of his wrath. And very faintly there drifted up the passageway the smell of the sea.

*He knows, he knows! I fooled him once that way, but not again. Woman or unicorn, he will hunt her into the sea this time, as he was bidden, and no magic of mine will turn him from it. Haggard has won.*

So the magician thought as he ran, all hope gone for the first time in his long, strange life. The way widened suddenly and they emerged into a kind of grotto that could only have been the Bull's den. The stench of his sleeping hung so thick and old here that it had a loathly sweetness about it; and the cave brooded gullet-red, as though his light had rubbed off on the walls and crusted in the cracks and crevices. Beyond lay the tunnel again, and the dim gleam of breaking water.

The Lady Amalthea fell as irrevocably as a flower breaks. Schmendrick leaped to one side, wheeling to drag Molly Grue with him. They brought up hard against a split slab of rock, and there they crouched together as the Red Bull raged by without turning. But he came to a halt between one stride and the next; and the sudden stillness—broken only by the Bull's breathing and the distant grinding of the sea—would have been absurd, but for the cause of it.

She lay on her side with one leg bent beneath her. She moved slowly, but she made no sound. Prince Lír stood between her body and the Bull, weaponless, but with his hands up as though they still held a sword and shield. Once more in that endless night, the prince said, "No."

He looked very foolish, and he was about to be

217

trampled flat. The Red Bull could not see him, and would kill him without ever knowing that he had been in the way. Wonder and love and great sorrow shook Schmendrick the Magician then, and came together inside him and filled him, filled him until he felt himself brimming and flowing with something that was none of these. He did not believe it, but it came to him anyway, as it had touched him twice before and left him more barren than he had been. This time, there was too much of it for him to hold: it spilled through his skin, sprang from his fingers and toes, willed up equally in his eyes and his hair and the hollows of his shoulders. There was too much to hold, too much ever to use; and still he found himself weeping with the pain of his impossible greed. He thought, or said, or sang, *I did not know that I was so empty, to be so full.*

The Lady Amalthea lay where she had fallen, though now she was trying to rise, and Prince Lír still guarded her, raising his naked hands against the enormous shape that loomed over him. The tip of the prince's tongue stuck out of one corner of his mouth, making him look as serious as a child taking something apart. Long years later, when Schmendrick's name had become a greater name than Nikos's and worse than afreets surrendered at the sound of it, he was never able to work the smallest magic without seeing Prince Lír before him, his eyes squinted up because of the brightness and his tongue sticking out.

The Red Bull stamped again, and Prince Lír fell on his face and got up bleeding. The Bull's rumble began, and the blind, bloated head started down, lowering like one half of the scales of doom. Lír's valiant heart hung between the pale horns, as good as dripping from their tips, himself as good as smashed and scattered: and his mouth buckled a little, but he never moved. The sound of the Bull grew louder as the horns went down.

Then Schmendrick stepped into the open and said a few words. They were short words, undistinguished either by melody or harshness, and Schmendrick himself could not hear them for the Red Bull's dreadful bawling. But he knew what they meant, and he knew exactly how to say them, and he knew that he could say them again when he wanted to, in the same way or in a different way. Now he spoke them gently and with joy, and as he did so he felt his immortality fall from him like armor, or like a shroud.

At the first word of the spell, the Lady Amalthea gave a thin, bitter cry. She reached out again to Prince Lír, but he had his back to her, protecting her, and he did not hear. Molly Grue, heartsick, caught at Schmendrick's arm but the magician spoke on. Yet even when the wonder blossomed where she had been—sea-white, sea-white, as boundlessly beautiful as the Bull was mighty—still the Lady Amalthea clung to herself for a moment more. She was no longer there, and yet her face hovered like a breath in the cold, reeky light.

If would have been better if Prince Lír had not turned until she was gone, but he turned. He saw the unicorn, and she shone in him as in a glass, but it was to the other that he called—to the castaway, to the Lady Amalthea. His voice was the end of her: she vanished when he cried her name, as though he had crowed for day.

Things happened both swiftly and slowly as they do

in dreams, where it is really the same thing. The unicorn stood very still, looking at them all out of lost, elsewhere eyes. She seemed even more beautiful than Schmendrick remembered, for no one can keep a unicorn in his head for long; and yet she was not as she had been, no more than he was. Molly Grue started toward her, speaking softly and foolishly, but the unicorn gave no sign that she knew her. The marvelous horn remained dull as rain.

With a roar that set the walls of his lair belling out and cracking like circus canvas, the Red Bull charged for the second time. The unicorn fled across the cave and into darkness. Prince Lír, in turning had stepped a little to one side, and before he could wheel back again, the Bull's plunging pursuit smashed him down, stunned, with his mouth open.

Molly would have gone to him, but Schmendrick took hold of her and dragged her along after the Bull and the unicorn. Neither beast was in sight, but the tunnel still thundered from their desperate passage. Dazed and bewildered, Molly stumbled beside the fierce stranger who would neither let her fall nor slacken her pace. Over her head and all around, she could feel the castle groaning, creaking in the rock like a loosening tooth. The witch's rhyme jangled in her memory, over and over.

"Yet none but one of Hagsgate town
May bring the castle swirling down."

Suddenly it was sand slowing their feet, and the smell of the sea—cold as the other smell, but so good, so friendly that they both stopped running and laughed aloud. Above them, on the cliff, King Haggard's castle splayed up toward a gray-green morning sky splashed with thin, milky clouds. Molly was sure that the king himself must be watching from one of the tremulous towers, but she could not see him. A few stars still fluttered in the heavy blue sky over the water. The tide was out, and the bald beach had the gray, wet gleam of a stripped shellfish, but far down the strand the sea was bending like a bow, and Molly knew that the ebb had ended.

The unicorn and the Red Bull stood facing each other at the arch of the bow, and the unicorn's back was to the sea. The Bull moved in slowly, not charging, but pressing her almost gently toward the water, never touching her. She did not resist him. Her horn was dark, and her head was down, and the Bull was as much her master as he had been on the plain of Hagsgate, before she became the Lady Amalthea. It might have been that same hopeless dawn, except for the sea.

Yet she was not altogether beaten. She backed away until one hind foot actually stepped into the water. At that, she sprang through the sullen smolder of the Red Bull and ran away along the beach: so swift and light that the wind of her passing blew her footprints off the sand. The Bull went after her.

"Do something," a hoarse voice said to Schmendrick, as Molly had said it long ago. Prince Lír stood behind him, his face bloody and his eyes mad. He looked like King Haggard. "Do something," he said. "You have power. You changed her into a unicorn—do something

221

now to save her. I will kill you if you don't." He showed the magician his hands.

"I cannot," Schmendrick answered him quietly. "Not all the magic in the world can help her now. If she will not fight him, she must go into the sea with the others. Neither magic nor murder will help her."

Molly heard small waves slapping on the sand—the tide was beginning to turn. She saw no unicorns tumbling in the water, though she looked for them, willing them to be there. What if it is too late? What if they drifted out on the last ebb tide, out to the deepest sea where no ships go, because of the kraken and the sea-drake, and because of the floating jungles of wrack that tangle and drown even these? She will never find them then. Would she stay with me?

"Then what is magic for?" Prince Lír demanded wildly. "What use is wizardry if it cannot save a unicorn?" He gripped the magician's shoulder hard, to keep from falling.

Schmendrick did not turn his head. With a touch of sad mockery in his voice, he said, "That's what heroes are for."

They could not see the unicorn for the hugeness of the Bull; but suddenly she doubled on her track and came flying up the beach toward them. Blind and patient as the sea, the Red Bull followed her, his hoofs gouging great ditches in the damp sand. Smoke and fire, spray and storm, they came on together, neither one gaining, and Prince Lír gave a soft grunt of understanding.

"Yes, of course," he said. "That is exactly what heroes are for. Wizards make no difference, so they say that nothing does, but heroes are meant to die for unicorns." He let go of Schmendrick's shoulder, smiling to himself.

"There is a basic fallacy in your reasoning," Schmendrick began indignantly, but the prince never heard what it was. The unicorn flashed by them—her breath streaming blue-white and her head carried too high—and Prince Lír leaped into the path of the Red Bull. For a moment, he disappeared entirely, like a feather in a flame. The Bull ran over him and left him lying on the ground. One side of his face cuddled too hard into the sand, and one leg kicked the air three times before it stopped.

He fell without a cry, and Schmendrick and Molly alike were stricken as silent as he, but the unicorn turned. The Red Bull halted when she did, and wheeled to put her once more between himself and the sea. He began his mincing, dancing advance again, but he might have been a courting bird for all the attention the unicorn paid him. She stood motionless, staring at the twisted body of Prince Lír.

The tide was grumbling in hard now, and the beach was already a slice narrower. Whitecaps and skipper's-daughters spilled up into the sprawling dawn, but Molly Grue still saw no other unicorn but her own. Over the castle, the sky was scarlet, and on the highest tower King Haggard stood up as clear and black as a winter tree. Molly could see the straight scar of his mouth, and his nails darkening as he gripped the parapet. But the castle cannot fall now. Only Lír could have made it fall.

Suddenly the unicorn screamed. It was not at all like

the challenging bell with which she had first met the
Red Bull; it was an ugly, squawking wail of sorrow and
loss and rage, such as no immortal creature ever gave.
The castle quaked, and King Haggard shrank back with
one arm across his face. The Red Bull hesitated, shuffling in the sand, lowing doubtfuly.

The unicorn cried out again and reared up like a
scimitar. The sweet sweep of her body made Molly
close her eyes, but she opened them again in time to see
the unicorn leap at the Red Bull, and the Bull swerve
out of her way. The unicorn's horn was light again,
burning and shivering like a butterfly.

Again she charged, and again the Bull gave ground,
heavy with perplexity but still quick as a fish. His own
horns were the color and likeness of lightning, and
the slightest swing of his head made her stagger; but he
retreated and retreated, backing steadily down the
beach, as she had done. She lunged after him, driving to
kill, but she could not reach him. She might have been
stabbing at a shadow, or at a memory.

So the Red Bull fell back without giving battle, until
she had stalked him to the water's edge. There he made
his stand, with the surf swirling about his hoofs and the
sand rushing away under them. He would neither fight
nor fly, and she knew now that she could never destroy
him. Still she set herself for another charge, while he
muttered wonderingly in his throat.

For Molly Grue, the world hung motionless in that
glass moment. As though she were standing on a higher
tower than King Haggard's, she looked down on a pale
paring of land where a toy man and woman stared
with their knitted eyes at a clay bull and a tiny ivory

unicorn. Abandoned playthings—there was another doll, too, half-buried; and a sandcastle with a stick king propped up in one tilted turret. The tide would take it all in a moment, and nothing would be left but the flaccid birds of the beach, hopping in circles.

Then Schmendrick shook her back to his side, saying, "Molly." Far out to sea, the combers were coming in: the long, heavy rollers, curling over white across their green hearts; tearing themselves to smoke on the sandbars and the slimy rocks, rasping up the beach with a sound like fire. The birds flew up in yelling clumps, their strident outrage lost in the cry of the waves like pins.

And in the whiteness, of the whiteness, flowering in the tattered water, their bodies aching with the streaked marble hollows of the waves, their manes and tails and the fragile beards of the males burning in the sunlight, their eyes as dark and jeweled as the deep sea—and the shining of the horns, the seashell shining of the horns! The horns came riding in like the rainbow masts of silver ships.

But they would not come to land while the Bull was there. They rolled in the shallows, swirling together as madly as frightened fish when the nets are being hauled up; no longer with the sea, but losing it. Hundreds were borne in with each swell and hurled against the ones already struggling to keep from being shoved ashore, and they in their turn struck out desperately, rearing and stumbling, stretching their long, cloudy necks far back.

The unicorn lowered her head one last time and hurled herself at the Red Bull. If he had been either true flesh or a windy ghost, the blow would have burst

225

him like rotten fruit. But he turned away unnoticing, and walked slowly into the sea. The unicorns in the water floundered wildly to let him by, stamping and slashing the surf into a roiling mist which their horns turned rainbow; but on the beach, and atop the cliff, and up and down through all of Haggard's kingdom, the land sighed when his weight had passed from it.

He strode out a long way before he began to swim. The hugest waves broke no higher than his hocks, and the timid tide ran away from him. But when at last he let himself sink onto the flood, then a great surge of the sea stood up behind him: a green and black swell, as deep and smooth and hard as the wind. It gathered in silence, folding from one horizon to the other, until for a moment it actually hid the Red Bull's humped shoulders and sloping back. Schmendrick lifted the dead prince, and he and Molly ran until the cliff face stopped them. The wave fell like a cloudburst of chains.

Then the unicorns came out of the sea.

Molly never saw them clearly—they were a light leaping toward her and a cry that dazzled her eyes. She was wise enough to know that no mortal was ever meant to see all the unicorns in the world, and she tried to find her own unicorn and look only at her. But there were too many of them, and they were too beautiful. Blind as the Bull, she moved to meet them, holding out her arms.

The unicorns would surely have run her down, as the Red Bull had trampled Prince Lír, for they were mad with freedom. But Schmendrick spoke, and they streamed to the right and left of Molly and Lír and himself—some even springing over them—as the sea shatters on a rock and then comes whirling together again. All around Molly there flowed and flowered a light as impossible as snow set afire, while thousands of cloven hoofs sang by like cymbals. She stood very still, neither weeping nor laughing, for her joy was too great for her body to understand.

"Look up," Schmendrick said. "The castle is falling."

She turned and saw that the towers were melting as the unicorns sprang up the cliff and flowed around them, exactly as though they had been made out of sand and the sea were sliding in. The castle came down in great cold chunks that turned thin and waxen as they swirled in the air, until they disappeared. It crumbled and vanished without a sound, and it left no ruins, either on land or in the memories of the two who watched it fall. A minute later, they could not remember where it had stood, or how it had looked.

But King Haggard, who was quite real, fell down through the wreckage of his disenchanted castle like a knife dropped through clouds. Molly heard him laugh once, as though he had expected it. Very little ever surprised King Haggard.

# XIV

NCE THE SEA had taken back their diamond-
shaped footprints, there was no sign that they
had ever been there, any more than King
Haggard's castle had been. The only difference was that
Molly Grue remembered unicorns very well.

"It's good that she went without saying good-by," she
said to herself. "I would have been stupid. I'm going to
be stupid in a minute, anyway, but it really is better like
this." Then a warmth moved over her cheek and into
her hair, like sunlight, and she turned and put her arms
around the unicorn's neck.

"Oh, you stayed!" she whispered, "you stayed!" She
was about to be very foolish then, and ask, "Will you
stay?" but the unicorn slipped gently from her and
moved to where Prince Lír lay with his dark blue eyes
already losing their color. She stood over him, as he had
guarded the Lady Amalthea.

"She can restore him," Schmendrick said softly. "A
unicorn's horn is proof against death itself." Molly
looked closely at him, as she had not done for a long
time, and she saw that he had come at last to his power
and his beginning. She could not say how she knew, for
no wild glory burned about him, and no recognizable

omens occurred in his honor, just at that moment. He was Schmendrick the Magician, as ever—and yet somehow it was for the first time.

It was long that the unicorn stood by Prince Lír before she touched him with her horn. For all that her quest had ended joyously, there was weariness in the way she held herself, and a sadness in her beauty that Molly had never seen. It suddenly seemed to her that the unicorn's sorrow was not for Lír but for the lost girl who could not be brought back; for the Lady Amalthea, who might have lived happily ever after with the prince. The unicorn bowed her head, and her horn glanced across Lír's chin as clumsily as a first kiss.

He sat up blinking, smiling at something long ago. "Father," he said in a quick wondering voice. "Father, I had a dream." Then he saw the unicorn, and he rose to his feet as the blood on his face began to shine and move again. He said, "I was dead."

The unicorn touched him a second time, over the heart, letting her horn rest there for a little space. They were both trembling. Prince Lír put his hands out to her like words. She said, "I remember you. I remember."

"When I was dead—" Prince Lír began, but she was away. Not a stone rattled down after her, not a bush tore out as she sprang up the cliff: she went as lightly as the shadow of a bird; and when she looked back, with one cloven foot poised, and the sunlight on her sides, with her head and neck absurdly fragile for the burden of the horn—then each of the three below called to her in pain. She turned and vanished; but Molly Grue saw their voices thump home into her like arrows, and even more than she wished the unicorn back, she wished that she had not called.

Prince Lír said, "As soon as I saw her, I knew that I had been dead. It was so the other time, when I looked down from my father's tower and saw her." He glanced up then and drew in his breath. It was the only sound of grief for King Haggard that any living thing ever made.

"Was it I?" he whispered. "The curse said that I would be the one to bring the castle down, but I would never have done it. He was not good to me, but it was only because I was not what he wanted. Is it my doing that he is fallen?"

Schmendrick replied, "If you had not tried to save the unicorn, she would never have turned on the Red Bull and driven him into the sea. It was the Red Bull who made the overflow, and so set the other unicorns free, and it was they who destroyed the castle. Would you have it otherwise, knowing this?"

Prince Lír shook his head, but he said nothing. Molly asked, "But why did the Bull run from her? Why didn't he stand and fight?"

There was no sign of him when they looked out to sea, though he was surely too vast to have swum out of sight in so short a time. But whether he reached some other shore, or whether the water drew even his great bulk down at last, none of them knew until long after; and he was never seen again in that kingdom.

"The Red Bull never fights," Schmendrick said. "He conquers, but he never fights."

He turned to Prince Lír and put a hand on his shoulder. "Now you are the king," he said. He touched

Molly as well, said something that was more of a whistle than a word, and the three of them floated up the air like milkweed plumes to the top of the cliff. Molly was not frightened. The magic lifted her as gently as though she were a note of music and it were singing her. She could feel that it was never very far from being wild and dangerous, but she was sorry when it set her down.

No stone of the castle remained, nor any scar; the earth was not even a shade paler where it had stood. Four young men in rusty, ragged armor wandered gaping through the vanished corridors, and turned around and around in the absence that had been the great hall. When they saw Lír, Molly, and Schmendrick, they came running toward them, laughing. They fell on their knees before Lír and cried out together, "Your majesty! Long live King Lír!"

Lír blushed, and actually tried to pull them to their feet. "Never mind that," he mumbled, "never mind that. Who are you?" He peered in amazement from one face to the next. "I know you—I do know you—but how can it be?"

"It is true, Your Majesty," the first of the young men said happily. "We are indeed King Haggard's men-at-arms—the same who served him for so many cold and weary years. We fled the castle after you disappeared into the clock, for the Red Bull was roaring, and all the towers were trembling, and we were afraid. We knew that the old curse must be coming home at last."

"A great wave took the castle," said a second man-at-arms, "exactly as the witch foretold. I saw it go spilling down the cliff as slowly as snow, and why we did not go with it, I cannot tell."

"The wave parted to go around us," another man said, "as I never saw any wave do. It was strange water, like the ghost of a wave, boiling with a rainbow light, and for a moment it seemed to me—" He rubbed his eyes and shrugged, and smiled helplessly. "I don't know. It was like a dream."

"But what has happened to you all?" Lír demanded. "You were old men when I was born, and now you are younger than I am. What miracle is this?"

The three who had spoken giggled and looked embarrassed, but the fourth man replied, "It is the miracle of meaning what we said. Once we told the Lady Amalthea that we would grow young again if she wished it so, and we must have been telling the truth. Where is she? We will go to her aid if it means facing the Red Bull himself."

King Lír said, "She is gone. Find my horse and saddle him. Find my horse." His voice was harsh and hungry, and the men-at-arms scrambled to obey their new lord.

But Schmendrick, standing behind him, said quietly, "Your Majesty, it may not be. You must not follow her."

The king turned and he looked like Haggard. "Magician, she is mine!" He paused, and then went on in a gentler tone, close to pleading. "She has twice raised me up from death, and what will I be without her but dead for a third time?" He took Schmendrick by the wrists with a grip strong enough to powder bones, but the magician did not move. Lír said, "I am not King

Haggard. I have no wish to capture her, but only to spend my life following after her—miles, leagues, even years behind—never seeing her, perhaps, but content. It is my right. A hero is entitled to his happy ending, when it comes at last."

But Schmendrick answered, "This is not the end, either for you or for her. You are the king of a wasted land where there has never been any king but fear. Your true task has just begun, and you may not know in your life if you have succeeded in it, but only if you fail. As for her, she is a story with no ending, happy or sad. She can never belong to anything mortal enough to want her."

Most strangely then, he put his arms around the young king and held him so for a time. "Yet be content, my lord," he said in a low voice. "No man has ever had more of her grace than you, and no other will ever be blessed by her remembrance. You have loved her and served her—be content, and be king."

"But that is not what I want!" Lír cried. The magician answered not a word, but only looked at him. Blue eyes stared back into green; a face grown lean and lordly into one neither so handsome nor so bold. The king began to squint and blink, as though he were gazing at the sun, and it was not long before he lowered his eyes and muttered, "So be it. I will stay and rule alone over a wretched people in a land I hate. But I will have no more joy of my rule than poor Haggard ever had."

A small autumn cat with a crooked ear stalked out of some secret fold in the air and yawned at Molly. She caught him up against her face, and he tangled his paws in her hair. Schmendrick smiled, and said to the king, "We must leave you now. Will you come with us and see us in friendship to the edge of your domain? There is much between here and there that is worth your study—and I can promise you that there will be some sign of unicorns."

Then King Lír shouted for his horse again, and his men searched for it and found it; but there were none for Schmendrick and Molly. Yet when they came back with the king's horse, they turned at his amazed stare and saw two more horses trailing docilely behind them: one black and one brown, and both already saddled and bridled. Schmendrick took the black for himself, and gave the brown horse to Molly.

She was afraid of them at first. "Are they yours?" she asked him. "Did you make them? Can you do that now—just make things?" The king's whisper echoed her wonder.

"I found them," the magician answered. "But what I mean by finding is not what you mean. Ask me no more." He lifted her into the saddle, and then leaped up himself.

So the three of them rode away, and the men-at-arms followed on foot. No one looked back, for there was nothing to see. But King Lír said once, without turning, "It is strange to have grown to manhood in a place, and then to have it gone, and everything changed—and suddenly to be king. Was none of it real at all? Am I real, then?" Schmendrick made no reply.

King Lír wished to go swiftly, but Schmendrick held them to a leisurely pace and a roundabout road. When the king fretted for speed, he was admonished to consider his walking men—though they, marvelously, never tired for all the length of the journey. But Molly soon understood that the magician was delaying in order to make Lír gaze long and closely at his realm. And to her own surprise, she discovered that the land was worth the look.

For, very slowly, spring was coming to the barren country that had been Haggard's. A stranger would not have noticed the change, but Molly could see that the withered earth was brightening with a greenness as shy as smoke. Squat, snaggly trees that had never yet bloomed were putting forth flowers in the wary way an army sends out scouts; long-dry streams were beginning to rustle in their beds, and small creatures were calling to one another. Smells slipped by in ribbons: pale grass and black mud, honey and walnuts, mint and hay and rotting applewood; and even the afternoon sunlight had a tender, sneezy scent that Molly would have known anywhere. She rode beside Schmendrick, watching the gentle advent of the spring and thinking of how it had come to her, late but lasting.

"Unicorns have passed here," she whispered to the magician. "Is that the cause, or is it Haggard's fall and the Red Bull's going? What is it, what is happening?"

"Everything," he answered her, "everything, all at once. It is not one springtime, but fifty; and not one or two great terrors flown away, but a thousand small shadows lifted from the land. Wait and see."

Speaking for Lír's ear, he added, "Nor is this the first spring that ever has been in this country. It was a good land long ago, and it wants little but a true king to be so again. See how it softens before you."

King Lír said nothing, but his eyes roved left and right as he rode, and he could not but observe the ripening. Even the valley of Hagsgate, of evil memory, was stirring with all manner of wildflowers—columbine and harebell, lavender and lupine, foxglove and yarrow. The rutted footprints of the Red Bull were growing mellow with mallow.

But when they came to Hagsgate, deep in the afternoon, a strange and savage sight awaited them. The plowed fields were woefully torn and ravaged, while the rich orchards and vineyards had been stamped down, leaving no grove or arbor standing. It was such shattering ruin as the Bull himself might have wrought; but it seemed to Molly Grue as though fifty years' worth of foiled griefs had struck Hagsgate all at once, just as that many springtimes were at last warming the rest of the land. The trampled earth looked oddly ashen in the late light.

King Lír said quietly, "What is this?"

"Ride on, Your Majesty," the magician replied. "Ride on."

The sun was setting as they passed through the overthrown gates of the town and guided their horses slowly down streets that were choked with boards and belongings and broken glass; with pieces of walls and windows, chimneys, chairs, kitchenware, roofs, bathtubs, beds, mantels, dressing tables. Every house in Hagsgate was down; everything that could be broken was. The town looked as though it had been stepped on.

The people of Hagsgate sat on their doorsteps wherever they could find them, considering the wreckage. They had always had the air of paupers, even in the midst of plenty, and real ruin made them appear almost relieved, and no whit poorer. They hardly noticed Lír when he rode up to them, until he said, "I am the king. What has befallen you here?"

"It was an earthquake," one man murmured dreamily, but another contradicted him, saying, "It was a storm, a nor'easter straight off the sea. It shook the town to bits, and hail came down like hoofs." Still another man insisted that a mighty tide had washed over Hagsgate; a tide as white as dogwood and heavy as marble, that drowned none and smashed everything. King Lír listened to them all, smiling grimly.

"Listen," he said when they were done. "King Haggard is dead, and his castle has fallen. I am Lír, the son of Hagsgate who was abandoned at birth in order to keep the witch's curse from coming true, and *this* from happening." He swept an arm around him at the burst houses. "Wretched, silly people, the unicorns have returned—the unicorns, that you saw the Red Bull hunting, and pretended not to see. It was they who brought the castle down, and the town as well. But it is your greed and your fear that have destroyed you."

The townsfolk sighed in resignation, but a middle-aged woman stepped forward and said with some spirit, "It all seems a bit unfair, my lord, begging your pardon. What could we have done to save the unicorns? We were afraid of the Red Bull. What could we have done?"

"One word might have been enough," King Lír replied. "You'll never know now."

He would have wheeled his horse and left them there, but a feeble, roupy voice called to him, "Lír—

little Lír—my child, my king!" Molly and Schmendrick recognized the man who came shuffling up with his arms open, wheezing and limping as though he were older than he truly was. It was Drinn.

"Who are you?" the king demanded. "What do you want of me?"

Drinn pawed at his stirrups, nuzzling his boots. "You don't know me, my boy? No—how should you? How should I deserve to have you know me? I am your father—your poor old overjoyed father. I am the one who left you in the marketplace on that winter night long ago, and handed you over to your heroic destiny. How wise I was, and how sad for so long, and how proud I am now! My boy, my little boy!" He could not quite cry real tears, but his nose was running.

Without a word, King Lír tugged at his horse's reins, backing him out of the crowd. Old Drinn let his outstretched arms drop to his sides. "This is what it is to have children!" he screeched. "Ungrateful son, will you desert your father in the hour of his distress, when a word from your pet wizard would have set everything right again? Despise me if you will, but I have played my part in putting you where you are, and you dare not deny it! Villainy has its rights too."

Still the king would have turned away, but Schmendrick touched his arm and leaned near. "It's true, you know," he whispered. "But for him—but for them all—the tale would have worked out quite another way, and who can say that the ending would have been even as happy as this? You must be their king, and you must rule them as kindly as you would a braver and more faithful folk. For they are a part of your fate."

Then Lír lifted his hand to the people of Hagsgate, and they pushed and elbowed one another for silence. He said, "I must ride with my friends and keep them company for a way. But I will leave my men-at-arms here, and they will help you begin to build your town again. When I return, in a little time, I also will help. I will not begin to build my new castle until I see Hagsgate standing once more."

They complained bitterly that Schmendrick could do it all in a moment by means of his magic. But he answered them, "I could not, even if I would. There are laws that govern the wizard's art, as laws command the seasons and the sea. Magic made you wealthy once, when all others in the land were poor; but your days of prosperity are ended, and now you must start over. What was wasteland in Haggard's time shall grow green and generous again, but Hagsgate will yield a living exactly as miserly as the hearts that dwell there. You may plant your acres again, and raise up your fallen orchards and vineyards, but they will never flourish as they used to, never—until you learn to take joy in them, for no reason."

He gazed on the silent townsfolk with no anger in his glance, but only pity. "If I were you, I would have children," he said; and then to King Lír, "How says your Majesty? Shall we sleep here tonight and be on our way at dawn?"

But the king turned and rode away out of ruined Hagsgate as fast as he could spur. It was long before Molly and the magician came up with him, and longer still before they lay down to sleep.

For many days they journeyed through King Lír's domain, and each day they knew it less and delighted in it more. The spring ran on before them as swiftly as fire, clothing all that was naked and opening everything that had long ago shut up tight, touching the earth as the unicorn had touched Lír. Every sort of animal, from bears to black beetles, came sporting or shambling or scurrying along their way, and the high sky, that had been as sandy and arid as the soil itself, now blossomed with birds, swirling so thickly that it seemed like sunset most of the day. Fish bent and flickered in the whisking streams, and wildflowers raced up and down the hills like escaped prisoners. All the land was noisy with life, but it was the silent rejoicing of the flowers that kept the three travelers awake at night.

The folk of the villages greeted them cautiously, and with little less dourness than they had shown when Schmendrick and Molly first came that way. Only the oldest among them had ever seen the spring before, and many suspected the rampaging greenness of being a plague or an invasion. King Lír told them that Haggard was dead and the Red Bull gone forever, invited them to visit him when his new castle was raised, and passed on. "They will need time to feel comfortable with flowers," he said.

Wherever they stopped, he left word that all outlaws were pardoned, and Molly hoped that the news would come to Captain Cully and his merry band. As it happened it did, and all the merry band immediately abandoned the life of the greenwood, saving only Cully himself and Jack Jingly. Together they took up the trade of wandering minstrels and were reported to have become reasonably popular in the provinces.

One night, the three slept at the farthest frontier of Lír's kingdom, making their beds in high grass. The king would bid them farewell in the morning and return to Hagsgate. "It will be lonely," he said in the darkness. "I would rather go with you, and not be king."

"Oh, you'll get to like it," Schmendrick replied. "The best young men of the village will make their way to your court, and you will teach them to be knights and heroes. The wisest of ministers will come to counsel you, the most skillful musicians and jugglers and storytellers will come seeking your favor. And there will be a princess, in time—either fleeing her unspeakably wicked father and brothers, or seeking justice for them. Perhaps you will hear of her, shut away in a fortress of flint and adamant, her only companion a compassionate spider—"

"I don't care about that," King Lír said. He was silent for so long that Schmendrick thought he had fallen asleep, but presently he said, "I wish I could see her once more, to tell her all my heart. She will never know what I really meant to say. You did promise that I would see her."

The magician answered him sharply. "I promised only that you would see some sign of unicorns, and so you have. Your realm is blessed beyond any land's deserving because they have passed across it in freedom. As for you and your heart and the things you said and didn't say, she will remember them all when men are fairy tales in books written by rabbits. Think of that, and be still." The king spoke no more after that, and Schmendrick repented of his words.

"She touched you twice," he said in a little while. "The first touch was to bring you to life again, but the second was for you." Lír did not answer, and the magician never knew if he had heard or not.

Schmendrick dreamed that the unicorn came and stood by him at moonrise. The thin night wind lifted and spilled her mane, and the moon shone on the snowflake crafting of her small head. He knew it was a dream, but he was happy to see her. "How beautiful you are," he said. "I never really told you." He would have roused the others, but her eyes sang him a warning as clearly as two frightened birds, and he knew that if he moved to call Molly and Lír he would wake himself, and she would vanish. So he said only, "They love you more, I think, though I do the best I can."

"That is why," she said, and he could not tell what she was answering. He lay very still, hoping that he would remember the exact shape of her ears when he did wake in the morning. She said, "You are a true and mortal wizard now, as you always wished. Does it make you happy?"

"Yes," he replied with a quiet laugh. "I'm not poor Haggard, to lose my heart's desire in the having of it. But there are wizards and wizards; there is black magic and white magic, and the infinite shades of gray between—and I see now that it is all the same. Whether I decide to be what men would call a wise and good magician—aiding heroes, thwarting witches, wicked lords, and unreasonable parents; making rain, curing woolsorter's disease and the mad staggers, getting cats down from trees—or whether I choose the retorts full of elixirs and essences, the powders and herbs and banes, the padlocked books of gramarye bound in skins better left unnamed, the muddy mist darkening in the chamber and the sweet voice lisping therein—why, life is short, and how many can I help or harm? I have my power at last, but the world is still too heavy for me to move, though my friend Lír might think otherwise." And he laughed again in his dream, a little sadly.

The unicorn said, "That is true. You are a man, and men can do nothing that makes any difference." But her voice was strangely slow and burdened. She asked, "Which will you choose?"

The magician laughed for a third time. "Oh, it will be the kind magic, undoubtedly, because you would like it more. I do not think that I will ever see you again, but I will try to do what would please you if you knew. And you—where will you be for the rest of my life? I thought you would have gone home to your forest by now."

She turned a little away from him, and the sudden starlight of her shoulders made all his talk of magic taste like sand in his throat. Moths and midges and other night insects too small to be anything in particular came and danced slowly around her bright horn, and this did not make her appear foolish, but them most wise and lovely as they celebrated her. Molly's cat rubbed in and out between her forefeet.

"The others have gone," she said. "They are scattered to the woods they came from, no two together, and men will not catch sight of them much more easily than if they were still in the sea. I will go back to my forest too, but I do not know if I will live contentedly there, or anywhere. I have been mortal, and some part of me is mortal yet. I am full of tears and hunger and the fear of death, though I cannot weep, and I want nothing, and I cannot die. I am not like the others now, for no unicorn was ever born who could regret, but I do. I regret."

Schmendrick hid his face like a child, though he was a great magician. "I am sorry, I am sorry," he mumbled into his wrist. "I have done you evil, as Nikos did to the other unicorn, with the same good will, and I can no more undo it than he could. Mommy Fortuna and King Haggard and the Red Bull together were kinder to you than I."

But she answered him gently, saying, "My people are in the world again. No sorrow will live in me as long as that joy—save one, and I thank you for that, too. Farewell, good magician. I will try to go home."

She made no sound when she left him, but he was awake, and the crook-eared cat was miaowing lonesomely. Turning his head, he saw the moonlight trembling in the open eyes of King Lír and Molly Grue. The three of them lay awake till morning, and nobody said a word.

At dawn, King Lír rose up and saddled his horse. Before he mounted, he said to Schmendrick and Molly, "I would like it if you came to see me one day." They assured him that they would, but still he lingered with them, twisting the dangling reins about his fingers.

"I dreamed about her last night!" he said.

Molly cried, "So did I!" and Schmendrick opened his mouth, and then closed it again.

King Lír said hoarsely, "By our friendship, I beg you—tell me what she said to you." His hands gripped one hand each of theirs, and his clutch was cold and painful.

Schmendrick gave him a weak smile. "My lord, I so rarely remember my dreams. It seems to me that we spoke solemnly of silly things, as one does—grave nonsense, empty and evanescent—" The king let go of his hand and turned his half-mad gaze on Molly Grue.

"I'll never tell," she said, a little frightened, but flushing oddly. "I remember, but I'll never tell anyone, if I die for it—not even you, my lord." She was not looking at him as she spoke, but at Schmendrick.

King Lír let her hand fall as well, and he swung himself into the saddle so fiercely that his horse reared up across the sunrise, bugling like a stag. But Lír kept his seat and glared down at Molly and Schmendrick with a face so grim and scored and sunken that he might well have been king as long as Haggard before him.

"She said nothing to me," he whispered. "Do you understand? She said nothing to me, nothing at all."

Then his face softened, as even King Haggard's face had gone a little gentle when he watched the unicorns in the sea. For that moment he was again the young prince who had liked to sit with Molly in the scullery. He said, "She looked at me. In my dream, she looked at me and never spoke."

He rode away without good-by, and they watched after him until the hills hid him: a straight, sad horseman, going home to be king. Molly said at last, "Oh, the poor man. Poor Lír."

"He has not fared so badly," the magician answered. "Great heroes need great sorrows and burdens, or half their greatness goes unnoticed. It is all part of the fairy tale." But his voice was a little doubtful, and he laid his arm softly around Molly's shoulders. "It cannot be an ill fortune to have loved a unicorn," he said. "Surely it must be the dearest luck of all, though the hardest earned."

By and by, he put her as far from him as his fingers' ends and asked her, "Now will you tell me what it was she said to you?" But Molly Grue only laughed and shook her head till her hair came down, and she was more beautiful than the Lady Amalthea. The magician said, "Very well. Then I'll find the unicorn again, and perhaps she will tell me." And he turned calmly to whistle up their steeds.

She said no word while he saddled his horse, but when he began on her own she put her hand on his arm. "Do you think—do you truly hope that we may find her? There was something I forgot to say."

Schmendrick looked at her over his shoulder. The morning sunlight made his eyes seem gay as grass; but now and then, when he stooped into the horse's shadow, there stirred a deeper greenness in his gaze—the green of pine needles that has a faint, cool bitterness about it. He said, "I fear it, for her sake. It would mean that she too is a wanderer now, and that is a fate for human beings, not for unicorns. But I hope, of course I hope." Then he smiled at Molly and took her hand in his. "Anyway, since you and I must choose one road to follow, out of the many that run to the same place in the end, it might as well be a road that a unicorn has taken. We may never see her, but we will always know where she has been. Come, then. Come with me."

So they began their new journey, which took them in its time in and out of most of the folds of the sweet, wicked, wrinkled world, and so at last to their own strange and wonderful destiny. But that was all later, and first, not ten minutes out of Lír's kingdom, they met a maiden who came hurrying toward them on foot. Her dress was torn and smirched, but the richness of its making was still plain to see, and though her hair was tumbled and brambled, her arms scratched, and her fair face dirty, there was no mistaking her for anyone but a princess in woeful distress. Schmendrick lighted down to support her, and she clutched him with both hands as though he were a grapefruit hull.

"A rescue!" she cried to him, "a rescue, *au secours!* An ye be a man of mettle and sympathy, aid me now. I hight the Princess Alison Jocelyn, daughter to good King Giles, and him foully murdered by his brother, the bloody Duke Wulf, who hath ta'en my three brothers, the Princes Corin, Colin, and Calvin, and cast them into a fell prison as hostages that I will wed with his fat son, the Lord Dudley, but I bribed the sentinel and sopped the dogs—"

But Schmendrick the Magician raised his hand, and she fell silent, staring up at him in wonder out of wide lilac eyes. "Fair princess," he said gravely to her, "the man you want just went that way," and he pointed back toward the land they had so lately quitted. "Take my horse and you will be up with him while your shadow is still behind you."

He cupped his hands for the Princess Alison Jocelyn, and she climbed wearily and in some bewilderment to the saddle. Schmendrick turned the horse, saying, "You will surely overtake him with ease, for he will be riding slowly. He is a good man, and a hero greater than any cause is worth. I send all my princesses to him. His name is Lír."

Then he slapped the horse on the rump and sent it off the way King Lír had gone; and then he laughed for so long that he was too weak to get up behind Molly and had to walk beside her horse for a while. When he caught his breath again, he began to sing, and she joined with him. And this is what they sang as they went away together, out of this story and into another:

" 'I am no king, and I am no lord,
And I am no soldier at arms,' said he.
'I'm none but a harper, and a very poor harper,
That am come hither to wed with ye.'

" 'If you were a lord, you should be my lord,
And the same if you were a thief,' said she.
'And if you are a harper, you shall be my harper,
For it makes no matter to me, to me,
For it makes no matter to me.'

" 'But what if it prove that I am no harper?
That I lied for your love most monstrously?'
'Why, then I'll teach you to play and sing,
For I dearly love a good harp,' said she."

## THE END